Dirty DADDIES

International Bestselling Author

JADE WEST

Dedicated to all you wonderfully dirty people out there.
I hope you enjoy the ride.

MICHAEL

The moment *Carrie Wells stepped* into my office five months, six days and four hours ago, I knew she was one beautiful package of trouble.

She dropped herself into the seat opposite, sitting just as she is right now, with the same world-hating scowl on her pretty face, the same hunch of her perfectly sloping shoulders, and the same nervous tap of her right foot. She told me back then, just as she will today, that she doesn't give a fuck about anything.

She doesn't give a fuck about claiming assistance and applying for college.

She doesn't give a fuck about the fact she's less than a week away from being homeless.

She doesn't give a fuck about the latest foster family she's run ragged these past few months.

Carrie Wells has a chip on her shoulder bigger than the file of case notes with her name on the cover. She has a wildness about her, and if those feral looks of hers could kill, I'd be a dead man right now, along with half of my colleagues in this building.

Her long black hair is glossy and thick, even though I'm sure it rarely sees a brush. The sprinkling of freckles over her nose give her a softness at odds with the rest of her appearance. Her teeth are surprisingly perfect given the generally dishevelled state of her.

They say she's from Romany descent, although little is known about her actual lineage. She offered to read my palm once, then cackled when I handed it over.

I don't know why she comes here. Half of me wishes she wouldn't.

Half of me.

The other half is in the pits at the knowledge that this is our last official session. In four days' time she will turn eighteen and her funding here will cease. I will refer her to other agencies, of course, but I doubt she'll turn up.

For all my efforts over the past few months, I've failed her. My words have been for nothing, my time has been fruitless. Carrie Wells will leave my office today in a far worse position than she was when she first stepped foot in here. Eighteen and soon to be on the streets. A failure of the system.

Who knows where she's going to end up.

I've got twenty minutes to make the last five months count, but she's barely even looking at me.

"How was your week?" I ask, as though I think she'll grace me with an answer.

A shrug. That's all she gives.

"How are things with Rosie and Bill? Did you apologise for the carpet?"

"I tried."

I take a breath. "You tried? Good. And what did they say?"

"Rosie gave me that prissy smile of hers. Bill said nothing."

She's wearing the same filthy boots she soiled their new cream carpet with. She tugs at the laces absentmindedly. There's a trail of mud through my office showing just how well she learned her lesson, but I don't care about that. Cleaning the floor isn't my job.

Carrie Wells is.

I'm a community support assistant for a non-profit organisation handling disadvantaged youths, and this gem of a girl is my client. One of twenty I've currently got on my books, and the only one that makes my heart race.

She shouldn't.

On paper she's still technically a minor with a history of substance abuse and behavioural issues. On paper she's a bad kid who doesn't want help from anyone.

But that's not true. If it was, she wouldn't be here. At least that's what I like to tell myself.

"They're gonna throw me out on my birthday," she says. "The minute I turn eighteen I'll be out of there."

"Maybe if you tried again… offered another apology…"

She sneers at me like I'm a total fucking imbecile. Like I have no idea how the world works.

She's right. I have no idea how *her* world works. I have no idea how it would feel to grow up in a world where no one gives a shit about you. Without a family.

"They're dicks," she snaps. "I hate them."

"You don't hate them," I begin.

"I do hate them," she insists.

"Rosie and Bill are good people, Carrie. They care about you."

"They don't give a fuck about me." She stares me right in the eye and I feel it in my gut. "They *hate* me. They've always hated me."

She strikes like a snake, launching her skinny little body at my desk in a heartbeat. I have to fight to keep my composure as she learns right over, my stance easy and non-threatened even though my heart is pounding.

She tugs up the sleeve on her grubby bomber jacket and shoves her wrist in my face.

"They did this to me."

They didn't. I know they didn't.

Someone was definitely responsible for the yellowing bruises on her pale skin, but it won't have been Bill and Rosie. Those bruises on her wrist have been a constant throughout her file.

Rumour has it they're self-inflicted, but I'm not so sure on that either.

"Bill and Rosie did this to you? Is that what you're telling me?"

She sits back down. "Gonna call the cops?"

"Is that what you want?"

"They wouldn't do shit if you did."

She's right about that. My agency called the police out ten times in a twelve-week period when she first landed on our books. Ten tall tales, ten instances of accusations with no substance to back them up. Her account of events changes every five minutes, just as they would today if I pushed her on them.

I fell into the sob-story trap myself on day one, even though my colleagues told me I was being played. I wasn't the first, and I sure won't be the last. The girl is difficult, but she's compelling. Her wildness is addictive.

I breathe through the silence as she examines her grubby nails. I wait patiently until she speaks again.

"Bill wants me."

"Wants you?"

"He looks at me."

"Bill wants what's best for you," I insist.

"He wants to fuck me. You do, too." Her eyes bore right through me, and I don't move. I don't look away, not because she's right – which she is – but because playing her game is the last thing she needs from me.

I've wanted to fuck her ever since our first session when her pouty little mouth sneered at me and told me I was just another *useless cog in the useless fucking system.*

I've wanted to bend her over my desk and fuck some manners into the snarky little bitch ever since she spread her legs in that very same seat and asked if I was hard for her. Asked if I wanted a go.

Asked if I knew she was wet for me.

Carrie Wells is a beautiful package of trouble, just like I said.

We have CCTV in this room. One false move and I'd be out of the job I've dedicated the last fifteen years to.

And I wouldn't make one false move. Of course I wouldn't.

Couldn't.

I'm waiting for it – the stream of obscenities as she loses her shit and tells me I'm disgusting. That I want to smell her. Want to taste her. Want her to rub her tight little pussy in my face.

I wait for her to tell me I'm an asshole and she never wants to see me again, that my help isn't worth shit.

But today she doesn't.

It's the breath she takes. The shaky little rasp of air that sets my nerves on fire.

It's the way she looks at her boots and not at me.

"They really are gonna throw me out this time," she whispers. "I said sorry, too. I mean, I'll be alright, I can take care of myself, find myself someone to bunk with, I just… I like my room there. I feel safe."

"Apologise again," I tell her, but she shakes her head. "Tell them how you really feel."

"No point."

One false move and she'll storm away and I know it. One stupid comment and she'll be out and away from here long before our remaining fifteen minutes is up.

I should ask her the standard questions. Tick the right boxes. I should be professional, just as I have been every other session up until now.

But I can taste it. The tiny little crack in her beautifully plated armour.

"Who really hurts you, Carrie?" I ask her, and those green eyes crash right into mine.

"Who do you think?"

"Tell me," I insist, willing that just this one time she'll finally be honest.

She fiddles with her grubby fingernails. "You think I do it to myself. Everyone thinks that."

My skin prickles. "Do you?"

She shrugs. "I trampled mud across Rosie and Bill's posh carpet. And I put that hair dye in with Rosie's washing. I did it on purpose, all of it. Maybe I hurt myself too."

"Why did you do those things?"

"I wanted them to be angry. I wanted to hurt them."

"And what about now? Do you still want to hurt them? Do you want to hurt yourself?"

"Maybe." Another shrug. "No."

Make or break. I take an audible breath. "This is it, Carrie, last chance saloon. Five months you've been coming here, and for what? Tell me how I can help you. *Let* me help you. Why come here every week if you aren't going to let me do anything to help?" I sigh. She says nothing. "Just tell me this, what *do* you want?"

"I want *you*," she says, and this time there's a guarded honesty in her eyes, a burn that matches the one I feel in my gut whenever I look at the wild creature across from me.

There's no snide smile on her mouth. No arrogant cock of the head. No fidgeting. Nothing.

My mouth is dry as a bone, and my cock is a fucking traitor to everything I stand for. Everything I believe in.

"You're why I come here and you know it," she says. "I wanted you since you saw my bruises and called the cops even though everyone said you were a jerk for believing me. I wanted you since you got angry they'd hurt me. You were angry, I saw it. And then you were angry with *me*, and I liked that too. Not angry like Bill and Rosie, not angry like that cop who came here and took my stupid statement. Angry like real angry. Angry like you wanted to hit me worse than any stupid bruises on my arms. But you didn't give up." She pauses. Breathes. "*That's* what I'm doing here." She uncrosses her legs and lands her muddy boots right back on the carpet. "And that's the only thing I wanted to say. That and thanks for trying. See you around, Mr Warren."

She's up and out of her seat before I've collected my words.

"Wait…" I say, but she holds up a hand. "Carrie…"

But there are only a trail of muddy boot prints in her wake.

My office door swings on its hinges behind her and there's already a pair of nervous eyes waiting on the other side.

I welcome in my next appointment and try to brush Carrie Wells from my mind.

We're done. Finished. I did everything I could. More than I should have.

Session closed.

She's not my problem anymore.

If only I could believe that were true.

CARRIE

I keep my head down as I stomp away from Michael Warren's office. They all hate me in here, all the pen-pushers and the snotty bitches behind the crappy reception desk. All their smiley rainbow *welcome* signs mean nothing in this place, not if your face doesn't fit.

They want the nice kids who speak when they're spoken to and say *thank you* whenever anyone throws them a scrappy crumb of nothing.

They want nice kids like the one outside Michael's office, with big sad puppy dog eyes and a smile for everyone. Those are the kids that get good homes.

Kids like me, not so much.

But I'm not a kid anymore. In a couple of days I'll be kicked out of the latest home I was palmed off on. Rosie and Bill will be glad to see the back of me, and I don't blame them. Not really.

They're good people. Kind.

I just… I can't stop myself shoving my shitty attitude in their faces until they break.

It doesn't matter who they are, they always break in the end.

I've been in fourteen homes since I turned ten. Fourteen sets of new

8

parents telling me to make myself one of the family. But I never do.

I don't belong in anyone's family. I don't belong in anyone's little Lego house or their neatly-mown back garden. I don't belong on any grinning school photos or in the county netball team.

I don't belong in this little shit hole of a town, with its backwater villages where everyone is in everyone else's business.

My ancestors were travellers, roaming the wilds and making a living from the land. I feel it in my blood – the urge to dance through the countryside and make my own way in a little wagon somewhere. Maybe I'll find my own kind, just as soon as I'm old enough to make my own way.

That's what I've been telling myself – that this is destiny. That I won't miss Rosie and Bill, not even a bit. That they mean nothing to me, just like none of the others meant anything to me. Not even Emma and Frank all those years ago who bought me the doll house and helped me set up all the pretty furniture Frank made me.

They thought it was me who hit their baby daughter, but I didn't. It was Eli, their eldest, but nobody believed a little liar like me. *Problems* – that's what they said. I had *problems*. Too many *problems* for Emma and Frank and their nice little family.

That's why I scratched his car to shit with one of his screwdrivers. *Problems*.

That's why I spat in Emma's face when she tried to say goodbye. *Problems*.

And that's why everyone ditches me when I get too much. So many problems.

I should have been nothing but a problem to Michael Warren too. Hell, I was a problem enough for the two colleagues of his I saw before him. They lasted weeks before they felt *intimidated*. But he was different.

I could shout in his face and he didn't turn me away. I could tell him what I thought and he didn't scowl and sigh and mutter about *problems, problems, problems*.

He could be angry, but he never kicked me out.

He could want to smack the attitude right out of me, but he didn't lose his cool.

I like Michael Warren, and I wish I'd told him before now, before our last ever session. Who knows, maybe a man like him could have actually helped a *problem* like me. Maybe if I'd have listened to him I wouldn't be kicked out of Rosie and Bill's.

Sometimes I even thought maybe he'd be the one I couldn't break, no matter what I said or what I did. No matter how far I pushed him, he was always there next week, at our scheduled time with my stupid dumb file on his desk and his stupid dumb questions trying to help me.

Maybe he really would have helped me, if I'd have told him the truth. If I'd have told him who really hurts me.

But it's too late for all that now. At least I told him how I felt about him, just once.

I hate this shitty little town with its shitty weather. Grey drizzle turns to full on rain and none of the shops want me in them, so I slip into an alley down the side of the bank and wait for it to ease up, cursing the fact these boots have holes in them and I threw the ones Rosie bought me back in her face a few months back.

I don't need your fucking boots. You can't fucking buy me, I'm not for fucking sale.

The memory makes me cringe.

She didn't see how I ran to my room and cried harder than she did. She didn't see how sorry I was after, even though my stupid mouth wouldn't let me say a word.

I whistle as a guy in a scummy brown hoodie walks on by. I know him. Eddie something.

He stops, squints at me, then smiles. He knows me too, by reputation if not by introduction.

"Carrie, right?" he asks and steps on in.

I don't have time for stupid hellos. I hitch my boot up against the wall, playing it as disinterested as I possibly can. "Got a smoke?"

He nods and pulls a pack from his pocket. Shitty menthols, but beggars can't be choosers. I take one and light it off his lighter.

"Got somewhere to be?" he asks and I shake my head. "Want to come for a drink?"

"I'm underage," I tell him. "Nowhere's gonna serve me. Not without ID."

He takes a long drag. "I'll be buying. You look eighteen."

His eyes are all over me, but that's nothing new.

"Few days and I will be eighteen," I tell him. "And then I'll be away from his shitty place and off on my own."

He laughs but there's no malice in it. "Sounds good to me, this place is a shit hole." He holds out his arm but I shrug it off. I really don't want to be touching him. He looks the sleazy type, but a drink's a drink if he's the one paying.

"You're buying?" I clarify.

"Sure am." He pulls out his wallet, a battered thing on a chain. "Got paid today, did some overtime."

Just as well. I'm in the mood for a few, just to drink this awful day with its crappy goodbyes away. "Alright," I tell him, "lead the way."

And he does.

I ignore my shitty phone buzzing in my pocket. I ignore the angry messages Rosie and Bill will be leaving me.

I ignore everything, because tonight Eddie something is going to buy me drinks and look at me like he wants me.

It's the best thing on offer to a *problem* girl like me.

Two

MICHAEL

I rarely drink, especially not on a week night, but completing my final writeup and filing Carrie's case notes into the archive room is more than enough to drive me to a few after work. I tidy my desk and take one final look at Carrie's muddy boot prints before shutting down my PC for the day.

None of us here are miracle workers. We do our best, but not every case on our books has a happy ending. I've watched kids grow into adults with even bigger challenges than the ones they faced in the chair opposite me. I've lost good kids to a life of drugs in Bristol or Birmingham once they've taken a one-way ticket out of our sleepy county for pastures new. You hear about them, the ones who didn't make it. It's not a rare event that we get enquiries from lawyers and prosecutors digging for background information for their criminal cases.

Some support workers can't handle the disappointment. For others of us, we take the rough with the smooth – finding encouragement in the kids that we do manage to make a difference to, even just a little. We use the disappointments to harden our steel, determined to do better next time. That's how I *should* be feeling about Carrie. That's how I *have* to feel about Carrie.

My best clearly wasn't good enough to reach her, not in five months. Maybe not in five years. Maybe not ever. Not within the framework of our agency guidelines, not with half an hour per week to work miracles and tick all the policy boxes.

It's a hard pill to swallow.

I wonder if she'll end up back in Gloucester. That's where she came from before she ended up staying with Bill and Rosie. I was at one of their earliest meetings with the agency, when she was first listed on our books. The foster agency thought the countryside may agree with her, the slower pace of life may help her edginess. I can't see that it has, but the thought was a good one.

Pam Clowes, one of my fellow support workers, pats my shoulder as I head out for the evening, giving me one of her kindly smiles that tells me *we can't win them all*.

In truth, we can't win all that many of them, not with so many factors stacked against us. We really are just small cogs in a big social machine, and our jurisdiction doesn't carry all that much weight. Support, that's all we can offer – giving kids an ear and a voice through us when it's needed, but what difference can that really make to a girl who doesn't want either?

Carrie told me once that the only home she'll ever have is on the road. That's the only time I've ever seen her face truly light up, and the image is burned in my memory for all time.

I'm strangely tempted to withdraw my savings and buy her a wagon, but even if she'd accept it, that would never do. It would be against every safeguarding practice in our handbook and then some.

Being fired would be incomprehensible – both for me and all the kids who need me. But just occasionally, in bed at night, I wonder if a wild spark like Carrie would be worth dropping everything for. You couldn't get more cliché a description of a mid-life crisis, so it's just as well I have my stable best friend, Jack, to talk me down.

I told him once, after too many whiskies, that if I was ten years younger – alright, *fifteen* years younger – I'd run away with a girl like Carrie. We could travel around on some magical gypsy adventure, she and I, in a little wagon working the land and selling sprigs of heather.

Jack told me I was a fucking idiot and sent me back to my apartment to sleep off my crazy admission, of course. I took it all back in the morning, but there's no fooling that guy. He knows me far too well.

His astuteness and his sensibilities are exactly the reasons I message him tonight.

He replies to my text before I'm even through the office doors.

She's gone?

My reply is hard even to type. *Gone. Done. Off my books.*

I can imagine his sharp inhalation of breath. My phone pings a few seconds later.

Drury's Tavern. I'll be there in fifteen.

I loosen my tie as I head across the street. Our little town of Lydney is only a small place but it's all I've ever known. Jack and I grew up around these parts, went to the same school then college, but I stayed local, studying social care while he aimed for the stars and landed a business management degree at Warwick.

I'm surprised he came back here, but it turns out it was a good career move on his part. He set up an insurance agency the best part of a decade ago and it's doing great. Big premiums in agriculture, he tells me, a niche market he's done well to crack. Just as well he's around, considering how much I've needed his sound words these past few months.

On the face of it our lives are very different now. I'm still living in a bland apartment in the centre of town – he has a sprawling house on the outskirts with plenty of land. I'm driving a safe old Ford, whereas he has a Range Rover with all the optional extras.

Jack's made it financially, but my work matters, at least that's what I tell myself.

I see him heading down the high street in the opposite direction before I've even made it to Drury's. He cuts a fine image in his tailored suit. The dark grey matches the salt and pepper of his hair, a stylish bastard even though he's ageing more noticeably than me. I guess that's what building up a business does to you.

I hold the door until he joins me, and he slaps me on the back as we head inside. Drury's is one of those typical small-town drinking holes. A dimly lit bar with a good selection of local ales and a random collection of tables and chairs that don't match, but it suits the place. We head to the bar, and Jack orders. The first slug of ale goes down a treat, and we head over to a table in the corner by the open fire. Jack kicks back and takes off his tie. He rolls it around his fist and slips it into his inside pocket, then he eyes me with that easy smile I've come to know so well over the years.

"Rough day, then?"

I breathe out a sigh. "Can't win 'em all."

"No," he says. "You can't. What's going to become of the little madam?"

I shrug. "Hopefully she'll be able to stay where she is. Hopefully she'll even change her mind about college."

He's never seen Carrie Wells, but he's heard enough to be as sceptical as I am. "Not your problem anymore," he tells me. "You did what you could."

"What if everyone just *did what they could* and it's not enough?"

He leans forward. "You need to rein in that social conscience, you'll find it easier to sleep at night."

"I sleep just fine," I lie.

"Dreaming of your wild princess, no doubt." His smile is bright. "We should hit Cheltenham for a night out, see if we can't hook you up with someone who isn't either far too young or determined to self-destruct."

The thought of meeting someone else seems distant. I've had no appetite for dating and all that crap since things ended with me and Molly last year. That's one thing Jack and I still have in common – we're both not-so-lucky in love. Jack was engaged for a while to some posh cow from Oxford who was far more interested in his business prospects than she was in him. That ended recently and explosively, but he doesn't seem too hung up on it.

In the main, while I was cooped up with Molly, Jack fucked around. I wouldn't even like to guess how many women he's had in his bed and in his life. But still, having taken very different roads, here we both are, single and ageing a little more every month.

"Maybe *you* should hit Cheltenham," I say. "The women there are more your type."

"The women there are *anyone's* type after a couple of large wines, don't let the pretentiousness of the place fool you." He swigs back his beer, then stares at me. "You'll get over this. Give it some time."

"There's nothing to get over. She was on my books and now she's not."

"You give a shit about her, that's likely more than anyone else can say about the girl."

"Sad but true." I sip my beer but my throat feels tight. My whole body feels tight. "I can't just let her walk away. She'll head straight into trouble."

Jack straightens in his seat. "Trouble that isn't your problem. You need to get a grip of this, Mike. She's gone."

"I achieved nothing."

He sighs. "Who knows what difference you made to her? It's impossible to say how our words impact another, and if your advice wasn't welcome now there's nothing to say she won't remember it later."

I raise my glass. "To your excellent words."

He raises his. "May you heed them."

My gut feels strangely bereft. A sense of loss below the struggle for rationality. Maybe I need a support worker myself after suffering the Carrie Wells effect.

I take a deep breath, attempting to quell my inner turmoil.

"She's gone," I say, as if saying it out loud will put a lid on it.

"That she is," he replies. "May she be blessed with a long and fruitful life, wherever that may take her."

"Far away from here most likely."

"You should hope so, for your own sanity," Jack says, and he's right.

I should hope I don't see Carrie Wells again. I should hope that she's picked up by other agencies and they manage to succeed where I've failed. I should hope that she finds happiness with a young, spirited guy her own age, someone decent and caring. I should hope that she finds the love she's so sorely missed in her life this far.

I should hope she's found it within herself to offer up a genuine apology to Bill and Rosie and ask for another chance. Maybe she has. Maybe they're all having a heart to heart right now down the road in Lydbrook, sharing a cup of tea in Rosie's warm kitchen.

But no.

Of course not.

I hear her voice before I see her. I'd recognise that cackle anywhere, full of life and mischief rolled together. The bar door creaks on its big old hinges and in stumbles a guy in a hoodie who used to be on our books a few years back. Eddie Stevens, son of a bricklayer who sold drugs from the back of his van over in Gloucester.

Carrie stumbles on in after him, and my beer catches in my throat.

Her pale cheeks are flushed pink and her legs seem bandy. Drunk. She's fucking drunk.

Eddie lurches into the bar and she follows him, points out a tequila bottle on the back shelf.

Jack turns slowly in his seat, looks from them to me and back again.

"Is that–"

"Yes," I say.

"Sweet Jesus," he mutters, "but she's–"

"Underage," I finish. "Yes, she is."

He slams a hand on my wrist as I rise from my seat. "Not. Your. Problem," he says and his grey eyes are icy.

I shake him off more roughly than I intend.

CARRIE

Eddie is an idiot, but he's fun enough and he's paying. He brought me a couple of beers out to the back of the George and Dragon, then we dashed into the Brewers Arms for one before stumbling down the street to Drury's Tavern.

I'm already past dinner time back at Rosie and Bill's, but who gives a shit. Not them, that's for sure. It's probably a relief.

Eddie swings open the big door of Drury's and I follow him in. I've been drinking on an empty stomach and it's gone to my head, but I don't care. Why should I? Nobody else does.

I've barely got enough bus money to get home to Lydbrook and the timetable is pathetic here. The last bus leaves about six, and I'm sure I've missed it already, but that feels hazy now. Maybe I can bunk up with Eddie tonight. I don't want him, but I'm sure he wants me, and that's bound to be enough to get me somewhere to sleep at least.

I'll kick him in the balls if he tries to grope me.

If he doesn't let me stay after that, I'll sleep outside. I've done it before. It wasn't great, but I lived, and I'd better suck it up since I'll likely be doing a lot more of it later this week.

I point to a bottle of tequila on the back shelf of the bar and Eddie raises an eyebrow.

"You sure we wanna be hitting the hard stuff? The night's young."

"Not being a pussy, are you?"

He gives me a smirk. "I'm no fucking pussy. You'll find that out later."

The barman eyes me as Eddie points to the bottle at the back, but Eddie slaps his wallet on the counter and I give my most confident expression. I'm almost old enough to drink, what's a few days?

Then come the words I've been dreading. I groan as the barman clears his throat.

"Do you have ID?"

Footsteps at my back give me shivers. "No," a voice says. "She doesn't."

I spin on the spot to launch abuse at the interferer, all ready to tell the nosey sonofabitch to mind his own fucking business, but as my stare crashes into Michael Warren's, and those dark green eyes bore into mine, I take a breath.

My drunk tongue won't function properly, my words feel garbled in my throat, but it turns out I don't need them, because it's him who does all the talking.

He pushes Eddie with a shunt that surprises me. "What do you think you're playing at?" he asks him, before taking me by the elbow and pulling me away from the bar. I wrench away on instinct, fists ready to fly, but Michael doesn't let go.

His grip is firm on my arms, his eyes serious and burning and… pissed at me.

He's really fucking pissed at me.

"What are you doing here?" he snaps. "You should be at home, making amends with Rosie and Bill."

"It's not my fucking home," I snap back. "Rosie and Bill are dead to me. I'm having fun with Eddie. *Fun*, Michael. I'm having a good fucking time."

"And that good fucking time is over now," he snarls, and the blood rushes to my cheeks. I've never heard him swear before.

I feel like the whole place is staring at me. Some posh guy in a suit shakes his head from the table in the corner and it gives me the rage, right in the pit of me. I hate people laughing at me. Judging me. Taking me for a fucking loser.

"This good fucking time is over when I say it's over!" I hiss, but Michael doesn't let me go. His grip tightens on my arm and he takes a step toward the door. I feel myself moving, even though my boots are dragging. He's strong, much stronger than I gave him credit for under that boring suit in his office. He's still wearing it, but he looks different with his tie hanging loose. He looks… wired.

"This is assault!" I screech, but Michael Warren must be as trashed as I feel, because he doesn't stop, doesn't even pause as he marches me out and presses me up against the brickwork outside.

"I'm trying to fucking help you," he tells me, and his breath is in my face. There's only a hint of ale, and he doesn't look drunk at all, not even a little bit. Fuck.

The cold air hits me hard and my legs feel like jelly. I should have grabbed something to eat from Rosie and Bill's before I came out here, I've had nothing since breakfast, and that was just a flimsy slice of toast.

I take a breath and it feels like the wind has been knocked right out of my sails. Not least since Eddie hasn't even poked his head out to make sure I'm okay.

"You can't *help* me," I tell him but my voice sounds weak and pathetic. I hate how it sounds.

"You won't fucking let me."

I shrug in his grip. "So? Just let me fucking go!"

He doesn't move. "You need to get home to Bill and Rosie."

"And I've fucking told you already! That's not my fucking home!"

"So where were you planning on staying tonight? With that loser Eddie Stevens? He's nothing but a waster."

I shrug again. "Eddie's alright. I like him."

"Eddie's a fucking prick," he snaps. "You think he gives a shit? You think a few drinks are worth spending the fucking night with a loser like that?"

I grit my teeth. "He's the best fucking offer I've got. *Nobody* gives a shit. At least I can get drunk and forget about it for a few fucking hours."

I hate how I'm doing this, acting like I'm so hard when all I want to do is ask him to take me home. To his home. Ask him to stay with me awhile, until I sober up. All I want to do is tell him I'm hungry, and I don't know how I'm going to get back to Rosie and Bill's, and I don't know what the hell I'm going to do when they throw me out, and I need him. I really need him.

But I don't.

I can't.

"I'm taking you home," he tells me, and my heart does a jump. I don't know whether he sees it in my eyes because he takes a breath. "To Rosie and Bill's," he clarifies and my heart drops.

"They don't want me–" I begin, but his hands squeeze my arms.

"Shut up, Carrie. Just shut the fuck up."

I'm so taken aback that I do.

Nobody's told me to shut the fuck up for a long, long time. It's all tight lips and careful language. All disappointment and tutting and sadness – not anger. Nobody actually pulls me up on my shitty behaviour anymore.

Because they've given up. Everyone's given up on me. But not Michael.

Not even now I'm not his problem anymore.

"My bus left already…" I tell him.

"I wouldn't trust you on the fucking bus anyway," he says. "You're coming with me. I'm driving you straight to their front door and handing you over."

I smirk. "But you've been–"

"Drinking?" he interrupts. "Thanks to you my first beer is still on the table."

I'm trying to summon up the voice to say thanks, or whatever I'm supposed to say to shit like this, but I don't get a chance. The door opens to my right and the posh suited guy steps out.

They stare at each other, him and Michael, and Michael loosens his grip on me.

I wish he hadn't. I liked the way he held me there.

"What the hell are you doing?" posh guy asks, and Michael groans.

"Taking Carrie back to her parents."

I can't bring myself to argue. It's a first for me.

They stare at each other a long time, and I fidget, scuffing my boot along the brickwork.

"Text me when you're done and make it quick. This is way out of order," the posh guy says, and I wonder for a second if they are… but they can't be, because I've seen the way Michael looks at me, even though he tries to hide it, even though he doesn't want to.

Posh guy leaves and I let out a sigh. "He your boyfriend? He's a bit stiff."

"He's a friend," Michael tells me. "We were having a beer."

I watch the guy walk up the street. He's hot for an old dude, looking ripped under that pompous suit he's wearing.

I kinda wish they were into each other, maybe I could, I dunno.

It's stupid. Dumb. I push the thought away.

"I don't want to go back to Rosie and Bill's," I say, but Michael shakes his head.

"You're out of fucking luck," he tells me, and he's not playing around. His voice is edgy outside of his office, edgy and deep and dangerous, even though I don't feel in danger at all. "I'm taking you home right fucking now."

I hate it when people touch me. I hate walking down the street attached to someone else, but when Michael takes my wrist in his hand and leads me across the street, I don't mind it at all.

Michael isn't like other people. Not like anyone I've ever met.

He won't be played. He won't be pushed away. He won't be screamed off me.

Not yet, anyway.

And I don't mind that at all, either.

Three

MICHAEL

don't let go of Carrie's wrist as I head across the High Street towards my apartment building's car parking area. I curse under my breath as I check for bystanders. This town is full of eyes and ears and there's every chance the fake news that I dragged Carrie back to mine will hit my office before I do in the morning. I could do without that, not least because I'll have questions to answer that won't look great on my employment file. I don't give a fuck what they say about me, but if stupid rumours were to impact the kids on my caseload… It doesn't bear thinking about.

I'm crazy for getting involved, but I can't stop. My feet take it upon themselves to keep on walking, my heart hammering while my mind spins with justifications for my actions, even though I know there are other ways to handle this.

I could've looked up Rosie and Bill's number and called them out to collect her. I could've opened up the office and made her wait in reception with me until they arrived.

I pull my car keys from my pocket the moment my car is in sight and switch off the central locking. Carrie tugs at my arm and I turn to realise she's staring up at my apartment block. It's nothing fancy, just a regular brick building. Mine is the top floor, and Pam Clowes, who works with me, has the ground. I really fucking hope she's not at her kitchen window.

She's not. Thank God for small mercies.

"Neat place," Carrie says, and I'd think she was being sarcastic if I didn't know her tone better.

"It's alright," I tell her, tugging her along the remaining distance.

"Which one's yours?" she asks, and I definitely shouldn't tell her that, but I do anyway.

I point out my living room window as I slip into the driver's seat. I'm relieved when she drops into the passenger side and buckles herself in without argument.

"Are you feeling sick? Queasy?" I'm already scouting the backseat for a paper bag or something but she laughs at me.

"I can handle my drink."

"Sure you can."

"I can," she insists, "I only had one or two, no big deal."

"Don't take me for a fucking idiot," I say as I turn the key in the ignition. "Good job I was there or who knows what state you'd have ended up in. You don't want to be associating with Eddie Stevens, he'll lead you nowhere good."

I pull the car out onto the main road, fighting the urge to stare at her and not at where I'm going. I know Bill and Rosie's place. It's a pretty white house set back from the lane into Lydbrook, the chocolate-box picture of tranquillity – which has no doubt been shattered since this bundle of trouble arrived on the scene.

"Do you want to call ahead?" I ask her, "maybe you should let them know you're on your way home?"

"They won't care."

It doesn't matter how many times she says it, I don't believe that's the case. I tell her so and she spins in her seat to glare at me.

"Why do you always have to see the best in people all the time? The world isn't like that, *Michael*. It's mean and shitty and nobody gives two fucking craps about a nasty little *gypsy* like me. You're a fool. A fucking idiot."

"Well, this *fucking idiot* gives *two fucking craps* about getting you back home safe, Carrie, so I guess the whole entire universe can't be entirely mean and shitty now, can it?"

She sighs. "Maybe the whole entire universe except you."

"I'm flattered you think I'm that exceptional a member of the human race, but I'm simply one of many trying to do their best. The world is full of us, maybe you could try letting us help sometime."

"I'll let *you* help," she whispers and I'm so surprised I do a double take. The evening light through the windscreen dances across her features, and her eyes look big and sad. She pulls her knees up and rests her dirty boots on the dashboard, oblivious to the mess she'll be making.

But I don't even care.

"*How* can I help?" I say, eyes firmly back on the road. "Just tell me, Carrie. Because I'll do whatever I can."

"You can take me away from this shitty place." Her voice is quiet and breathy.

I remind myself she's a drunk young woman who probably doesn't mean half of this.

"I mean it," she says, as though she can read my mind. "You and me. It could be an adventure."

"You'll have plenty of adventures with plenty of people," I tell her. "But right now you need to be settled and safe. I can speak to the right agencies, we can get you set up somewhere, even if it's not Bill and Rosie's. I'm sure I can speak to the college, too."

The thump of her fist on the window takes me aback. "I don't *want* any of that. I want *you*."

"And I'm your caseworker," I tell her. "I have a duty of care to your wellbeing."

"Not anymore," she says, and I'm pleased to pass the sign for Lydbrook. My neck feels itchy under my collar, my palms sweaty on the wheel.

She points out Bill and Rosie's on the right, but I'm already turning. I pull onto their driveway and their Labrador starts barking from the porch.

Carrie is out of the car in a heartbeat. She gives me nothing but a cursory *thanks* before she slams the passenger door and heads to the house alone, but that's not how this ends.

I follow her, catching her on the doorstep just as she's trying the handle.

It's locked.

It surprises me, but it is.

She hammers on the wood with her fist.

"Do you not have a key?" I ask.

She shakes her head. "They don't want me to have one."

Don't trust her with one, more likely. I shouldn't blame them, knowing her, but I can't help but feel hurt on her behalf.

It's Bill who comes to the front door. He looks drawn and grey as he answers, his face a grimace until he sees me standing alongside his ward.

"Michael," he says, ignoring her completely.

I shake the offered hand. "Carrie needed a ride home."

He doesn't even look at her. "Up to no good, no doubt. Drinking. Drugs, probably."

I don't think Carrie does drugs. Call me naive, but I've seen plenty of youngsters who do. She's never struck me as one of them. Especially not given the way she so poorly handles her alcohol.

He steps aside to let her pass and she brushes by with her arms folded tight.

"Say thanks to Michael," he barks and she throws him the finger on her way upstairs.

"Already did, asshole."

I cringe as a door slams after her.

"She's... got some challenges..." I begin, but Bill waves me silent.

"She's got more than some challenges, Michael. The girl's a devil woman. We can't take it anymore, Rosie's nerves are shot."

I take a breath, trying to find words, but he's shaking his head.

"Don't even try, Mike. I've already told the agency *no*. We can't do it anymore. It's not fair on any of us. I'll have her here until her birthday, but after that she's on her own. The housing will have to find her somewhere, emergency accommodation or something. Maybe she could go to one of those drugs hostels."

"She's not on drugs," I say. *Not yet, anyway.* "And she won't let me help her, not with the agencies. If you throw her out, Bill, she'll be on the streets. Nobody will take her in, not unless she goes through the proper channels."

He steps out onto the porch and pulls the door closed behind him, shunting his dog inside with his boot.

"She's not our problem," he tells me. "And she's not yours, either. Believe me, Michael, the girl's bad news. We've had nearly fifty kids here over the years, some of them good, some of them with issues. She's the worst. She steals, she lies, she smashes things. She has no respect. She throws everything back in our faces. She spat in Rosie's stew last Sunday. Spat in it and laughed."

I feel a lurch in my stomach as he rubs his temples.

"She's got some issues," I say again and he sighs.

"We're out," he says.

"Bill, maybe if I could speak with Rosie, maybe we could..."

"We're OUT," he repeats, and he's serious. Deadly serious. "The girl is a vicious little bitch. She's a fucking nightmare. A disgusting, vindictive little shit."

His hate knocks me sideways. Hate and disgust, and something else.

He wanted her, I can see it in his eyes, just like Carrie said. But whatever was there is done and gone. He's at the end with her, that much is obvious.

"Bill, please," I begin, but he holds his hand up.

"Thanks for bringing her back out here," he says. "You're a good man. A better man than me." He slaps a big hand onto my arm and grips hard, and for a moment I wonder about Carrie's bruises. Her allegations.

He smiles his usual, kindly smile, and I realise I'm not even vaguely objective, not anymore. She's suckered me in and I'm reeling. Lost on this crazy fantasy of the wild girl with her drunk whispers.

"Be careful," he tells me. "She's..."

"She's what?"

"She's spiteful, difficult. She's nasty. But she'll hook you into her shit if you're not careful. She knows how to play a game, that one."

I've no doubt she's all of those things, and I've no doubt Bill got caught up in the allure of the girl, but saying anymore would be wasting my breath. These people are done. Nothing I say here will make any difference, I know when a battle's been lost – and Rosie and Bill are definitely done with this one.

As I say my goodbyes and walk back to my car, I assure myself that I'm just a guy doing my job, just as I do for all those on my books. Just as I would care for any other kid who needed a ride home after a stupid drinking session.

I assure myself that Carrie is just a girl who's off my caseload now. That maybe Bill and Rosie will sort her out somewhere to go before they really do throw her out onto the streets. I tell myself Bill is just having an off day, that they're frustrated and probably worried.

But none of this is true, and I know it the moment I look back and see Carrie's face at the upstairs window.

It's her eyes. So sad.

Her smile, melancholic and broken – a rare sliver of honesty under her bravado.

She holds up a hand and waves goodbye, and I realise how small she looks up there. She's not short, it's not that. It's her frame, willowy and wasted and... fragile.

Carrie Wells looks fragile, and she's looked many ways over the months but fragile isn't one of them.

Our eyes meet and hold. My breath feels tight in my throat.

The pain of failing her hits hard, right in my gut, and I sigh as I realise all over again that she's just a kid who's had a rough start. A girl who doesn't yet know how to make better choices. Who doesn't trust. Who doesn't even know how.

A girl who needs some stability.

A girl who needs love.

But I can't be the one to give it to her.

I'll try again with the agencies in the morning. I'll set up some new referrals and hope upon hope Carrie lets someone help her.

I wave goodbye, and I really have to mean it.

For my own sanity.

CARRIE

Bill doesn't even care that I hear him. In the early days they would whisper or talk about me behind closed doors where they didn't know I was listening. But not now.

Now Bill and Rosie don't give a shit that I know what they think of me.

Bill's words carry loud and clear. The little window in the room I sleep in is open, and his voice reaches me perfectly. So does Michael's.

The girl is a vicious little bitch. She's a fucking nightmare. A disgusting, vindictive little shit.

Bill, please...

Of course the answer was no. I knew it would be. They hate me, both of them, and I don't blame them.

I didn't spit in Rosie's stew though, I just pretended to. She wouldn't believe me when I said I hadn't really. She threw the whole lot in the sink and told me I was a *horrible girl*. And then she cried.

She flapped her arms about and called for Bill and told him she was done with me, that they were all done with me.

And I shrugged and said I didn't care, that I didn't give a fuck about her shitty stew, either. I said it tasted like shit and she'd done us all a fucking favour by throwing it out.

I don't know when to stop when I start, that's the problem.

I don't know how to stop the way I feel about Michael, either.

I watch him watching me. He looks as defeated as I feel deep inside. He looks like he doesn't want to leave, even though I know he really didn't want to bring me here.

It's probably just because he's one of those *good guys*. There aren't many of those about, but if they really exist, he's definitely one of them.

I hold up a hand and wave, hoping he'll wave back. Maybe he'll smile.

Michael's got a great smile. He's got a great scowl, too. He looks so fiery and hardcore when he gets angry, and it comes more natural to him than he seems to think it should.

He doesn't have any idea how hot he is. Most hot guys know it. Even most of the not-so-hot guys think they're God's gift around here, but Michael is the real deal and he doesn't have a clue.

His hair is messy even though I'm sure he tries to keep it looking smart. It's probably not even a style, not on purpose, but it looks just right on him. Dark and messy and cute. Cool, even though I'm sure he doesn't mean it to be.

I think most guys look like dicks in suits, but he looks just right. He only has three ties, and one of those is a shitty garish purple one that makes me smile when he's not looking. Once I saw him walking through his office, and he had stripy socks on, that made me smile too but he thought I was laughing at him.

On the surface he seems so professional and in control, strong and supportive and awesome at what he does. But I can't help but notice this other side of him, the side maybe I shouldn't see.

The gawky, kind of cute side. The side that doesn't match even though he tries. The side that breaks the rules and brings me home when I've been drinking, and swears at me. The side that looks at me the way he's looking at me now.

He does wave and my heart aches for him. It's a sad goodbye.

He hovers for a minute before he gets into his car, and I wonder what he's thinking.

I wonder if he believes everything Bill said about me. I wonder if he knows now that I wasn't lying when I said they don't give a shit about me anymore, and there was no way an apology would make any difference to them now.

Like it or not, I'll be on my own in a few days. *Welcome to adulthood, Carrie.* I can hardly wait.

I watch his car pull away and keep watching the road until he's long gone. The day is drawing in outside and I love the way the birds sing around here.

I love Bill and Rosie's house, even though I would never say it to their face. I love their dog, Harry, even though I never fuss him when they're around to see it. I walk him through the fields at the back of the garden but they don't know that. I always hang his leash up exactly as they left it, and I've never been caught yet.

They'd just think I was up to no good if they did catch me, so it's our little secret, Harry and mine.

Michael's place looks small and clearly has no garden. There would be no birds singing and no fields to walk in and no Harry, and loving those things is in my blood, being Romany and all, but even so, I'd still consider giving up my dreams of a wagon and the open road if he'd let me stay with him.

I hear Bill and Rosie in the kitchen downstairs loading up the dishwasher. My stomach rumbles, but they don't offer me anything to eat, and I don't expect them to.

I missed dinnertime.

I'll have to sneak downstairs when they're in bed and grab something from their pantry. They've started hiding stuff from me these past few weeks, but I know Rosie keeps some chocolate in her sewing tin.

They've already got a kid lined up to replace me, I heard them on the phone to the agency talking about it. I think he's called Leo.

I hope he's a better kid for them than I've been, and I hope he likes this place as much as I do.

The thought of leaving here makes me feel more upset than it should. I ball my hands into fists and choke back stupid tears that I don't deserve.

I could've stayed if I was better.

I could've stayed if they hadn't seen the bruises on my arms and thought I was into drugs or self-harm, or a load of other things that made them look at me in those ways I hate.

Pity and fear and disappointment.

Maybe I wouldn't have been such a bitch to them then.

I'm not into drugs and I'm not into self-harm, I'm just sick of telling people that when they never believe me anyway.

I have to wait a long time for Rosie and Bill to go to bed, and when they do I find Rosie has moved her chocolate stash from the sewing tin.

There's a note on the side, scrawled out for me.

If we don't deserve respect enough for you to join us for dinner, you don't deserve to eat our food.

She's left a couple of slices of bread out for me, but I can't even find the butter. She's hidden it. She's hidden everything.

The tears sting, but I don't let them fall.

I'll be gone before morning, eighteen be fucked.

And I won't even be sad.

I pack up a backpack of my clothes and my few stupid trinkets, and I kiss Harry goodbye before I leave. I have to ditch out of the living room window because the front door is locked, but I'm as quiet as I can be, as quiet as a mouse.

And then I'm gone.

Four

JACK

wait for a text from Michael letting me know he's done dropping his drunk infatuation back home where she belongs, but it doesn't come. I despair for the guy and his midlife crisis.

This thing with Carrie Wells, it isn't like him. Mike is responsible and considered. He plays by more rules than he should in life, certainly more than I do, and if there's one he should choose to break it's definitely not this one.

I'm about to call the crazy sonofabitch when I hear his car pull up outside. He's had the same car for over a decade, I'd recognise the sound anywhere.

I've already opened the door when he reaches my doorstep. He brushes past me without a word, and I follow him on through to the kitchen to grab the beer we didn't manage at Drury's.

I hand him a bottle and he slumps himself against my kitchen island.

"They're going to throw her onto the streets," he says, and I sigh.

"Not. Your. Problem."

"I've been working with her for over five months," he tells me, like I don't know already. "I can't just turn my back on her, not like that."

"So refer her to someone who can help. Again."

He takes a swig of beer. "I doubt she'll co-operate. She doesn't trust anyone."

"You tried. That's all you can do."

"I guess you're right."

He doesn't believe me, and I know it. It's written all over his face. In Mike's sweet deluded mind he's on a one-man mission to eliminate all youth problems in our poor rural county. He thinks *I* work hard, but I have nothing on him. I leave my work at the office every evening, he lives his 24/7. He never forgets those kids on his books, never forgets a face or a sad story.

For all my sighs and grimacing and talk of cold, hard reality, I admire him for it. My work is based around simple risk analysis, working out the right insurance premiums for the right clients. His is emotional, turbulent. Difficult.

Yet I'm the one who lives in the big country pad with a Range Rover. Go fucking figure. Society has this shit upside down.

"You have to let this go, Mike," I say and the guy practically flinches.

"I'll let it go when I know she's safe."

"And if she isn't safe? If she ends up clearing off back to Gloucester and slumming it on the streets?"

He shrugs. "Then I'll keep trying."

"You'll follow her around the back alleys like a stalker? Bring her a hot soup every evening?" I stare at him. "Or smuggle her into your bedroom and hope your neighbours don't talk?"

His eyes flash with disgust. "I never would."

I can't help but smirk. "If you say so. That girl's all woman, Michael. She's definitely all of eighteen, in spirit as well as in body, give or take a few measly days."

"She was my client."

"A pretty one, if a little uncouth."

I'm underplaying it. For all I've heard about Carrie Wells over the past few months, the descriptions didn't do her justice. She's stunning. Even a grotty bomber jacket and grubby boots can't hide that. Her eyes are pale and piercing, her nose has a pixie quality about it that matches the rest of her. She's fey and feral, and totally not the kind of girl either of us old farts should be ogling.

"She's beautiful," Mike says, and his eyes have this worryingly wistful quality about them. "It'll get her into trouble."

"*More* trouble."

He groans. "Eddie Stevens is a waste of space, we both know it. She'd have ended up in his bed tonight if I hadn't stepped in."

"You don't know that." I take another swig of beer. "And Eddie Stevens *is* a waste of space, but he was another one whose corner you were fighting a few years back. You don't always win the fight and you know it. She's another one, you just gotta let it go."

"Eddie Stevens was different," he tells me. "Eddie still had his family. Eddie's problems weren't nearly so marked as Carrie's."

I'm talking to a brick wall. Mike's whole body is tense. His brows are heavy and his shoulders look rigid. I'm never worried about him, not really, because he's the kind of guy who never does anything crazy. I'm the one who makes the impulsive decisions. I'm the risk taker. But right now, looking at him, I've nothing but dread at the prospect of leaving for a conference in Berlin tomorrow.

"Are you gonna be alright?" I ask him. "I can cancel…"

He holds up a hand. "Of course I'll be alright."

"I can go next year if you need me around. I'll send Tom instead of me."

He shakes his head. "Christ, Jack, don't be so fucking melodramatic. I'm sure I'll survive without doing anything too radical for the ten long days you're away."

I hope he's right.

I could send Tom Holland, my product manager, but I've already lined up seminars I want to attend, plus the networking opportunities are going to be good this year. This conference is for proper business, not just a jolly out of the office. I'm still not feeling entirely easy about the prospect of leaving, though.

Michael doesn't have all that many friends. He has his work and he has his colleagues – a drink out with them for birthdays and Christmas and leaving parties, but that's about all. Being with Molly for so long cut off his already limited social circle, and to be honest, I'm surprised they didn't survive long distance since the two of them were so ingrained in their relationship. I thought they'd be together forever, for better or worse. The split came as a shock.

I thought he was good with it, and good with being single, but this thing with Carrie leads me to believe he's not so happy with his life outside work after all.

He'd say this is ridiculous, and he's perfectly happy with his lot. He'd say he's too engrossed in his work to socialise all that much outside of it. Plus, he'd say he has family. He sees his folks every month down in Devon – they surprised us all when they opted to retire to the coast, not least Michael – but I guess the weekend trips are a good change of scene for him.

If you traced both of our family trees back through the ages they'd have this place right through them. We're from these parts, my parents are still down in Coleford, just a few miles away. Michael's got cousins here, and an elderly aunt and uncle at the care home in Lydbrook, but besides that it's really just us for him here now.

I pick up my tablet and thumb through my emails, checking my flights again for tomorrow. My schedule is rammed, back to back meetings in London before I fly late evening. I'm seriously considering firing an email off to Tom to get him to take my place at everything when Mike sighs at me.

"Seriously, Jack, what do you think I'm going to do? Elope with her? She'll be at Rosie and Bill's for a few days and then I'll do my best to hook her up through the proper channels."

"And that's it? No ridiculous maverick stunt moves? No smuggling her into your apartment?"

He smiles like I'm a crazy man, but he's the crazy man these past few months. "I'm sure I'll be able to hold things together until you get back."

"Fine." I put my tablet back on standby then finish up my beer. I open the fridge as he finishes his. "Are you having another? A goodbye drink before I head overseas?"

It's nice to see him relax a little. "As long as you don't mind an overnight guest."

I hand him a fresh beer. "When have I ever minded an overnight guest? Stay the whole week if you want, keep an eye on the place."

That would suit me well enough and he knows it. This place is too big to be empty, not so much in that I'm worried of a burglary attempt, it's just old. A little rough around the edges. Places like this need to be kept an eye on.

He pulls his keys out of his pocket and my front door key jangles on his keyring. "I'll make myself at home. Scope out your porn subscriptions on your big screen."

He's not even joking and it makes me smile. "Might as well get the best out of them, I pay enough. At least it might keep you out of trouble."

Somehow I doubt that.

Call it instinct, but there's a niggle in my gut. Something that tells me I'm walking away from a disaster about to happen.

It eases off a little as we move to the living room and kick back with beers as usual. Talk of Carrie eases up, and it leaves me no reason to red flag my travel plans.

So I keep my schedule intact.

We drink and make the same old in-jokes we've always made. We talk through the same old stories we've relived a thousand times, and at the end of it all, when it's past two sensible men's bedtimes on a work night, we head upstairs and I finish up my packing for Germany.

I'm gone before him in the morning, and I hover one last time on the driveway. I fire off a text before I drive away, one last passing message before he's on his own for the next ten days.

Don't do anything bloody crazy.

I just hope he heeds the advice.

CARRIE

I walked for hours before I was too tired to keep going. I wake up feeling groggy, my neck stiff from using my backpack as a pillow. It takes me a second to remember where I am.

Shit.

I'm in one of the old bike sheds at the back of Lydney Primary School. My arms feel stiff as I stretch them and my feet are like blocks of ice in my crappy boots. I'm starving hungry, too. My belly rumbles the minute I sit up, and I have to fight back the panic as I realise I don't have either food or money to help fill it back up again.

Part of me wants to go back to Bill and Rosie's and say sorry. Maybe if I asked kindly enough, maybe if I begged… but there's no way I'm gonna beg those dicks. No way.

They hate me and I hate them. I can take care of myself, just as my ancestors did.

I get to my feet and shake them out a bit, trying to get back the feeling. I'm not scared of the outdoors, it's in my blood to belong here. I'm not scared of being alone, either. I'm not scared of anything.

It's just… I don't know what it is. I don't know why one night away from a warm bed makes me feel so weak and small, but it does. I fucking hate that it does.

I take my bottle of water from my backpack and I'm disappointed to find there's only a couple of sips left. I'll need to find a tap and fill it up, and then I'm going to need to find something to eat and work out a plan to get out of here.

There's only one place I can head, and it's going to take some walking, but I can make it. I'll need to stay off the main roads in case Bill and Rosie call the cops and tell them I'm missing, but I can't imagine they care enough to do that.

She's a fucking nightmare. A disgusting, vindictive little shit.

They'll probably be glad I've gone. They'll probably hope I'm dead in a ditch somewhere just so I never show back up there.

We're right in the middle of woodland here, and I'm sure I can keep off the main routes as I head back towards Gloucester. It's got to be twenty miles away at least, and my boots aren't the best for long distance, but I'll need to get there before dark if I want to call on Eli. Like I said, I'm not scared of anything, but the alleys around his place after dark sure make me edgy.

I'm edgy around him after dark, too, but beggars can't be choosers. Hopefully he'll have something for me to eat at least.

If I had any credit left on my mobile I'd consider calling ahead, but I don't.

It'll be a risk showing up there without something to give him, but Rosie hasn't left any cash around for weeks now. I'll have to turn up emptyhanded and there's fuck all I can do about that unless I take to breaking and entering before the morning's out.

I dip into the public toilets on the way through town to fill up my bottle.

It's still early and I've hardly slept. My face looks pale and drawn and my eyes look sunken. My hair is a crazy mess and looks little better for me running my fingers through it. It'll have to do as it is.

I try to keep my spirits up as I set off. I'm going to take a route across the countryside, so at least there's that to look forward to. I conjure up crazy fantasies as I walk, imagining that I'll run into a travelling community with traditional wagons. Maybe one of them will be a distant relative and there could be a big happy reunion. Maybe they'll cry and say they've been looking for me my whole life. Maybe they have dogs, too. They'll surely have dogs, and horses.

I'm happily lost in the fantasy as I stumble upon Michael's apartment block. I hold my breath as I pass the entrance to his car park, and all thoughts of my long-lost traveller family disappear at the prospect I could knock on his door for real and ask if he really can help me after all.

My heart will almost let me. *Almost.*

I'm almost at the rear door of his block when I think better of it.

He'll just take me back to Bill and Rosie's.

Once I realise that cold fact, it's easy to turn away, even though I don't want to.

It's only when I'm on my way out again that I register there's no sign of his old blue Ford. I guess he didn't come home last night, and I don't know why I feel so miserable at the thought of him being with a girlfriend somewhere, but it quickens my pace as I power on.

Of course he has a girlfriend, why wouldn't he?

He's old. Older than me. He must be at least forty, and that means he could be married or anything for all I know.

Maybe he laughs about me with her. Maybe he tells her I'm just a *fucking nightmare*, and a *vicious little bitch*. Maybe that's why he was always so cool and calm when I asked him disgusting questions in his office.

Most people hate that, it makes them uncomfortable. Bill left the house and slammed the door behind him when I told him I knew he wanted to lick my pussy, but not Michael.

Maybe Michael doesn't give two fucks about my pussy, because he's riding some gorgeous bitch of his own every fucking night after work.

What nobody gets is that this crap is all talk with me.

I've messed about with guys, but nothing serious. I've had boyfriends, but they were only stupid young pricks who didn't mean anything.

I've not been anywhere near an actual man, and I nearly crapped myself the one time Bill finally did answer my question and told me that *yes, he did want to lick my pussy*. He hated me even more after I laughed in his face and told him I was gonna tell Rosie and call the cops.

I didn't do either, but that didn't matter to him. He's been gunning for me ever since.

My phone starts bleeping in my backpack when I'm a couple of miles outside Lydney. One incoming call and then silence. I check out the handset and find the voicemail icon, but I haven't got enough credit to listen.

It doesn't matter anyway. I'm on my own now, on the road and happy for it. I'll only stay with Eli a short while, just enough time to try to earn a bit of cash and find a way to join some travellers somewhere.

He always promised we could go together one day, but over the past few years – since he's been dealing drugs – I don't think he has any intention of really coming with me. He never says he gives a shit about me anymore either.

I wonder if it was always all just a load of empty words. Promises made out of thin air meaning sweet fuck all.

I have to double up on socks by lunchtime, and my belly is rumbling worse than ever. I pick some blackberries from a hedge but they don't do shit to stop the hunger. My water runs out not long after and fuck knows where I'm going to find another tap to fill it back up. I consider knocking on someone's door and asking to borrow their bathroom, but I'm too worried they'll call the cops on me.

By the time I reach the outskirts of Gloucester my feet are so blistered I'm limping. My shoulders are aching from my backpack and my lips are dry as fucking paper.

My mind is so numb that all I can do is count my steps to keep on walking.

One. Two. Three.

Twenty-nine.

On and on and on until I'm in well into the city.

I drop my backpack to the floor when I finally get to Eli's. I hammer his door with all the strength I have left in my hands, and even then it takes him a minute to open it.

He used to be pleased to see me, but not anymore.

He leans out and looks behind me, checking for other people – like I've ever brought anyone along to this shithole with me.

"What you doing here?" he asks, like my backpack doesn't speak for itself.

"I left," I grunt. "Gonna let me stay or what?"

He takes a drag on his skinny roll-up and I hold up my fingers for him to give it to me, but he doesn't. "Bring any cash?"

I knew this was coming, and I knew I'd feel like crap to say no. I shake my head. "Rosie's been careful. She even hides the chocolate now."

He laughs and I'm not sure it's not at my expense. "Stupid bitch."

I wonder if he's talking about her or me. Maybe both of us.

"Can I stay then or what?"

He smirks. "Or what?"

I fold my arms. "I don't fucking *need* you, Eli. I'm here because I want to be, not because I'm fucking desperate. I can take care of myself."

"You can't take care of yourself enough to outsmart that snooty fucking bitch and bring me some fucking cash though, can you? How you gonna pay your way?"

I shrug. "I don't need her cash, I'll make my own."

"Oh yeah? You gonna be earning your keep?"

I nod. Grit my teeth. "I'll pull my weight."

I stare at him, taking in the tattoos on his neck, the buzz of close cropped hair on his scalp. The way he could be such a looker if he wasn't always so filthy and scruffy.

I bet they say the same about me.

"Alright," he says finally. "You can stay, but you better make it worth my while."

The place smells rancid as I step foot in there, but I'm done caring about any of that. He doesn't offer to take my backpack and I don't expect him to. I don't expect him to do shit for me other than give me somewhere warm to sleep tonight and maybe a bit of food in my belly.

I set my backpack down and take a seat on his grimy armchair, choking back the sadness that this is really it for the time being.

I've almost convinced myself it's going to be fine when I see the package of white powder on the coffee table.

I've almost convinced myself I made the right decision when he snorts up a big fat line of it.

I hate him when he snorts this shit.

I hate the person it turns him into.

But it's too late for all that now. I'm just grateful when he makes me a sandwich.

Five

MICHAEL

I *have to use my lunch* break to make agency calls on behalf of a girl who's no longer on my books. I take a bite of my sandwich, cursing that I'm spending so much time on hold. I've a lot of people to speak with, and not a huge amount of time to do it in.

The result: more of the same old shit.

They'll need her to register. They'll need some form of ID. They'll need to do an assessment.

They'll be able to do none of those things unless Carrie actually agrees to toe the line.

I'm exasperated by the time I look up Rosie and Bill's number at the end of my shift. One last shot, that's what I tell myself. One last attempt to reason with them and get them on side enough to keep her room open for her until we can get her into these appointments.

It's Rosie who answers. She sighs as she registers it's me.

I launch quickly into my monologue, telling her I know how hard they've worked with Carrie, how much time they've put in, and how difficult this has been on all of them, but if she could just find it within herself to give this one final push…

It's another sigh that cuts me off.

"You're too late," she says. "She's gone."

My mouth drops before I reply. "Sorry?"

"She took off this morning. Left with all her clothes and everything."

"And where has she –"

"Don't know, don't really care," she interrupts, and it pains me.

"She didn't say?"

"Didn't see her. She'd slipped out the living room window before Bill and I got up."

I'm lost for words, my pulse heavy in my temples. "Have you called the police?"

She tuts like I've insulted her. I probably have.

"Of course we did. They won't do anything until she's been missing forty-eight hours, not given the trouble we've had before. By then she'll be eighteen. Not our problem." She pauses. "And not yours, either."

Her tone is kind but it's pointed. I've known these people a long time, and they know me. "She's not on your books anymore, is she?" Rosie asks, already knowing full well she isn't.

It's my turn to sigh. "No, not officially."

"Then I think it's about time we all let her go, Mike. We've all tried."

Not hard enough.

I can't say that to her, not given how hard they've worked for those in need over the years, so I don't.

"You'll let me know if you hear anything?"

She tuts again. "You'll be the first to know. It's not a long list."

I say thanks, and I'm surprised at how clammy my palms feel when I hang up.

Gone.

She's really gone.

The thought of her being alone out there is a kick to my gut. She could be cold, hungry. Lost, for all I know.

We're surrounded by miles of woodland – she could be trekking through there for days. She could trip and break and ankle. Those boots of hers have seen better days. They wouldn't hold up to that.

I've grabbed my car keys before I've regained my composure. And I'm driving the streets before I've even contemplated what my strategy is.

There isn't one. She could be anywhere.

I head out towards Gloucester, scouring the verges for sight of her. Nothing.

I double back and drive the country lanes through the forest. Nothing.

I pass through Lydbrook three times, asking dog walkers if they've seen her around. Nothing.

Finally, I drive into the heart of Gloucester itself, not caring that the night is closing in and I haven't stopped for dinner. I wander streets I shouldn't be wandering, asking questions of those settling down outdoors for the night.

I'm crazy and I know it.

I shouldn't be doing this, and not even Jack is around to talk some sense into me.

Finally, after stopping at all the picnic areas through the forest on my way back home, shining my flashlight around like a madman, I accept defeat for the evening.

I grab some instant noodles and eat them in a daze. I do internet searches on my work laptop, even though I know my history is logged, and I ring the local police and hospitals before I allow myself to get some sleep.

Nothing.

Carrie Wells has gone.

I don't sleep a wink.

CARRIE

The sleeping bag at Eli's stinks of weed like the rest of the place. I know they say it's nature's herb and all that, but it's always smelled like crap to me. It's only ever made me sick and giggly. I don't really do giggly, so I'm better off without the shitty stuff.

Eli says it will *chill me fucking out*, but I do *chilled* even less than I do giggly. He stays up late with the TV on loud. The room is full of the stench, and when I hunker down under my grotty covers that's when I come to realise *everything* smells of it here.

I probably smell like it here.

He has a couple of cats that he doesn't let out. Their litter tray stinks even worse than the weed. Some random ex-girlfriend left them here, he told me once. He hardly feeds them, so I share my ham sandwich with them, loving the way they purr as they settle down under the covers with me.

Maybe I can take them on the road with me, but they'll probably run away.

I wouldn't blame them.

I'd run away from here too if I didn't need to stay warm for the night.

Eli isn't coming on the road with me, not like he promised. We talked about it earlier, but he'd already been snorting his white stash by then. He told me he wasn't ditching this place for a crappy fucking gig in a caravan somewhere. He told me he doesn't love me, either. I already knew that. I already knew all of it.

He says I'm going to have to pay my keep before I leave here, that food doesn't come cheap even though I've only had a couple of slices of bread and I had to tear the crusts off because they were mouldy. It just reinforces everything I already know.

People are dicks, and nobody gives a fuck. Not Bill and Rosie, and not Eli either.

I'd leave tonight if the memory of my ice-block feet this morning wasn't still fresh. I'd wait until he passed out and slip past him, maybe try to find some cash to take with me on the way. Cash or drugs to sell. I'm sure I could get a decent price for them, just to set me up.

"Ain't you gonna watch this with me?" he grunts, and I curse that he knows I'm still awake.

"I'm fucking tired. Walked all last fucking night."

"Yeah, well, you'll be walking all through this fucking one if you keep speaking to me like I'm a soft fucking asshole."

It stings to bite my tongue.

"Lee's coming over," he tells me, and I cringe inside. "He's looking forward to seeing you."

"He can go fuck himself."

Eli laughs. "He's hoping you'll do that for him. Says he'll give you a tenner towards your caravan fund."

Lee Davis was a mistake of mine. A stupid idiot who told me I was special.

Like I said, I've never been anywhere near a real man. Lee Davis is nothing but a joke. A druggie joke who thinks he's a hard man. He's not. I punch harder than he does.

Still, how it ended between us is all the incentive I need to get myself up and out of there. I move the cats and climb out of the sleeping bag. I head to Eli's grotty bathroom and put on another couple of layers under my clothes.

He doesn't even look at me when I head back through and pick up my backpack.

"Where do you think you're fucking going?"

"I'm gonna make a move," I say. "Gonna head down south. See if I can get to the coast."

He laughs, points to the armchair. "Sit your skinny ass back down."

I head for the front door regardless, hissing under my breath as he catches me. He moves fast for a stoner. That'll be the coke. His breath is hot and fucking gross. I give him the finger even as he pins against the wall.

"Fuck off," I hiss. "I'm fucking leaving."

"You always were a snotty fucking bitch," he says. "I told you. Lee's coming. He wants to see you."

"And I don't want to fucking see him."

"Tough fucking shit," he says and then his eyes soften, just a bit.

For that moment he's the Eli I always knew. The boy who could convince me to do anything, just with a smile, even though I knew I'd get all the blame for it.

"There's some pasta in the cupboard. Why don't you make yourself a proper dinner?"

I glare at him. "I can't pay you for it."

He shrugs. "We're friends. We help each other."

Friends.

That's a fucking joke.

But I'm hungry, even after a crappy sandwich. I know it's cold outside and I don't want to walk through those alleys on my own, not right now when I'm already tired enough to drop.

"Alright," I say and he smiles.

"That's my cute little sis."

He ruffles my hair and I cringe.

I'm not his sister and I never have been.

He lets me go and I drop my backpack. I head through to the kitchen with a sigh and he takes his TV show off pause.

"Make me some as well while you're at it," he says. "I'm fucking starving."

I was only pretending when I spat in Rosie's stew, I'm not tonight.

MICHAEL

Three days and three long nights.

I've been calling every agency I can think of through my lunch breaks and driving around the streets looking for her every night, despite knowing full well that she's probably long gone. I wonder how she celebrated becoming an official adult. I wonder if she celebrated at all.

I found myself at Rosie and Bill's front door last night, just to check in person that they hadn't heard anything. Their eyes said it all. They told me she's a lost cause and it's sad I haven't accepted that yet. But I haven't.

I can't.

We've never had Carrie Well's mobile number on her case file, simply because she refused to give it to anyone, me included. It was Rosie's parting gift to me, followed up with the assurance that there's no way the *madam* will answer, but it still felt like I'd been handed the Holy Grail as I left their doorstep and headed back to my car. I pulled over before I was even back in Lydney, my heart thumping as I keyed her number into my mobile.

Rosie was right, of course. The call rang straight to voicemail.

They've gone straight to voicemail ever since.

When the office is quiet and my meetings are done for the day, I sit back in my chair and stare at my handset. Nothing from Carrie, and only a string of unanswered texts from Jack in Germany. I haven't replied because I daren't. I can't lie, and the moment I tell him Carrie has taken off somewhere and I'm on a one-man mission to locate her and solve her housing crisis, he'll either have me committed or fly back home to scream some sense into me.

If Carrie would just pick up her pissing messages and think to let me know she was safe, life would be a whole lot easier. I've left several voicemails – all of them perfectly professional requests that she please let me know she's still breathing. All of them guarded and work-focused – mentioning my calls with the housing agencies and how I'd appreciate her contacting me to push things forward.

Maybe I should try a more personal approach, but that would be more than my job would be worth should it ever reach the ears of my superiors.

So I don't call again. I drive instead. My usual route, which up until now has proved utterly pointless. Another evening of fruitless searching. Picnic areas and back alleys and meandering lanes through the middle of nowhere, all for nothing.

I'm on autopilot as I drive back from Gloucester, contemplating whether I really do need to put this search to bed and move on. I'm thinking I should fill Jack in on what's been happening and hope that his common sense manages to hammer its way through my thick skull.

I've all but decided this needs to be my final night scouring the streets for an adult woman who clearly doesn't want to be found, when I notice a figure walking along the hedgerows by Forest Oak Farm. I slow down, but only a little, well aware that it's probably just some random out walking their dog after dark, but my heart is in my throat when I see the backpack swinging heavily from the woman's shoulder. It's a she, it's definitely a she, and she's limping. I close the distance and a pale face turns to me, illuminated by my headlights for long enough that I recognise the glowering stare. Her long black hair is whipping in the evening wind, her mouth angry and tight as she glares at the stupid idiot with his lights on full beam.

I slam on the brakes in a heartbeat, and the car skids to a halt just past her.

She must recognise the car, that's the only explanation for why she waves her arms and tries to run for me. I'm already out and rushing in her direction when she limps onto the tarmac.

Her backpack crashes from her shoulder and she's about to crash down with it as I grab hold of her and keep her steady. She weighs nothing in my arms. My poor lost Carrie is nothing but a limp little bird with hollow bones. I'm holding her so tight I'm worried I'll crush her, but she holds me right back and lets me support her without squirming. Her eyes are sunken and tired, even in the moonlight, and her lip is split and dried with crusty blood, but despite any of that she's the most beautiful thing I've ever seen.

"I've got you," I tell her as she digs her fingers into my arms. "Are you hurt?"

"Sprained my fucking ankle this afternoon."

She struggles in my grip, trying to hitch her backpack back up, but I hold her firm. "You've been bleeding," I tell her, nodding to her lip as she stares right up at me.

"I'll live."

"I left you messages."

"Got no battery, no minutes left, either."

I pick up her backpack and sling it over my shoulder, being careful not to let her go for even a second. I take a step towards the car but she digs her heels in, even though it makes her grimace.

"I'm not fucking going back there!" she hisses. "I'm eighteen now, I don't fucking have to. They don't fucking want me there anyway!"

I stop. Think. And she's right. Of course she is.

There's no room waiting for her now at Bill and Rosie's. There's no room waiting for her anywhere, not this time of night.

"So where were you going if not to Bill and Rosie's?" I ask. "Why were you heading this way?"

She looks away from me, staring into the shadows of the hedgerow so intently I think she must have spotted something. I look to my right but there's nothing there.

"I was coming to *you*," she whispers, and my pulse races.

"To me?"

She nods. "Had nowhere else to go, did I?" She still won't look at me. "I mean, I know you wouldn't want me around either and all that, it's just... I needed somewhere to get warm..."

"And you were coming to me? To my place?"

She sighs. "You don't have to make me feel like a total fucking dick."

But I'm not. I never would.

"I'm glad you thought you could come to me," I say, and her pretty mouth curls into a snide smile.

"Like I said, had no other asshole I could call on."

Even exhausted and limping with a cut lip and nowhere to go, the girl has to be a brash little shit. Maybe I'd be taken in by her bravado if I couldn't feel the way her fingers are grasping my arms for dear life.

I'd be a fool to believe this could mean anything. I'd be a fool to believe these feelings I have for her could be real, and even if they were, that they could ever amount to anything. But my mouth is dry and my breath is short and my heart is thumping so hard I can feel it in my temples.

"So, what's it gonna be, Michael?" she asks. "You gonna take me to yours, or do I have to keep on limping down this road all fucking night?"

I hoist her back onto her own two feet and she winces at the pain.

"I can't take you to mine," I tell her. "Pam lives on the ground floor. You're not officially on my books anymore, Carrie, I shouldn't be…"

"Aww, you don't want poor Pammy to think we're fucking? Is she your girlfriend or something?"

I sigh. "She's my colleague." I help her along the road to the car. "A wrong impression could cost me my job, Carrie. I have kids to take care of, kids who need my help, just like you."

She stiffens in my arms. "I'm not a fucking kid."

She steadies herself against the car as I drop her backpack onto the back seat and open the passenger door for her. She sucks in breath as I help her inside.

She's staring straight through the windscreen as I get behind the wheel.

"If I can't stay with you, I gotta keep running," she says. "I have to get out of here."

"Running from who?" I ask, but she doesn't answer.

"Carrie, where the hell have you been? People have been worried sick about you." I set off on the empty road, shooting her sideways looks just to make sure I'm not dreaming all this.

"Nobody's worried sick about me."

"You think I'm driving these roads in the middle of the night for my health?"

She shrugs and it makes me sigh again.

"I'm driving these roads for *you*, Carrie. To look for *you*. I've been out here for days."

Her eyes burn in the darkness. "You have?"

"Yes, I have."

"You've really been looking for me?"

"Every spare fucking minute."

She laughs that vivacious cackle of hers. It zips up my spine, even though it's more muted than usual. "Guess you weren't looking fucking hard enough then, were you?"

CARRIE

Michael puts the car heater on and it's warmth feels amazing on my cold feet. I want to tell him thanks, but the words won't come. I want to reach out and touch his hand, but I'm scared he'll pull away.

So I sit still, staring straight ahead as he drives us fuck knows where.

He's nervous and it's obvious. His fingers keep tapping the steering wheel as we head back to Lydney. It's weird to be in a car again, travelling roads in a flash that would've taken me hours on foot. I'm guessing he really must be taking me back to his, no matter what *Pam* might have to say about it, but he turns right when he should turn left onto his road and carries on down the High Street.

"Where we going?"

"A friend's."

I stiffen in my seat, and even that stupid small movement sets my ankle off hurting worse. "What kind of friend?"

He glances in my direction and I feel a weird flutter in my belly. "You met him briefly. The guy in the suit from Drury's."

"The posh guy? Can't see *him* giving me a warm welcome."

I can't believe he's taking me there, to hang out with some rich snob who probably thinks I'm just a useless piece of shit. I'm tempted to open the car door, bail out and hope for the best, just to save myself the awkwardness, but I could do without any more injuries right now.

"He isn't going to know about it, not yet anyway. He's away on business."

Even fucking better. I groan. "You're going to break into his house while he's away and let me squat there? Some friend you are."

That makes him smile. "I have a key, which hardly makes it breaking in. I'm house sitting. And you won't be squatting. You'll be a guest."

That makes me smile too. "I don't think I'm the kind of guest he'd want there, somehow."

"It's only going to be for a few days, Carrie. I'll be sure to smooth it over with him when he's back."

A few days. The thought of being back on the road after that isn't great. Maybe it'll be different when my ankle eases up.

I dare to ask the question. "And then what? When he's back?"

He shrugs. "We'll work something out."

I want to ask him *what* we'll work out. Whether he'll be coming with me wherever I end up going. Whether him looking for me every night means that he likes me just as much as I like him.

I'm eighteen now, and it's nobody else's business if we like each other, it's nobody else's business what we do.

I'm not usually happy with vague answers and letting other people decide what I will and won't be doing, but it's different with Michael. He says we'll work something out, and for once in my life I really want to believe him.

It felt so nice in his arms, so warm and safe. I wish he was still holding me. I've always felt alone, but never so much as I have these past few days. I've always felt like I should be on the road, but I've never tried to run so fast as I have these past few nights. It's nice to let all that go, even if it's just for a little while.

A few days.

Maybe a few days will just have to do. Maybe a few days will be long enough to convince him he should come away with me.

We drive straight through Lydney and out the other side. The big houses are out this way and I know most of them by sight. I used to wander past sometimes when I had a couple of smokes after my sessions with Michael. People might think I'm a filthy gypsy who belongs in a wagon, and I do – but these houses are nice enough to make even a traveller like me dream a little dream. Michael indicates left and pulls onto the driveway of a big white farmhouse. It's not where I'd have imagined posh-suit man to live and I'm secretly impressed. I'd have put him down as a minimalist apartment kinda guy. One of those dicks who thinks a cream rug and a piece-of-shit modern art makes you a *somebody*.

"This is Jack's place," Michael tells me, like I need it pointing out.

I wait in the car until he comes around to my side, and my heart does a stupid sappy jump when he opens the door and helps me up again. I hold on a little longer than I need to, just to feel the warmth of him, hoping I don't stink too bad from a couple of days without a shower. I probably do.

He takes my backpack from the back and helps me to the front door. It's a big solid oak thing with an iron knocker. Very grand. Maybe this place really does suit posh guy after all.

Michael jangles his keys under the porch light until he finds the right one. It turns in the lock with a click and the door swings open into the darkness.

Michael seems to know his way around. His hand lands right on the switch for the hall light, and he supports me right on through to the kitchen where he hitches me up onto the worktop. For once in my life I keep my muddy boots away from dirtying everything. Despite what Bill and Rosie would believe, I don't really want another cream carpet incident. Especially not now I've nowhere else to go. I dangle my feet in the air until Michael drops down to slip by boots off for me.

I grit my teeth as he examines my sprained ankle.

"It's swollen," he says, once again pointing out the obvious.

"It'll be fine in the morning," I bluster, hoping to fuck I'm right about that. He takes a tea towel from a drawer and some ice from the dispenser on the fridge, then makes me up a weird icepack which he holds on the swelling.

"*Nurse Michael*," I laugh, but he doesn't laugh with me.

He looks so serious when he meets my eyes, and there are those flutters in my belly again.

"Does that feel okay?" he asks and I nod. I know he means the icepack, but it's not that that's making me tingle warm tingles, it's the feeling of his fingers against my skin.

The strength in his grip as he supports my sore foot makes me feel so cared for.

Relief rushes over me. Relief that I don't have to walk any further. Relief that I'm not going to be cold tonight. Relief that there was someone out there who really did give a shit about me.

"What happened to your lip?" he asks. His hair is messier than usual and a stray wisp hangs over his forehead. I'd love to reach out and brush it away.

"Fell over," I lie.

"A likely story," he says and follows it up with a sigh. He moves the icepack along my calf and I grimace. "Can you wiggle your toes?"

I wiggle my toes.

"Not broken," he says. "That's good."

"Maybe you really are a nurse," I comment and this time he smiles.

"I've done plenty of first-aid courses in my time, Carrie. Part of the job."

I wish I'd sprained my lungs instead, maybe then he'd have given me mouth to mouth. It crosses my mind to hold my breath and pretend I've fainted, just to feel his lips on mine. I hope I'm not blushing like a fucking sap at the thought.

"We need to talk," he says. "We need to work out a plan of action from here on in." He pauses and all I can think about is how green his eyes look under the kitchen lights. "But not tonight. Tonight you should eat and drink and rest up." He places my hand on the icepack. "Keep that there."

I can't hold back the rush of panic as he gets to his feet and leaves me on the counter. "Where are you going?"

"Only to put some food on, don't worry," he tells me, and I hate the way he's seen through my armour. He opens posh guy's big kitchen cupboards and talks me through the contents. So many things. Way more things than Rosie and Bill ever had at theirs.

He heats up a pan of soup at my request, because that's all I think I can stomach right now, and I watch him like I've never seen him before. His shirt is crumpled and his jacket has a patch of dry mud on the elbow. It must be from me. He has really fine hands, long fingers like he should be a pianist or something, not some charity worker. His jaw has a shadow of stubble and it really suits him. The lights in here are harsh and show the fine lines around his eyes, but they really suit him too.

I'm not sure if it's my belly rumbling, or the butterflies, or a bit of both, but I think I love this man. It's the most crazy stupid thing to be thinking in some stranger's house while my ex-charity-caseworker stirs a pan of chicken soup, but it's true.

If I'm honest – which I rarely am – I think I've loved Michael for months. I think I've loved him since the day he called the cops and argued with them that I could be telling the truth about my bruises.

I haven't loved anyone since the Evans family threw me out all those years ago. I don't think anyone's loved *me* since then, either. Not any of the families I've been palmed off on, and definitely not Bill and Rosie. And not Eli, no matter what crap he comes out with when he wants me to do something for him. But here, now, I think Michael could love me one day. Maybe.

He looked for me.

He called me and left me messages.

He made me an icepack for my ankle and stopped me from falling.

I feel in a lump in my throat and I'm so scared it might turn into stupid tears that I pretend it's a cough. Michael gets me a glass of water and that only makes it worse.

He's about to step back to the pan when my hand moves on its own. I watch my fingers clasp around his wrist, and he freezes dead. He doesn't even breathe. I'd feel it on my face if he did.

"Thank you," I say, and my voice is thick with that stupid lump in my throat.

His wrist turns in my grip and his fingers take mine. I close my eyes to stop the tears and focus on how warm his hand feels.

"You're welcome, Carrie," he says, and that's it. Just like that. Like it's a simple answer to a simple thank you, when what I really want to say is that I need him. I want him. That I wasn't lying when I said I wanted us to run away together.

He's back at the pan before I can say one single word, let alone all the others I want to say.

I choke them down after the stupid lump in my throat.

MICHAEL

Carrie devours her soup like a starving person. She dips the bread right into the bowl and I watch with fascination as she dips her fingers right in after it. She cleans the bowl, the spoon squeaking against ceramic as she scrapes up every last drop.

I could watch her forever, and it surprises me, because I don't remember ever feeling like this about Molly – not even back in the early days when things were new.

Even with tangles in her hair and an obvious layer of grime on her skin, Carrie Wells is a beautiful creature.

I've seen plenty of teenagers grow into attractive young women and never considered any of them as anything other than wards in my care, but this girl is different. Everything about her is different.

She's unusually quiet as she places the empty bowl at her side, eyes fluttering as she struggles to stay awake. She shouldn't be here, and yet having her here feels ridiculously good. Maybe Jack is right and this is a midlife crisis. Maybe I'm just a stupid old idiot with a stupid infatuation, but it's only now the panic of losing her has eased that I realise how tightly wound I've been these past few days.

"You should get some sleep," I say and she nods.

She's limp as I help her down from the side. Her eyes are closed all the way through the house and upstairs, her body nestled into mine, her head pressed against my shoulder as she limps along in whatever direction I guide her.

Jack's house isn't really set up for guests. Aside from the master bedroom, the other upstairs rooms are used for storage and laundry. The room I usually sleep in has a small single bed amongst a load of old suitcases. It does me just fine whenever I'm visiting, and I hope it'll do just fine for Carrie.

"I should shower..." she mumbles as I ease her onto the bed, and no sooner she's said it than she's wriggling out of her jacket and the couple of layers underneath. My breath is shallow as I watch her strip down to just a cami top and underwear. She winces as her jeans catch on her ankle and I'm forced to drop to my knees and help them off. Sleepy hands rest on my shoulders. A thumb brushes my neck and it feels electric. I pull away before I run the risk of doing something despicable, and without a word she pulls up her knees and wriggles herself under the covers, shower seemingly forgotten.

Her hair is so dark against the white bedding, and her skin looks so much dirtier against the clean sheets.

"Where are you gonna sleep?" she asks.

"Downstairs," I say. "I won't be far."

"You can stay..." she whispers. "There's room for two." She backs into the wall and pats the bed to prove her point, but I couldn't.

I just couldn't.

"If you need me, you can holler," I tell her. "I'll hear you from downstairs."

I hate the flash of rejection across her face. I hate the way she stiffens as though she's done something wrong.

I hate how it feels to deny myself the pleasure of her body against mine.

"I'm not a kid," she says, and I have to clear my throat.

"I know. I hope you had a good birthday all things considered."

"I had a shit birthday, like always. I've no reason to celebrate, just me congratulating myself on being alive another year. Big fucking whoopee."

I don't know what to say, so I hover, standing over the bed of a barely dressed girl while she stares up at me. While she wants me.

I know she wants me. I've felt it in every touch of her fingers. In every flash of her eyes. In every moment her body pressed so perfectly to mine.

"Goodnight, Carrie." The words feel like glass. "I have to work in the morning. If I'm gone before you wake up, help yourself to food. I'll be back when I finish."

"I'm not a kid, Michael," she says again and there's a roughness to it. "I'm not in your office. I'm not a pile of notes in your crappy folder. I'm a woman. And you should stay."

"I can't," I insist, and with the words come the same nervousness I felt every week with her across the desk from me.

Her unpredictability. Her dramatic mood shifts.

Her impulsive gestures.

I know it's coming before it happens. The sweet, sleepy Carrie who slipped between the covers disappears before my eyes, and in her stead is a siren from the deep. Her eyes are hooded but piercing, her breath is short and fast. She turns down the covers until I can see the swell of her tits over her cami. She hooks a finger in the fabric and tugs it down, offering me up the lacy cups of her bra.

"Tell me you don't want me," she whispers, and it's not a request, it's an order.

"This isn't–" I begin, but she shakes her head.

"You're hard. I know you are."

My hand covers my crotch instinctively, knowing full well she's right.

"You need to sleep."

"Stay," she says, and I have to close my eyes to block her out.

"Carrie, I can't." My voice is as firm as I can muster. I hear the hitch of my own breath as I fight for resolve.

And she changes again. Just like that.

She pulls up her cami and rearranges the covers on top of her. I'd believe I'd imagined the entire interaction if it wasn't for the glint in her eyes.

"A goodnight kiss, then." She says, and my dick fucking aches with the strain. "Just a peck, to say thank you. For the soup. And the other stuff."

Just a peck. To say thank you. And then a sharp exit.

I lower myself over her, my arms rigid to keep my distance. Her fingers are lightning-fast, slipping inside my jacket and up my chest before I even lower my face to hers, her pretty mouth perfectly angled to meet mine.

It's not a peck. Her fingers twist in my hair and hold me tight. Her lips press to mine and stay there, and so do I.

I'm not a man who gives into desire. I'm not a weak man who can't control his urges. But I'm not the man I recognise as me as Carrie Wells sweeps her tongue across my mouth and begs for entry. I'm one heartbeat away from kissing her like I've never kissed anyone before in my life. I'm one breath away from tearing her grubby clothes from her and fucking her the way I've been dreaming of fucking her since the moment I first fucking met her.

She arches her back as if she knows it. She moans against my mouth as though she knows I'm about to break.

But I don't.

It takes every scrap of resolve to pull away. I take a breath as I gather myself, ignoring the throb of my cock and the heat I'm packing under my suit.

"Goodnight, Carrie," I say.

And this time I mean it.

Seven

MICHAEL

I'm in the office early, attempting fruitlessly to bury myself in paperwork to numb the guilt I feel at wanting a girl less than half my age.

I know I can't act on it. I know both my professionalism and my sense of moral judgement won't go down without one hell of a fight, no matter what my dick has to say about it.

None of my colleagues have even arrived for the day when I receive the latest *WTF* message from Jack. I type out a response and delete it three times straight. What can I possibly say to him?

Found Carrie. She's in your house with a bloody lip and a swollen ankle. Hope you don't mind?

He'd be on a plane home before the morning was out.

I send him a simple *everything's fine* and curse myself for it. I've got less than a week to find Carrie a more permanent place to stay, and I'm at a brick wall with all the agencies without her cooperation.

Jack's place is the only viable option for now, although the thought of Carrie trampling muddy boots all over his living room carpet does little to ease my anxiety.

It appears I'm switching one set of stresses for another. At least I know she's safe for the time being.

That will have to do for now.

I send her a text message at lunchtime telling her I'll be back early evening, wondering how the hell things are going to be in the cold light of day after having given her the brush off last night. She's volatile. Unpredictable.

Intoxicatingly wild.

I'm seriously out of my depth here and I feel it right through me. I consider calling Bill and Rosie and letting them know she's been found safe, but I'm already well aware they are beyond caring about her current whereabouts. I could confess the sorry situation to my co-workers and hope they don't judge me too harshly for going maverick on an epic scale, but I don't.

I tell myself it's for Carrie's sake, making sure she can find her feet before she's shunted into a load of agency meetings, but I know it has just as much to do with my own inability to let go of this time with her as any of that.

My gut is one big knot as I drive to Jack's place straight after work. I plead for good fortune under my breath as I make my way to the front door, trying not to contemplate the carnage that might be waiting on the other side.

Muddy boots could be the least of my problems. She could have taken it upon herself to redecorate his living room with ketchup for all I know. Nothing would surprise me, having seen her case notes.

I breathe a sigh of relief as I find her in front of Jack's huge TV. Her hair is shiny and full, cascading down over her shoulders to pool on the leather sofa. Her skin looks fresh and clear, her eyes bright as she watches some crappy reality TV show. Her knees are gathered to her chest, a collection of crockery discarded on the living room floor.

"Hi," I say, but she barely gives me a glance. "How was your day? How's your ankle?"

She shrugs then wiggles her foot. "Told you I'd live."

The coldness in her tone takes me aback. The memory of her lips pressed to mine feels alien and distant. This is another face of Carrie Wells, one that should be familiar to me from weeks of grunts and silent treatment, but in my office it never felt personal. Not like it does now.

I clear my throat. "Did you sleep well?"

"The bed's shit," she says. "Too springy."

It is springy, she's right.

"What did you have for lunch?"

She shoots me a glare that damns me for interrupting her TV show. "Sandwich. Soup. Bar of chocolate. Any other questions?"

I take a breath. "Are you ready to talk about where you've been these past few days? Who did that to your lip?"

She rolls her eyes. "No. I'm not ready to talk about where I've been these past few days. Who even cares?"

"I do."

Her eyes are fierce. "How about you? Are *you* ready to talk about why you're too much of a pussy to act on what you want?"

"It's not like that," I begin, but she groans and turns the volume up. "Carrie…"

"It *is* like that!" she hisses.

For all of my patience over the months and all the relief of having the girl back safe and sound, I feel the simmer of impatience under my cool. I don't lose my temper with the people I work with. I subscribe to the philosophy that people are always doing the best they can with the resources they have available. That in Carrie's world right now she's making choices based on choices she's been making all her life up until this point. That she doesn't mean what she says, it's just that she doesn't have a framework for more effective ways of social interaction.

Even so, I want to give the bratty little cow a good slap for her rudeness.

I take a breath to compose myself and she laughs at me.

"Don't like being called a pussy? Then don't fucking act like one."

"This isn't my office," I tell her, and my voice doesn't sound like mine.

"No, it's your posh friend's place and you put me in here."

"Yes, I did. Because you needed somewhere to stay. You still do. Last night has nothing to do with anything. You needed help, I was there."

"There with a fucking hard on in your pants. Admit it, that's why you came to rescue me, right? That's why you even give a shit?"

I can't keep up with this. I stare in morbid fascination as Carrie's glare burns right through me. Angry with me for not fucking her? Angry for not breaking my principles? Angry that I want to?

"This is impossible," I say to her. "This conversation is impossible."

She folds her arms. "You want me to leave?"

"No," I tell her. "I don't want you to leave."

"Then let me watch my fucking TV show," she says.

CARRIE

I don't know why I'm being like this. I don't know why I'm pushing him away as soon as he's walked through the fucking door, but bitchy Carrie is running the show and I can't stop myself talking shit at him.

I feel a weird satisfaction in the way he looks so confused. Hurt. He looks hurt, and that's satisfying too.

I don't know why I want him to think I'm a lazy useless bitch. I only put the TV on when I saw his car pull into the street and I don't even watch this shitty show. I don't know why I used a different plate for every sandwich and left them piled up around me for maximum mess. I don't know why I'm being such a terrible cow to a man who's only ever tried to help me.

Because he doesn't want me.

Because he doesn't love me.

Because he'll never love me.

The urge to give him the finger and tell him to fuck off out of my life is strong. I feel it twisting in my belly, the urge to make him leave me and get this over with.

I could scream in his face that he's a useless prick who probably can't keep it up, but I'm not sure that would do it. The words are on the tip of my tongue, but they won't come out.

He sighs at me and turns his back, and that's when I feel the rage build up. He's heading to the kitchen with an announcement that he's going to make coffee when I spring to my feet and follow him into the hall.

"Did you tell those stupid cunts you found me?! Did you?!"

He turns on the spot and raises an eyebrow. "I assume you're referring to Rosie and Bill?"

I fold my arms. "Yeah, those *cunts*."

I both hate and love the way he shakes his head. There's an anger in his eyes, but he hides it well. "Enough of the language."

My laugh is my bitchiest one. "*Enough of the language,*" I parrot. "Do you think you're my fucking dad or something? Do you want to be my fucking daddy, Michael?"

He takes a step toward me and my skin tickles. "Stop it, Carrie."

"Or what?" I goad. "Is Daddy gonna spank me?" I'm cackling as I spin to present my ass, giving myself a decent slap as he approaches. *"Oh yeah, spank me, Daddy. Teach me a lesson."*

I've gone too far and I know it. My heart drops as I register I'm losing him, but I can't take it back. I don't know how.

He looks at his watch, his mouth a tight line. "Well, as long as you're settled in here, Carrie, I'll make my way home for a while. I'll get onto the agencies in the morning for appointments in the afternoon, if that's what you'd like? Do you want to be out of here? What *do* you want, Carrie?"

You.

I want you to love me.

I want you to tell me to stop being a prissy little bitch because it won't make any difference, you'll still love me.

I shrug. "Whatever. This place will do until I find somewhere better."

"You want me to help you find a place of your own, yes?"

His eyes are so angry but so genuine. He's trying to understand the impossible.

When I was in one of my first foster homes they took me and this other kid to choose new beds. They chose the beds, but we could choose the headboards. The other kid was excited, said she wanted a bright blue one to match the flowers on our wallpaper. I wanted a blue one too, but I was jealous. Jealous of the way the other kid seemed part of the family already when I didn't feel like anything at all.

So I told them I didn't want a shitty blue one, even though I did. I told them I wanted a bright red one that didn't match at all. I loved how shocked they were, I loved how they couldn't hide their disappointment that I was going to wreck their perfect colour scheme.

Are you sure you don't want a blue one? they'd said. *You said blue was your favourite.*

I wished I could tell them yes, I do really want a blue one, but I couldn't. Not even right to the end when they smiled and shrugged and got me the stupid red one.

I hated that day.

I was mean all the way home because I was jealous and upset, even though it was my own dumbass decision. I hated that red headboard when it arrived, but I hated the blue one even more.

That's why I drew on it in marker pen and pretended it was an accident. That's why I kicked it as hard as I could until the studs came out of it and the shitty thing fell apart.

And it's like that now.

I'm telling him I want to leave here when it's the very last thing I want to do. I'm trying to make him think I don't give a shit for his help, when it's the best thing that's ever happened to me.

"Do you want me to go?" he asks, and his eyes are still trying to read me.

I force my eyes to burn into his. "Not bothered either way."

"Okay," he says, and I want to die inside. "I'll come back tomorrow. Use the landline and call my mobile if you need anything." He hands me a business card and I toss it on the side as though it means nothing.

"I'll be fine."

"Good," he says. "I'm glad you're feeling better."

But I'm not.

I'm feeling fucking awful and it's all my own fault.

I stand in the hallway with my arms folded when he leaves. I won't even look at him, not even when he pauses in the doorway.

I hate the slam of the door behind him. I hate the sound of his car starting up.

I hate the way I leave it too late to run after him and his car is already turning the corner.

I hate... *me*.

Eight

JACK

thought I'd be able to breathe easy when I finally received a reply from the silent sonofabitch back home. I let out a sigh of fucking relief as his name flashed up, until I saw the ridiculous message.

Everything's fine.

Just those two measly words after days of nothing.

Like fuck *everything's fine*. It's the most bullshit excuse for a text message I think I've ever had from him. I'd laugh at how ridiculous it was if I wasn't already worried sick about the state of his affairs in my absence.

I've been trying to ignore it – trying to blank out the prospect of that sappy idiot losing his mind over some pretty piece of trouble while I'm in a different time zone.

It's only when I realise I haven't registered a damn word in my latest conference session that I call up my calendar and check what events I'd be missing if I left for home early. I curse under my breath, because fucking dammit, there's at least three presentations I've marked on my *must see* list over the next few days. But it's pointless. Really fucking pointless.

I try Mike's phone again one last time after the session ends. He doesn't answer, which only cements my decision.

I've got to get back there, and it has to be ASAP. Jesus fucking Christ.

Having seen the state this girl's got him into these past few months, it's all too easy to imagine him going batshit about her disappearance. The fool could be hunting her down all over the country by now. And then what? What if she never resurfaces? Will he spend his whole life chasing after a pretty little ghost with a shitty attitude?

Not on my fucking watch.

I email Tom, telling him to book a flight out in my stead and take notes on everything I'm going to be missing. It's the best I can do.

I book a seat on the first flight back in the morning and then I curse Mike's midlife crisis for taking me away from business.

I'm about to send him another text to warn him of my changed plans, but I don't. My fingers hover over the keypad, my mind scoping out the prospect of a load of vague-arsed return messages playing down whatever crap he's got going on over there. No. If there *is* anything going down, then I'd rather walk straight into the heart of the craziness and see it in all its ugly glory. At least then I'll know what I'm dealing with.

Carrie Wells. I shake my head. Pretty girl, but is she ever worth all this?

In my educated opinion – considering I've bedded almost every attractive woman our local vicinity has to offer – I'd say a categoric *no*. So what if she's pretty? So what if she has a look in her eyes that tells you she'd be a fucking wonder in bed? She's got problems coming out of her ass and a bad attitude to boot. Scrap that, a *terrible* fucking attitude to boot. I saw it clear as day while she was trailing around Drury's after Eddie fucking Stevens.

I sigh to myself as I book a cab for the airport in the morning. Bright and early, just as I like it.

Carrie Wells. Would I go there? Would I want a piece of sweet, feral, teenage pussy? Would I want to see those pretty eyes staring up at me as I shoved my cock down her throat to quiet that smart little fucking mouth?

I allow myself a laugh before I head into my next seminar.

In my educated opinion, *no*. I fucking would not.

She'd never be worth the aggravation. No member of the female populous I've ever encountered would be.

My business associates haven't assembled yet for the next event, so I take a coffee from the side cabinet and stare at the projected intro screen. I'm always early, it's a trait of mine. My father always said that opportunity waits for no man. It's the man at the front of the line who gets awarded the best choices, and it must have stuck with me far better than some of the other bullshit advice he gave me early on, because I'm always at the front of the line in life.

I love my dad. *He'd* say a lot of his advice was bullshit too. The thought makes me smile as I sip my coffee.

They've used a decent blend. I like that.

Michael thinks I'm where I am in life because I work harder than the others. He thinks it's because I'm smarter than the others too, but I'm neither of those things. I had to work my ass off to get grades high enough to get into Warwick University, but from that point I worked smart, not hard. I came out with a mediocre business degree but a shit-hot attitude for business itself. I made sure my networking was on point, made it my business to be in the right place at the right time, ahead of all the others hungry for a piece of the same pie. And it worked.

It continues to work over a decade later.

Michael gives everything to his profession because he loves it. He pursued his career because of the meaning he takes from helping other people find their feet.

I give only what my business absolutely needs and maybe a little beyond, everything on top of that is the reason I have staff. But insurance was never my calling, clearly. Nobody loves risk analysis. I set up on my own because I knew I didn't want to work for anyone else; it's that simple. I couldn't stomach a future divided into work weeks and days off on loop, on and on until retirement, when you finally get to do the shit you want with your own time, just as long as you've banked enough to afford your club memberships and your winter heating bill.

I guess you could say I like to lead rather than follow. You could also say I like to be in control of my personal situation at all times, hence why this infatuation of Michael's perplexes me somewhat.

Why do people go so fucking insane over random members of the opposite sex?

Are we really still slaves to base level hormonal instincts? Really? Are we?

I like to think not, which is probably the reason I've dated over a hundred women and only popped the question to one of them. Diana didn't even live with me, it was long distance. It would probably never have made it to the proposal stage if she'd lived anywhere near my doorstep.

I don't regret not tying the knot. I don't regret never having that one special person that I've opted to label my own above all others, even if my mother still whines on about grandchildren over Sunday dinner. I watched Michael and Molly live in a state of romantic mediocrity for years and it didn't nothing whatsoever to raise the green-eyed monster in me. I think I'd have been bored to death if I'd been in his shoes.

Carrie Wells – the little minx that pushed my poor sensible friend off his sensible rocker.

I'm still shaking my head at the insanity of it all as the other delegates filter in.

CARRIE

Michael didn't come back last night. I thought maybe he'd call or text, but he didn't. I sat by the landline with his business card in my hand, flipping it over and over and wishing my stupid dumb mouth would open up enough to tell him I'm sorry. But it wouldn't.

I hate TV, so the minute Michael left I turned it right back off again. I don't get why people like the stupid thing so much. Almost every house I've ever set foot in has a stupid screen blaring somewhere. I've spent loads of time watching people stare at moving pictures on a box like big dumb shits, and I just don't get it.

When you've been in foster care as much as I have, you come to know it's an easy option to palm off every kid that ever wants attention. *Why don't you just behave and watch some TV? Why don't you sit down in front of the TV and be quiet? Why don't you just watch the kids channel like every other kid we've ever taken care of?*

Because TV is a fucking life-stealer, you dumbfucks. TV is a fucking sedative for your fucking brain.

Know what burns more calories, watching TV or staring at a blank wall? Staring at a blank wall, because at least then your brain has to make moving pictures for its fucking self.

I want to put my boot through posh guy's big fucking screen, because even looking at it reminds me how I pushed Michael away last night. But I don't. Because I like it here, even though I know I won't be able to stay.

I'm never allowed to stay anywhere, not for long. But for now I'm gonna make the most of it, because posh guy's house is amazing – the best house I've ever been in. If you look through the back windows, especially from upstairs, you can see for miles, a patchwork of fields and trees and sheep. I wonder if posh guy has any animals here. There's no dog, which is sad because this place would be the best place ever to have a couple of Labradors. I can't see a cat, either, and there's no cans of petfood in the cupboards. The guy must be an idiot for not having pets here. If I lived here I'd have a whole zoo in my backyard.

It looks like it's gonna be a nice day today, even if the ground is still bound to be boggy from the rain last night. I got up early because that springy bed makes stupid squeaks every time I roll over, but that's alright. I like getting up early. It makes sense that travelling is in my genetics, because there's nothing I like more than exploring as the sun comes up outside. I hate being cooped up while there's a big open world out there.

I'm so desperate to get out into it that I don't even grab any breakfast. I lace up my boots and head through the back door, wondering just how many of the fields I counted from the window belong to this house. I bet it's all of them. Most of them at least.

I have to climb over some fences, but my ankle holds up just fine. I scrabble through a couple of broken hedgerows and find a little stream that's just perfect for hopping over.

Being in the middle of nowhere excites me. Being just me amongst the magic of nature is the thing that makes my soul happy. The hours disappear so easily out here. I find I'm smiling, even though I still feel like shit about Michael. I find I'm twirling, laughing, calling to the birds in the trees. They probably think I'm as crazy as I feel, but my blood is pumping and my hair is flying all around me and I love it. I really love it.

And then I see something. A bedraggled something flapping around on the ground by the hedge at the far side. I head over to get a closer look, and it's a crow, a big black one with beady eyes that glint as it stares at me. My heart drops as I see he's got his leg caught in some wire, and I hate posh guy for having such an amazing place and not taking care of the maintenance. The fence is crap down here, all broken and battered, and nature's suffering, yet again, for humanity's dumbfuck ignorance.

Even in boots I can move quietly when I need to. I'm slow and steady, making sure I talk to the bird real softly as I make my way over. He flaps hard but he can't go anywhere. His eyes don't leave mine at all, and when I get there he caws at me but doesn't freak out like I thought he might.

His feathers are muddy and trashed. His leg looks sore where the wire's cut him, but it seems like he can still move it.

I don't know where posh guy keeps a tool kit and I wouldn't want to head all the way back to the house even if I did. This crow needs freeing right away, so I crouch down, crawling along the last bit, right through the mud, until I can get a proper look at things. I sigh in relief to find I can do this. I really can do this by hand.

I'm careful. Really careful.

I put my hand on the crow's wings and hold him to the ground, just enough to steady him. My fingers free up some slack on the wire and gently, really gently, I twist it free of the bird's leg.

I'm quick when I've done it, bundling the bird into my arms before he can attempt to fly away. I'll need to look at him, maybe wash him down with something and try to straighten up his mangled feathers.

I feel like I'm carrying the most amazing treasure on the planet as I head back to the house. The crow doesn't fight me, not when he's held safe under my arm. It's like he knows I saved him, and it figures, because they're super smart birds. Smarter than some people, I'm sure, because so many people are fucking idiots.

I don't really have a plan for once I'm inside, so I just shut the back door behind me and hope the crow stays calm when I put him on the kitchen island.

He doesn't.

The moment I let him go he flaps about and takes off right through to the dining room.

Fuck.

I haven't got time to take my boots off, be fucked with posh guy's carpets. I haven't got time to do anything but chase after the bird and hope he doesn't wreck everything before I've even had the chance to help his foot.

He settles on the top of some big display cabinet, so I grab a dining chair and climb up after him. He's gone before I reach him, and as he takes off he dislodges one of the ornaments on the top shelf. The big garish glass thing tumbles before I can catch it, smashes on the floor into a billion pieces of gaudy coloured glass.

Fuck. It's not even lunchtime and I'm already trashing the fucking place.

The sound of smashing glass freaks the poor crow out worse, and he shits himself, dumping big globs of crap over the dining table before he heads through the door back into the hallway.

Fuck. I should've fucking closed that.

My boots crunch over the broken glass and trample a load of it with me.

I see the sparkles in the carpet as I chase the bird around the house, finally cornering him in the living room where he settles on a big framed-mirror behind the sofa.

He stops. Stares at me.

And I know he's thinking, watching, working me out. It's like he can see right into me.

"I'm sorry I scared you," I whisper. "I'm just trying to help your foot, that's all."

He blinks and his eyes are so black.

"I just want to help," I tell him. "I'm not gonna hurt you."

I'm so pleased when he doesn't fly off again. It's pure instinct to step up onto the sofa and balance myself on the back cushions.

I can almost reach him here. He shuffles along the frame but he doesn't fly away.

"I'm a friend," I say. I'm so gentle as I stretch out and reach for him, I really am.

I'm close. So close. Moving so slowly I daren't even breathe in case I startle him.

My heart is beating fast, a big smile on my face as I realise he's really going to let me catch him.

And then there's a bang.

The loud fucking bang of the front door being barged open.

The crow freaks out and takes off, and he craps again on his way. He's flapping around the room, knocking fucking ornaments from the mantelpiece in his frantic flight, causing a real fucking commotion because some dumbfuck thumped the fucking door wide open.

I hear footsteps in the hall, and I'm raging. I'm fucking raging.

I know it must be Michael, because who fucking else would it be?

I know it's *his* heavy fucking footsteps clumping through the hall, oblivious to the fact he's just fucked my perfect fucking crow-bonding effort.

"You're a noisy sonofabitch," I hiss as I try to head the bird into the corner. "Next time, try to swing the front fucking door right off its hinges, why don't you?!"

My stomach tips right over itself when it's not Michael's voice that answers me.

Nine

JACK

Carrie Wells is in my fucking living room. Large as fucking life.

Her piercing eyes are as wide as fucking saucers, her pretty mouth flapping harder than the bird flapping around the ceiling.

My eyes don't know where to look first, at her, at the crow in my fucking house, or at the state of the place around her. My white carpet is filthy with muddy boot prints. The cushions on my perfect white sofa have been trampled, and they're covered in mud too. There's bird shit splattered over the front of my TV, my mantelpiece is in fucking disarray with several of my picture frames smashed on the top.

And her, covered in shit, mud and feathers, a picture of horror as she stares right back at me.

"The door!" she yells, but I'm too fucking dumbstruck to move. The crow flaps straight over my head and out. She races after it, and I hear her angry wail before I find her in the open front doorway. Her eyes are wild as she glares at me. "You let him out! He needed his foot taking care of and you let him out!"

When my voice comes back it comes back hard.

"What the holy living fuck is going on here?! What the fuck are you doing in my fucking house?!"

I know as soon as I've said it. Of course I fucking know.

I dig my mobile from my pocket and thumb straight through to Mike's number.

The girl takes one last look at the sky and groans as she accepts defeat. She closes the door behind her and heads back in like she owns the fucking place.

"If he dies, it's *your* fault," she snaps.

I've got the call connecting tone in my ear even as she says it. "My fucking fault?!"

"He was tangled in *your* crappy fucking fence!"

I hold up a hand to signal her to shut the fuck up, and she folds her arms as she waits. Her muddy boot taps on the floor, and it really shouldn't be a pleasure to watch her red mist fade away, but it is. There's a beautiful trepidation in her eyes as she soaks in the mess. I watch her gaze travel over the trail of boot prints to end with a long hard look at her boots. She lifts up the soles as if the mud needs explanation, and when her eyes meet mine again they are full of nerves at odds with her cocky stance.

Mike's phone rings to voicemail. I take a breath before I unleash my fury down the line.

"You'd better get here. Now. I'm in my fucking living room with your missing fucking person. Get here, Mike, before I call the fucking police."

Carrie Wells is a sight to behold as the colour drains from her cheeks. "You gonna call the cops?" she asks, and her whole body tenses, as though she's about to make a dash for it.

I hang up the call. "I should. It looks like the place has been fucking ransacked."

She shakes her head. "I haven't taken anything."

I gesture around me. "My house is fucking destroyed. Why the fuck are you even in here?"

She takes a step forward. "Michael tried to help me. I had nowhere to go." She pauses. "It's not his fault. He doesn't know about the crow, I was just trying to save it."

I'm rarely lost for words, but she has me stumped. I don't know whether to march her off my property or laugh insanely at this whole fucking spectacle.

"I'll clean up," she says, and I cover my face with my hands in disbelief.

"You'll clean up?!"

"Yeah," she tells me. "I will."

I point to the smashed frames on the mantelpiece. "And what about the damage? What about the fact I've got a total fucking stranger on my property? *In* my house?"

She's quiet while she thinks, chewing on her bottom lip like she wants to draw blood. "I'll pay for it."

"Do you *have* any money?" I look her up and down. It's a marvel that her beauty shines through the state of her tattered, filthy clothes. Her boots are grubby and old, and I can see a flash of pink sock through a hole in the toe.

She shakes her head. "Not yet, but I can earn it. When I get a job I'll pay you back."

I can't stand to look at the living room anymore so I step out and close the door behind me. The hall is also covered in boot prints and so is the kitchen. I dare to peek into the dining room and groan in disbelief to see the rainbow shards of what used to be my prized glass sculpture.

I hear her footsteps behind me. "I'll pay for that, too."

I swear under my breath. That sculpture was almost ten grand, a stupidly extravagant purchase at an auction house down in London.

I should order her to fuck off out of my house and never fucking come back. I can't believe she's even still here, following me around while I uncover more and more of her fucking catastrophe.

But Michael.

Even now, knowing that the stupid sonofabitch invited a whirlwind of trouble into my empty house without my knowledge, I can't bring myself to send her running. He'd only fucking follow.

"How long have you been here?" I ask her.

"Two nights."

My shoes crunch on broken glass. "Two nights?" The shock is numbing me to the anger. "Just as well I didn't stay away another fucking week."

"He was trying to help," she says again. "Michael, I mean. He found me on the road." She holds up her foot. "I sprained my ankle, couldn't walk."

"So he brought you here?"

She shrugs. "Someone called Pam lives in his block. He said he couldn't take me there."

"Pam Clowes," I say absentmindedly. "Yes. She'd have his job for it."

"It was only for a few days, he said. Just until we sort something else."

I can't help but register her word choice. *We* sort something else. I wonder what the fuck's really been going on here. Are they physical? Has this midlife crisis become more than a crazy pissing pipe dream?

I want to ask her but I don't. I'll ask him instead, just as soon as he fucking gets here.

"I'm sure he'll be here as soon as he can," she says, as though she's a mind reader. I wonder if the gypsy rumours are true. Maybe she's got some weird psychic gift in that pretty head of hers. I feel uncharacteristically self-conscious, because despite all this – despite the shit-storm of chaos around me, and the cold, hard horror of finding an intruder in my house – I'm thinking how much prettier she is sober and in the daylight. I'm thinking how glossy her hair is and how it ripples as she moves. I'm thinking that her eyes are more fey than human, and her freckles look surprisingly cute when she's angry.

I'm thinking that I can see why a girl like Carrie Wells has sent a man like Michael Warren fucking crazy.

"Can I wait for him?" she asks, as though she suddenly needs my permission for shit.

"You better had," I say. "You both owe me one fuck of an explanation."

She shrugs. "I told you what happened. I didn't have anywhere to go, Michael brought me here. I went out for a walk and found a crow in your busted fence, tried to help it and you let it go."

I sigh. "And you trashed my whole fucking house in the process, yes?"

She shrugs again. "Not the upstairs. It didn't go up there."

But *she* did.

I wonder if she's been sleeping in my fucking bed, too. Like bastard Goldilocks.

I wonder if they've *both* been in there.

The thought of her splayed out in my bed makes my mouth water, and I don't get it. I really don't fucking get it.

"I didn't mean to trash anything," she tells me. "You should take better care of your fences."

"*And* who I leave a fucking key with it seems."

She drops to one knee to unlace her boot, kicks it off and does the other. Too little, too fucking late.

I watch as she places them neatly on the mat by the kitchen door, then rummages under my sink for some cleaning products. She's a vision on all fours, her jeans riding low on her ass, loose enough at the waist that they show the top of her pale blue knickers. Her hair hangs free from her shoulders and gathers on the floor tiles, and her feet are tiny in silly pink spotty socks at odds with the rest of her grubby attire.

She glances up at me over her shoulder, and the involuntary image of me pounding her from behind jars my senses.

"Can I use this on the table?" she asks and holds up a random bottle of polish.

I nod.

She gets back to her feet, cloth in hand, and I wonder how much cleaning the girl has done in her life considering she thinks she'll get started with a bit of table polish. It'll take a damn sight fucking more than table polish to clean this place up.

I'm gawping like a fucking idiot when she strides past me into the dining room, and it's only instinct that possesses me to grab her by the waist before she treads on broken glass. She gasps at the contact, stiffening in my grip as her bright blue eyes stare up at me. I imagine how well the colour of her knickers go with her eyes when they're the only thing she's wearing.

"The glass," I say, "you'll cut your feet."

"Surprised you care."

"Blood's harder to get out than mud," I say and she thinks I'm serious. Her eyebrows pit until I smile.

I can't believe I'm fucking smiling.

"He really didn't mean it," she tells me. "Michael, I mean. He's been nice to me."

I wonder *how* nice Michael's been.

I wonder whether he's had his hands inside the cami top I'm staring down into. I wonder if his mouth has been on her. I wonder what she tastes like.

I'm usually unmoved by attractive women. I'll fuck them and enjoy it, but they make little lasting impression. Blonde, brunette, redhead; they're usually much of a muchness. As long as their body is tight and their pussy is wet, that's good enough for me.

Carrie Wells isn't like any of the attractive women I've ever seen. Her eyes are much older than her years, glinting with the promise of both a potty mouth and a massive chip on her shoulder. She dresses like a tomboy, a loose bomber jacket obscures her surprisingly tight cami. I get the impression that stripping the layers will show more and more woman the deeper you go.

She's all woman. There's no doubt about that.

Her scruffiness only adds to her femininity, as odd as that sounds.

"Let me clean up," she says, and I let out a breath as I release her.

She tiptoes around the broken glass, being careful with her feet as she sprays polish over the table. I watch her scrub the bird crap from the top. Her fingernails are grubby. They're also bitten to shit.

I can't believe I'm doing it, but I grab the brush and pan from the utility room and work to clear the glass from the dining room carpet. I tell myself it really is to save it from bloodstains, but I'm saving her feet and I think she's well aware of that, too.

She doesn't say a word as she goes about her cleaning and neither do I.

I'm almost relieved as I hear Michael's car pull onto my driveway.

Almost.

The other part of me wishes I'd never called him.

Worryingly it seems the Carrie Wells delusion might be fucking contagious.

Ten

MICHAEL

should've called Carrie last night. Or I should've at least tried. Even better, I should've turned back up at Jack's and told her I'm not going to be pushed away by her sticking her middle finger up to everyone trying to help. I should've told her that if things were different, if I was ten years younger and hadn't spent the last five months with her on my books, that I'd be falling into bed with her in a heartbeat, for right or wrong.

I should've told her I care. That I care too much.

Jack's right; this is a midlife crisis and it's getting the better of me. I can't get her out of my mind, and it takes every scrap of determination to stay focused on my meetings through the morning, knowing full well she's at Jack's getting up to Christ knows what.

If she's even still there.

The idea she's taken off again sends a chill up my spine.

I'm talking through career options with a kid called Brooklyn when I feel my phone buzz in my pocket. I hope it's her calling. I hope it's her who's left a voicemail when I feel the second buzz go off.

I ignore it until Brooklyn's session is wrapped up, of course I do, but my fingers are clumsy on the handset once he's out through the door, racing to retrieve my call log.

My heart drops when I see Jack's number appear on screen.

Shit.

I sigh as I press to hear his message, feeling like such an asshole for keeping him in the dark through this. His house isn't a hostel, and his friendship is worth more than keeping secrets of this magnitude, even for the sake of just a few days.

His voice is gruff enough to take me aback. His message chills my blood.

You'd better get here. Now. I'm in my fucking living room with your missing fucking person. Get here, Mike, before I call the fucking police.

I check the call time. Forty minutes ago.

Fuck.

Holy fucking fuck.

I grab my jacket from the back of my chair and make a dash for it, hating how frazzled my explanation sounds when I ask Pam to please cover my appointments for the rest of the afternoon.

She looks worried, and I feel like more of an asshole by the second.

"Are you alright, Mike?" she asks, and I count on looking as fucked up as I feel when I tell her I think I've got food poisoning.

She nods. "You don't look well."

I don't feel well, either.

I make a sharp exit, barely even offering her a goodbye in my haste to be out of there.

I jump into the car and speed off for Jack's, drumming my fingers on the steering wheel all the way. *Please, for fuck's sake, don't call the police. Please, for fuck's sake, don't let her run.*

Every set of traffic lights conspires against me, and the usual five-minute journey takes over ten. My tyres screech as I pull onto his driveway, stopping just short of bumping his Range as I kill the ignition and bail out.

I don't knock, just charge on in and expect to find a war breaking out, but it looks as though it's already happened.

Muddy boot prints everywhere, and oh fuck how I cringe inside. I stare open-mouthed at the state of the living room, cursing as I spot the smashed frames on the mantelpiece.

I'm calling his name as I charge down the hallway, following the boot prints through to the kitchen and on through again to the dining room.

I take a breath as I find them, my heart thumping with the relief that she hasn't gone running. Not yet, anyway.

"I can explain," I begin, but Jack's face looks like thunder. "This isn't Carrie's fault."

"Which fucking bit of it?" he snaps, and I cringe again as I notice this room has hardly fared better than the others.

Carrie's voice is breathy when she speaks. "I tried to save a crow. His leg was stuck in a fence. He freaked out, flew everywhere."

I try to take in the story, breaking out in a cold sweat when I notice Jack's sculpture is missing from the top of the display cabinet. I notice the brush and the pan full of glass at his feet and the furniture polish in Carrie's hand.

No.

Oh God, no.

"I'll pay for the damage," I say, and Jack sneers at me.

"Yeah, just PayPal me your retirement fund, why don't you?"

Carrie looks on blankly and I hope he doesn't elaborate and tell her how expensive that ornament was.

He doesn't.

"This is so fucking out of order," he snaps and I nod because it is.

"I'm sorry," I say, which is the truth of it. "I was in a corner. I was trying to do the right thing."

"The *right thing* would have been to book her into a fucking hotel, Mike. The *right thing* would have been to let me know you're using my fucking house as emergency accommodation. The *right thing* would have been to fucking tell me you found her in the fucking first place."

I nod through all of it. Yes, yes and more yes.

I feel like a fucking idiot, more off the rails than even I fully realised.

"It isn't his fault," Carrie offers and her simple defence makes my heart pang.

"It *is* my fault," I counter. "This was my decision, Carrie didn't ask to come here."

"The crow's *your* fault," Carrie tells Jack and I will her to shut up before she talks herself into a bigger hole than we're in already. "You need to fix your fucking fence. It's dangerous."

It's a three way stand-off, all of us staring and nobody speaking a word.

Jack's pissed, his shoulders rigid and his eyes dark as he looks from one of us to the other, but he hasn't called the police, and Carrie is still standing here, still staying put amongst the chaos.

I gesture her toward me. "I'll book you into a hotel in Coleford. You'll be safe there. Get your things and wait in the car for me, I'll be out just as soon as I've finished up talking to Jack."

She dithers, and it breaks my heart that she doesn't want to leave here, not even with Jack on the warpath.

I hand her the car keys and she heads for the kitchen without argument. It's a first.

"Wait," Jack says, and we both look at him. "Coleford?! What the fuck is there for her in fucking Coleford?"

I shrug. "I don't think it's a good idea to book her a room in town."

I'm thinking of her hobbling through the night on a mission to escape something. I'm thinking about her running when she bumps into Bill and Rosie, or drinking herself unconscious with Eddie Stevens just as soon as he realises she's back.

"I don't want to stay in Coleford," she says and her eyes are wide as they crash into mine. "I want to stay with *you*."

Jack groans. He turns a full circle with his hands in his hair and then he points a finger between us. "Is this a *thing*?"

"A thing?" I ask, but Carrie's already nodding.

I forget what little filter she has.

"It's not a thing," I say, even though it pains. Carrie looks as though I've struck her all over again, and that pains worse. I sigh as I look at her. "I care about you," I say. "Very much. But this can't be a... *thing*, Carrie. It wouldn't be right."

Her cheeks flush, her mouth closed tight as she hugs her arms around herself. I'd give anything to touch her, but I can't.

"Well?" Jack asks. "Is it a fucking thing or isn't it?"

I shake my head. "Christ, Jack. You know me. Do you even need to ask?"

"Of course I need to fucking ask," he says. "And I need to know what the fuck you're planning on doing from here."

It's the tone of his voice – the edge of interest under the anger. The hair on the back of my neck bristles, my blood running cold.

His eyes flit to her and linger too long, and I notice the brush and pan again, notice Carrie's pink socks and the speed in which Jack must have composed himself enough to clear up the glass from the floor.

He's a good man. One of the best. But Jack's hot-headed, it takes him an age to calm down when he's riled up, I've seen it more times than I can count over the years. But not now.

Because he wants her.

I've never seen Jack all that interested in anyone, but he's interested in Carrie.

My Carrie.

Only she's not my Carrie. She's just a girl who needs my help.

Our help.

Jack's right about Coleford. It's not fair to hole a girl up alone miles from anyone she knows. It's not fair to shove her into an impersonal hotel room and expect her to stay cooped up there while you try to sort her life out around your day job.

Carrie's still hugging herself. Her eyes are still all on me. A strange thrum of possessiveness threatens to eat me up even though I've no claim and I never will have.

"What do *you* want to do?" Jack asks Carrie and this time she shrugs.

I can't believe he gives a shit about what she wants after she's brought a one-woman wave of destruction down on his home.

The Carrie Wells effect.

If I'd have put money on anyone being immune, it would've all been on Jack, but it seems I'd have been wrong.

"You've really got nowhere else to go?" he asks her and she shakes her head.

"I'll clean up my mess," she says. "Just like I told you I would."

I'm on the verge of uttering the unthinkable and telling her I'll take her back to mine, Pam be damned, when Jack lets out a sigh.

"You can stay," he tells her, then looks at me. "Just for a few days until you sort something out with the housing agency. But no more secrets, and no more fucking crows."

My jaw flaps, stumbling over words that should be grateful but feel like glass.

"I can stay?!" Carrie asks and she looks so happy that all thoughts of bursting her bubble fade to nothing.

"For a few days," Jack says, but she's nodding. Smiling.

"No more crows," she says. "I promise."

She's never promised me anything. I wish she would.

I thank Jack and I mean it. I force my stupid jealousy aside and push myself to be the better man. The man I should be. The image of conscience and professionalism that I've been holding myself to my whole adult life.

And then we get to cleaning up the rest of the terrible fucking mess in his house.

I wait until Carrie's out of earshot before I give Jack my thanks for the second time, man to man.

He nods. Tips his head and there's that edge again. The one that makes me feel sick.

"I'm not doing it for you," he says, "I'm doing it for *her*."

Eleven

CARRIE

Posh guy *isn't so much* of a dick as I thought he would be. I normally hate rich people – they look down their noses when I pass them on the street like they're so much better than me. But being rich doesn't give you a free pass out of Dumbville. Having money doesn't make your shit smell any better than mine.

I thought I'd hate this guy, Jack, but I don't. Even though he's a negligent asshole with his fencing, and his temper is as hot as mine, he doesn't seem like an absolute total douche.

I feel a weird sizzle when he's close, and it's not just because he's a proper man – like Michael –but because he's different to everyone else I've ever met. A *different* different to Michael.

Michael is strong and calm and considered. Michael looks at me as though I'm someone who could be somebody someday. He looks at me as though I'm more than my shitty reputation, like I have my own mind and my own brain and my own reasons for acting like I do.

Michael gives me hope I've never dared to have before – that there maybe someone out there strong enough to hold me tight and not let go. Who can see through all my shit and call it out for what it is – a stupid, shitty way of coping with being alone.

Jack, on the other hand, he seems like the guy who'll see through all my shit and hold me firm, keep me right. Jack seems like the kind of guy to not take any shit at all.

His features are harder than Michael's. His hair is cropped short and his jaw is solid. His eyes are dark and heavy and his nose is slightly Roman. He's put together well for a guy who's clearly greying. He's got to be at least forty, too.

I guess they've been friends a long time, him and Michael. I'm good at reading people, because knowing people's ways is in my blood, and it's obvious these guys really give a shit about each other. The way people should give a shit about each other but rarely do.

Even though Jack has every right to be seriously pissed at both of us, he shakes his head and helps us out, cleaning up the crow shit and picking up the feathers from the sides.

I wonder why he came back early. I wonder why he didn't call the cops and make a big fucking scene.

I'm really relieved I can stay. It makes me scared how relieved I am, because good things hurt so bad when they're taken away, and I'm not sure I wanna go through that. I'm not sure I can stand losing Michael before he's even been mine.

I'm not sure I'll be able to stand losing this house, with its big airy windows and it's lovely green fields. I'd find it so easy to fall in love with this place.

And to fall in love with being around these guys, too.

I feel safe as I work alongside them, even though they're both pissed at me for different reasons. I've never had people pissed at me before who've knuckled down all the same and helped me sort my crap out.

They don't have to help me clean up this mess, but they do.

Jack doesn't have to give me a roof over my head for another few days, and I don't know why he is, but I'm grateful. I'm grateful he cared enough to sweep up the glass and not call the cops on me. I'm grateful he cared enough not to make Michael pay for my stupid fuck up.

I work as hard as I can, because I'm not lazy and I want them to know it. I get carried away in the moment sometimes, and I don't always think about the practical stuff, but I'm not a slacker.

I didn't mean to trash Jack's pretty house, it's just that I cared about saving the crow more than I cared about his carpets.

I hope he knows that.

I hope Michael knows that too.

Michael fills up a tub of soapy water and attacks the white living room carpet with a scrubbing brush. He doesn't stop scrubbing, not even as I drop to my knees alongside him and place my hand on his.

"I can do it," I say, but he sighs and carries on. He flinches when I turn his face to mine, closing his eyes as my fingers brush the shadow of stubble on his jawline. I hate the way he shies away from me touching him. If he hadn't then I'd have tried to kiss him again like I did last night.

"Let me do it," I insist and he lets go of his grip on the brush.

"I should've called last night," he tells me, staying put on his haunches as I continue what he started. I glance up at Jack as he heads past us into the hallway with a pan of more broken glass. I wait until I'm sure he's out of earshot.

"You should've *stayed* last night," I tell him. "You should've stayed with *me*.

We both wanted it."

"This needs to stop," he says and my heart pains. When he's serious he means it. He always means it. I both hate and love how he always means what he says.

I play ignorant. "What needs to stop?"

He brushes my hair away from my forehead and smiles one of those sad smiles. *It's not you, it's me.* Such a fucking cliché.

I hope he doesn't insult me by fucking saying it.

"I care about you," he says. "I care about what happens to you. Fuck, Carrie, I was worried sick about you. But I can't let this turn into anything it shouldn't be."

"Anything it *shouldn't be?*" My tone comes our sharper than I mean it. "Who's to say how this should and shouldn't be?! Who makes up the rules?!" My eyes burn into his. "Did *you* make them up? What about what *I* think should and shouldn't be?"

I stare right at him, all thoughts of scrubbing muddy boot prints drifting into nothing.

"I want you," I tell him. "I want to be with you. When I'm with you, I feel like we fit. I feel like you could get me, even when I don't get myself." I pause. "And I feel like I could get you too."

"We do fit," he says. "And that's a good thing. We can be friends, Carrie. I'd like to be your friend."

I'd laugh if I wasn't so fucking mortified.

Fucking friend-zoned by the hot older guy I've been getting myself off over for months.

It stings bad.

"Friends?! You want to be my fucking friend?!"

"Yes," he says, and he's got that serious edge to him again. "I'd very much like to be your friend, Carrie."

"And that's all, *just* friends? No matter what?" My eyes search his for a chink in his armour, but he looks so sure.

"Just friends," he says. "And I'll be your friend no matter what. I'm on your side, Carrie, always. You can count on me."

I hear Jack's footsteps in the hallway, and I'm too fucking proud for either of them to see me upset like a silly little cow, so I grit my teeth, shrug my shoulders and act like I don't give a shit about Michael Warren anyway.

"Fine," I tell him. "Just fucking *friends* it is then."

I turn my back on him and scrub that carpet until I get blisters.

They don't hurt nearly as much as my heart does.

JACK

I try to work out if they've fucked or not. Michael's got stronger control over his fucking dick than I have if he hasn't fucked the girl already.

Whatever heated exchange they're having on my living room carpet dries up as I return. You could cut the atmosphere with a knife as Carrie scrubs the carpet like a lunatic.

Oh how quickly things change.

This morning I boarded a plane with the sole intention of putting an end to Michael's Carrie Wells insanity for good. This evening I've invited the crazy girl to stay in my home, not for Michael's sake, but for hers.

Hers and maybe mine.

I'm rarely excited by anything, but I'm excited by her.

When I was a kid, I loved going to watch daredevil stunts with my dad. I loved the guys on bikes doing flips in the air and the people getting shot out of cannons. I loved magic shows where the pretty assistant always got sawn in half in a box.

It always felt so exhilarating – the inevitable buzz of adrenalin that zipped up my spine at the thought that something could really go wrong. As though I was dancing with danger just by looking on from the sidelines.

That's how Carrie Wells makes me feel – only I'm not on the sidelines with Carrie Wells, I'm right in the fucking arena.

Being around her feels like dancing with danger. It's all in her eyes. In her wildness. In the way she gives no fucks for social norms and conventions.

It's in the way I know she won't be tamed, but I want to try anyway.

I don't fucking know why, but I do.

I'm watching the clock until sensible Michael heads home for a sensible sleep before work tomorrow. I'm wondering how much work of my own I'll get done knowing this exotic sprite of destruction is loose in my house tomorrow.

Michael hovers a long while before he leaves. He declines a beer as we finish up the cleaning. He declines a coffee too, stating – as predicted – that he needs a decent night's sleep in order to give his meetings the best of himself tomorrow.

He's always trying to give the best of himself.

If he hasn't fucked Carrie Wells yet, that'll be the reason why. His own inflated sense of decency.

I tell him I'll see him soon when he finally heads off for the night. Carrie nods her head but says very little, even though he prompts her for a *goodnight*.

I can't keep up with their exchanges. One minute they're falling over themselves to take the blame for each other, the next they won't even look each other in the eye.

She looks shocked as I hand her a cold beer from the fridge.

"I think you've earned it," I tell her and clink my bottle against hers.

"Just cleaning up my mess," she says but swigs it back with a smile.

I pull out a stool from the kitchen island and take a seat. She follows suit, propping her grubby elbows on the freshly wiped marble like we haven't just spent an age making this house presentable.

I'm not like Michael with his super reasonable approach to life. I like to hammer down the ground rules and make sure everyone knows where I stand on things.

I'm direct and I give no fucks for anything less.

"Let's get a few things straight," I say and she cocks her head at me. "I may be letting you stay, but I'm not a total fucking moron. If you want to stay under my roof, you'll be treating the place with respect."

"I've got more respect than you have for the place," she tells me. "When was the last time you checked on your land?"

I shoot a look at the window, staring at the blackness beyond. "You mean my fields?" I shrug. "Fields pretty much take care of themselves last time I checked, with a little helping hand from the sheep in them."

"That's your problem," she says. "You don't know your own land. You have no respect for it. You like the house but not what comes along with it. Maybe you should be a city boy instead."

Her assumptions rile me and my tone lets her know it. "You think *you're* from the land? From a tribe of nature in harmony with the soul of these parts? Is that what you think?"

She raises an eyebrow. "Something like that actually, yeah."

I take another swig of beer. "Listen, sweetheart, if you cut my family tree it would bleed the sap of this fucking county and all the years we worked the land here. I'll show you, if you like? Agriculture runs all the way back through my bloodline on the very same soil my house rests on now. I belong in a city no more than you do, I'm just better at blending in."

"So why are you so fucking useless with the gifts you have, then?" she asks, and it takes me aback.

"Why didn't I fix a fucking fence, you mean? I have hundreds of fences. Miles of hedgerows and brooks and ditches. You think I'm going to keep an eye on every part of it all the time?"

"You should," she snaps, and I laugh.

"If you're so bothered about my fences, why don't you head out there and fix them up for me?"

I'm surprised when her confidence shrivels. She spins her bottle in her fingers and looks at the table, not at me.

I feel a tiny shiver of enlightenment, as though I've lifted up a pebble in a rock pool and found a desperate little crab underneath.

"Well?" I prompt. "You could head out there and fix them up for me. I'd say that was a fair exchange for a roof over your head, no?"

Her eyes meet mine but they're guarded. "You mean like a job? An actual job?"

"I mean like contributing to your keep. Doing what you can to keep the place together. If you're staying here too, you should be invested in keeping the place looked after, don't you think?"

"But I'm only here for a few days…" she says. "I'll hardly have time…"

I'm surprised to find I'm not even trying to fool myself into thinking she'll be gone in a few days.

"Then you'd better work quickly, hadn't you?"

She nods. "I can fix a fence, you'll see. I'll make it good as fucking new. *Better* than fucking new."

"I hope so," I say. "Carrie, I'm a fair guy. I like things to run smoothly.

I believe in order and taking control of life and making your own luck. I'm happy to give you a shot here, but there will have to be ground rules. I'm not talking Michael-type ground rules, either – I'm no fucking social worker out to fix the world and everyone in it."

"Ground rules like what?"

"Ground rules like don't fucking take the piss out of me, treat the place with respect, and do what's expected of you."

"And what'll be expected of me?"

I smile and finish up my drink.

"I'll let you know when I've worked that out," I tell her. "Goodnight, Carrie, I have work in the morning."

I've reached the stairs before I hear her call goodnight after me.

My hand is down my pants before I've even reached the top stair, because I've no delusions of fucking morality when it comes to women I want to fuck.

Unlike poor fucking Michael.

I fire a text message off to him before I take a shower, man to man.

And then I shoot my load over my bathroom tiles while thinking about Carrie's pretty little blue knickers.

MICHAEL

I should be long asleep when the text message sounds.

It's Jack, of course, not Carrie.

My heart thumps at the possibility that she's already decimated his patience. Maybe she's already descended into hissing monster Carrie and he's thought better of his offer. Maybe it wouldn't entirely be such a bad thing, having to bring her back here.

Maybe I could hide her from Pam long enough to figure something out. Maybe having her around could work, even if I won't allow myself to cross the line with her. Maybe I'd even be able to help her through her shit without having to check all the right boxes at work.

I open the message, expecting the worst – but it's nothing like that.

Man to fucking man, Michael, are you gonna fuck the girl or what?

My reply is instant, even though my gut aches with it.

Of course I'm fucking not.

It takes a while for him to reply. I'm just about drifting off to sleep when the phone bleeps at me.

But you want her? I'm talking for real here.

I don't let myself go there because I daren't. I daren't allow myself to admit how I really feel about Carrie Wells, because once I do that there'll be no going back. I can't allow myself to contemplate the serious potential of crossing the line with a girl less than half my age, a girl who depends on me to help her through this shitty time in her life. A girl who's had nobody constant who'll stand strong in the face of all her whims and tricks and silly games.

A girl who needs to know she can rely on me to be her friend above all other things, even if I'm in love with her.

I'm in love with her.

Fucking in love with her.

I've never felt so alive as I feel when I'm around her, and if I let myself entertain the possibility that this could be, even for a second, I'm not sure I'll ever be able to live my normal life again.

So I don't.

I say the right thing.

The sensible thing.

No, I don't want her and you shouldn't either. She's barely even eighteen, Jack. She's a girl who needs care, not fucking cock.

I don't get a response to that one.

And I don't get any fucking sleep either.

Twelve

JACK

Carrie Wells is a one-girl whirlwind of backchat in my once peaceful home. She's noisy and obnoxious, messy and disorganised with no respect whatsoever for timekeeping.

Every evening I head home from work nervous of what the fuck I'll find there, and yet I'm still excited when I turn the key in my front door.

Michael's right, of course. There's no way he should contemplate fucking Carrie Wells, and neither should I.

But I am contemplating it. I'm contemplating it every fucking minute.

Still, I do try to talk myself down from pursuing that tight little pussy of hers, simply because I have no idea where that kind of crap would lead any of us. The girl is a loose cannon, and I've never been one for commitment. I'm rarely still interested in a woman after she's spent the night in my bed, and where would that leave our living arrangement if it comes to a *thanks, but no thanks* next morning?

You know what they say: Hell hath no fury like a woman scorned – and Carrie Wells is both crazy and furious enough to make Hell's own demons shit a ton of bricks. I really don't need that kind of insanity on my plate, not while she's holed up in my house.

But that's really not what concerns me at the heart of it, not if I'm being totally honest with myself.

What concerns me most of all, is that this excitement I feel around Carrie Wells *would* survive a night in my bed, and escalate all the more because of it.

There's no doubt she's craving some kind of stability, and as grotesquely adult and responsible as it is, I feel a strange compulsion to help the girl find her own straight and narrow and keep her on it.

I know that helping Carrie has been Michael's job for the past five months, and I know he's been giving it his all, but whereas Michael usually has the experience to excel in this kind of one-on-one coaching, I can't help but feel he's slightly off the mark with this one.

Scrap that, I think he's well off the mark with this one.

Call me arrogant for forming an opinion after just a few days in her company, but I really think I'm onto something.

Where Michael is trying the calm, stable and supportive routine, I think he should be giving her an earful of shit. Where Michael seems like he wants to wrap her broken bits in cotton wool, I think he should be putting a heavy foot down on her bad behaviour,

In short, I think Carrie Wells needs discipline as well as support. Probably even more so.

I think she needs a heavy hand to keep her in line, and I think she'd flourish for it.

I think she'd even like it.

I know Michael's hands were mostly tied at work. He had boxes to tick and guidelines to adhere to. He had allocated time slots to make a difference and the clock was always ticking.

But not anymore. Not here.

Not for any of us.

I strongly doubt Carrie's ever been given boundaries by someone who isn't intimidated by her craziness. I doubt she's ever been made to understand the concept of tough love.

Maybe not even any love.

I see it in her eyes when they meet mine over our late night beer. I hear it in her voice when she tells me she doesn't need anyone and doesn't give a fuck what I think of her approach to loading up the dishwasher so insanely high it's almost impossible to close.

She's a bag of backchat and bluster, pushing and poking me for a reaction whenever I'm in her company, but I see enough to get a sense of the troublesome girl with the raven hair.

It's not that Michael isn't around enough to draw his own conclusions about what Carrie needs. He heads over every evening when his workday is done to check in on her. He makes calls to various associations about her living arrangements and talks her through the paperwork, even though she's thoroughly disinterested in everything he's doing for her.

Carrie gives him nothing because she's a snotty bitch who's punishing him for sticking to his morals. I see it even if he can't.

That's why I decide to broach it with her after the first swig of beer goes down a treat this evening.

"Straight up answer," I begin. "Why are you being such a fucking bitch to him?"

She raises her eyebrows like she doesn't know what I'm talking about, but I laugh in her face.

"Cut the crap, Carrie, we both know you're freezing him out. You want to humiliate him for giving a shit about you. Why?"

"You're fucking mad." She taps the side of her head. "You're seeing shit that isn't there."

"*You're* fucking mad if you think I can't see right through you," I tell her. "I just want to know why."

She shrugs. "Because he's a fucking dick."

I shake my head. "Nice try, sugarplum. We both know the guy's not a fucking dick. Just a couple of days ago you were desperate to confess your undying devotion to him in my living room. Now you act like he's the biggest loser piece of shit you've ever met."

"*He* treated *me* like the biggest loser piece of shit he's ever met."

I take another swig of beer. "What do you mean?"

She folds her arms.

"Carrie, what do you mean?"

She groans. "Why can't you mind your own fucking business?"

I'm not going to let this go. No fucking way.

"It's hard to mind my own fucking business in my own fucking house, Carrie."

"Yeah, well, it's hard to be nice to a guy who says he doesn't want you."

I raise an eyebrow. "He said that?"

She nods. "*Friends*, that's what he said we can be. Such fucking bullshit."

"Friends isn't the same thing as saying he doesn't want you."

She kicks my stool with her boot. "'Tis as far as I'm concerned. He can go fuck himself." She tips back her drink. "I don't want him anymore anyway. I don't give a fuck that he blew me out."

I know she must be lying, but my hands feel clammy all the same.

"You don't want him anymore?"

Her eyes aren't just piercing tonight, they're dangerous. Her guarded stare gives me the fucking shivers.

"So, what do you want?" I prompt.

"I want you to shut the fuck up," she snaps.

But I won't, because she's sucking her bottom lip as she spins her bottle in her fingers. I won't, because the sight of her sitting there makes my cock twitch in my pants.

Because I don't want her to want Michael, not anymore.

I want her to want me.

I want her to look me in the eye and ask *me* to stay the night, even though it would be crazy.

And I think she knows it.

"He cares about you," I tell her.

"He can fuck off," she says, and this time she looks like she really means it.

I can't fucking keep up with the girl.

CARRIE

I know Jack and Michael both think I'm being a lazy bitch who doesn't give a shit, not for all the advice they're trying to give me, and not for the way they sigh and shake their heads and try to work me out. I tell them nothing about the work I'm doing on the fences while they're busy in their day jobs. I tell them nothing about the way I leave Jack's place every morning and dig around the outbuildings for supplies as soon as his big fancy car pulls off the driveway.

I keep my mouth shut because I've never done this kind of shit before and I don't want to look like a total fucking idiot for getting it wrong. I've never hammered in fence posts and strung wire fencing, and trimmed back overgrown hedgerows and measured out planks before. I check out videos on my phone through Jack's Wi-Fi whenever I'm grabbing a quick sandwich for lunch, and I may not have any swanky grades from school, but by the end of the first week of sorting out Jack's neglected grounds, I think I might be okay at doing this stuff.

I think I might even be good at it.

My fences don't look half bad, and they're strong, too. I've tested them out by vaulting them and clambering over them and trying to wiggle them in the ground. My muscles are aching and I feel like I've run a marathon by the time Friday afternoon comes around, but there's a weird glow in my belly.

I did something good.

Something I'm actually proud of.

And although I'm nervous about showing them, just in case I'm wrong and they tell me I've made a right mess of it all, I'm excited about surprising them. I'm excited about proving to them I'm not just some loser who's watching daytime TV in Jack's house every day.

It still hurts that Michael doesn't want me. It still hurts that he blew me out when I thought there was really something between us.

It's been days now since he told me he's not interested. He's still kind but he's guarded, and when he's trying to talk me through whatever crappy agency he's working out my fate with next, all I can think about is the way he's so tense. It's like he thinks I'm going to jump him any second. Like I don't know what *I'm not interested* means and stand a chance of making more of a tit out of myself than I already did with him.

No fear there.

And then there's Jack. Jack who I first thought was nothing but a douche with a load of money. Jack who I thought for sure would chuck me onto the street and never want to see me again.

Jack who now gives me a beer every evening and talks straight, no bullshit and no dicking about. He says what he thinks, and what he thinks is that I'm being a bitch to Michael without good reason.

He doesn't know how much it stings to want someone who doesn't want you back.

But now things are getting complicated, because a few weeks ago I thought all I ever wanted was Michael. The way his eyes are firm but kind. The way he doesn't want to let me down. The way I know his calmness would disappear the minute his suit came off and I got my mouth around that big dick I know he's packing. I've seen the promise of it when he's hard but tries to hide it.

I've been checking him out for months and liked every single thing I've seen.

But here, in Jack's place, with a whole other proper man to scope out every evening, I realise that it's not just being grateful that has me feeling butterflies every time I hear his car in the driveway after work. It's not just wanting some company that has my heart racing every time he grabs me a beer out of the fridge.

Jack's eyes aren't kind, not like Michael's. They're tough and raw and brutal. His words are blunt but fair. And the way he wears his suit is different to the way Michael wears his. Michael has an almost scholarly look about him, like he's some kind of boffin professor or something. Jack's looks like he was born to wear it.

I don't like suits but I like them on Jack.

I like them on Michael, too.

I like the way both of these guys are put together, and in bed at night I think of both of them.

It breaks my heart to think I might not get either, but I'm not done yet.

Michael doesn't want me and he's made sure I know it, but Jack…

Jack looks at me. Not just like Bill and Eli and Eddie Stevens looked at me. He doesn't try to sneak a peek every time I'm sitting opposite him in a low cut top. He doesn't try to check me out in the shower when I leave the bathroom door slightly open – and I do.

Jack looks at me like I'm a proper woman, even if he isn't about to make a move on me. He looks at me as though he could tear my clothes off and fuck me hard and know what the fuck he was doing, even if he isn't going to. And I *am* a proper woman. I'm eighteen and I'm not sorry for the fact that I want to get fucked by a guy who can't keep his hands off me.

But Jack hasn't made a single move. Doesn't even hint that he wants to.

I wish he would, but he doesn't.

I've almost finished up a fresh section of fencing when the sky turns grey. I work quickly, because I planned to take pictures of this bit all finished up. I'm panting and sweating by the time the rain starts, and when it starts it starts hard.

I'm soaked through by the time I've hammered in the last few nails, skidding through the mud up the bank as I gather up my things and try to get a decent shot of my finished railings. My boots are definitely past it. Their grip is useless as I try to keep my footing, and my arms are too full of tools to keep my balance. I go tumbling, tits first into a sloppy pile of mud, and if I were an indoor kind of girl I'd be pissed, because my clothes are plastered with mud and sheep shit and fuck knows what else. My open jacket did little to protect my cami and bra, and any other colour than white would have definitely been a better choice for doing this kind of work in if I had all that many options to choose from. But I don't.

I can't stop laughing as I pull myself up. The rain on my muddy skin feels amazing. Getting so up close and personal with the outdoors sings to my soul, even if I am filthy now. I ditch my jacket in the mud and spin on the spot, not caring that my muddy hair is plastered to my scalp, or the rain is trickling down between my tits, or that I can taste the earth on my tongue.

It's a moment I want to keep forever, so I dig my mobile out of my pocket and angle it for a selfie. I hardly ever take photos of myself, and it feels weird. I make sure I hold the camera up high so you can see the fencing down below behind me, and I blink the rain from my eyes and give a smile.

And then I see how low my cami is now it's wet through. I see how you can see the scrappy lace of my old bra and the shape of my nipples poking through the fabric.

I think about Jack and Michael seeing me like this.

I think about Jack wanting me and Michael seeing how wrong he was for turning his back on having what could have been his.

I think about them getting hard when they see how much of a woman I really am under my baggy clothes and messy hair.

So I tug my top down just a bit more. Just enough that the camera shows more than it should. And then I smile a dirty smile and take the photo.

By the time I've finished up ditching Jack's tools back where I found them, it's later than usual. The lights are on in the kitchen when I kick off my muddy boots by the back door, and the kettle is already on. My heart is pumping as Jack steps in from the hallway, and my cheeks burn up as he does a double take at the state of me.

"What the–" he begins, and marches his way over.

"I've been out," I tell him.

"No shit," he says. He reaches behind me to grab a couple of mugs from the cupboard.

"I fell," I tell him and he cocks an eyebrow.

"You look like you've been mud bathing."

I fold my arms across my filthy tits. "I've been working."

"Working?"

I nod, already feeling self-conscious about the big reveal I've been planning for days.

It feels so much more stupid now it's nearly here.

I notice Jack's only pulled out two mugs. "Where's Michael?"

"Leaving do. Some temp worker from his office. He'll be over tomorrow."

My heart drops. "Tomorrow?"

Jack nods. "Will probably be a late one, these crappy socials normally are."

"Only if you want to stay at them." I can't help feeling rejected, even though it's stupid. I can't help feeling like he should be as excited to get here as I am excited to see him, even though I hate him now.

"He'll be over in the morning," Jack says. "Give the guy a break, will you? He's been fawning around you all pissing week already."

He hasn't been fawning around me at all, just trying to get me some shitty council accommodation, but I don't say it.

I must look sad because Jack tips his head and sighs. "If you miss him so fucking much, maybe you should stop being such a cow when he's here."

"It's complicated," I say and he laughs.

"*You're* fucking complicated, Carrie." He stirs my tea, and I love the way he knows just how I like it now. He puts in just the right amount of milk and hands it over. "Where did you go?"

I gesture to my top. "For a browse around the shops, where does it look like I've pissing been?"

"Good. I'm glad you got out for some fresh air. Better for you than watching crappy daytime TV all your life. That shit will rot your brain, you know."

And that's when I decide to show him. Michael be damned.

I reach inside my pocket and pull out my mobile, and my fingers are shaking as I call up the gallery app. "I don't watch fucking TV," I tell him as I select the very first photo I took of my fencing. "I've been working."

"Working?"

I nod and shove the handset at him. "Working, yeah. Sorting *your* shit fucking fencing out."

I hold my breath as he flicks through the images, trying to pretend I'm not nervous as he checks it out. But I am nervous. I feel like my whole fucking soul is exposed to him.

If he says it's shit, I'll want to cry and I know it. If he says it's no good, I'll have to run away and never come back, because I'll never want to see those fields again, even though I love them.

"You did this?" he asks and his eyes burn right into mine.

I nod. "Yeah."

"All of it?"

I sigh. "Think I called out a maintenance crew? *Yes*, Jack, I did all of it."

He keeps flicking through the images. "This is incredible. You've done every bloody paddock."

I shake my head. "Not every one. There's some at the top that need fixing up, but I'll do them. I'll finish up next week."

He looks between me and the phone, and he's impressed. My heart soars as I see it. He's definitely impressed.

"I don't know what to say," he says.

"You could say thanks," I tell him, and hate the way my tone is so fucking snarky all the time.

"Thank you," he says and I feel like a bitch. "You've done an amazing job. I'm blown away." He's still flicking through the images, and I cringe as I register how many I've taken. So many fucking pictures of fences and bits of wood and fields from different angles. My memory card is jammed full of them. "I'll pay you," he adds. "You've more than earned it. This is worth way more than a bit of food and lodging."

"You don't have to pay me," I say, and I don't want him to. I don't want it to feel like they're his fields and I was just a nobody doing him a favour.

I worked so hard because, just for these few days, it felt like they may be mine too. Like they're a part of me now.

Like I belong in them.

I take a breath as I notice him swallow. His thumb hovers. And I know where he is. I just know it. He's reached the end of the gallery, and the selfie I took just a few minutes ago.

His eyes flick from the phone to my open jacket and my soaked cami top. They darken when they meet mine.

"This is a dangerous game to play," he tells me, and my heart races. I grit my teeth instinctively, because that wasn't quite the fucking reaction I was hoping for.

"What's a fucking dangerous game?"

He spins the handset, like I haven't seen the picture already. But it's worse than I thought. My top looks even lower than I remember. You can pretty much see the dark circles under my bra.

I look like a slut.

A wet, muddy, filthy little slut.

"Was this for Michael?"

"Of course it wasn't for fucking Michael," I sneer. "Michael doesn't fucking want me, remember?"

"Then who?" he asks. "Who were you going to show this to?"

"No-fucking-one," I lie.

And just like he usually is, with his calling bullshit on every fucking thing, he looks me straight in the eye, so fierce it fucking burns, and then he says it. He just fucking says it.

"If you wanted me to see your tits, Carrie, you should have just shown me your tits. No need for the theatrics. I've seen plenty of them in my time."

He thinks I'm playing stupid slutty games, and I am.

He thinks I wanted him to see me, and I do.

The self-consciousness burns, and my stomach does a flip, because I do want him to see me. I want him to see me and be as impressed as he was about the fencing. I want him to look at me like he did a few minutes ago when he thought I was amazing.

"You think I took that so you could see my fucking tits?!" I hiss, like he's well fucking off the mark.

"Didn't you?"

I shrug. "Don't give a shit either way. You can look if you want."

"I wasn't looking," he says. "You showed me."

"I ain't shown you nothing. Can't even see my fucking nipples."

He flips the phone in my direction. "Yes, Carrie, I can see your nipples perfectly well, thank you." His eyes go straight to my top, and they're still poking through the fabric. I know they are. My cheeks burn. He hands back my phone, and even though I'm burning up I hate that it's over.

Jack sips his tea like nothing's happened, but it has. It has to me.

I've nothing to go on but one single second of his first reaction, because he's been cool as fucking ice for the rest of it. But he swallowed. He swallowed and his eyes widened, just for a second. But it's enough.

It's enough to take a chance on.

It's enough to take a risk on his stupid fucking comment.

So without a word I slip my jacket from my shoulders and tug my straps down. I pull my muddy cami down over my tits and pull my bra down with it. And I stand there, with fierce eyes as Jack takes a step back.

I stare as he stares, nerves dancing as his gaze rests upon my naked tits, nipples still pointy from the cold.

And then I try to come out with some snarky comment. Just like I always do.

Only there isn't one there.

For the first time ever, my smart mouth stays shut.

Thirteen

JACK

should have known by now to expect the unexpected from Carrie Wells. I should have known that my suspicions were right and there was more going on with her than vegging in front of my TV every day, stacking up plates as though she's been having a one-girl feeding frenzy, even though the fridge is still stocked full.

I should've also known better than to tell her she should've just shown me her tits if she wanted to, and not contemplated the possibility she would follow through with it.

But here I am, standing open-mouthed as Carrie pulls down her grubby white top and bares her perfect pale tits to me.

She's confident at first, cocky even. Her shoulders are back and proud as she juts out her sweet rosy nipples.

And I was wrong.

I have seen plenty of tits in my time, but I haven't seen it all before. I've never seen a pair of tits that make my mouth water like this pair.

She has a beauty mark to the side of her right nipple. There's a smear of mud above her left. And they're beautiful. Perfect.

She's fucking perfect.

They're bigger than I'd have expected from her frame, sitting high and proud and just right for a decent handful. My mouth waters, my cock fucking throbs in my pants, and I'm on the edge of fucking losing it. A breath away from shunting her against the kitchen sink and tearing the rest of her clothes off her.

But I can't. I can't because of Michael.

"Well?" she says, but I can't say a fucking word.

I watch her bravado slip away in a glorious heartbeat. Brash, sharp-mouthed Carrie disappears before my eyes, her shoulders dropping as she registers how exposed she is in the middle of my kitchen, in front of a man who wants to break and show her how fucking beautiful those tits are, but can't.

"You said I should show you..." she says, and her voice is unsteady. I've never heard her as unsteady as she is right now.

"I said it was a dangerous game you were playing," I tell her.

"I like dangerous games."

And so do I. But not now.

Not without knowing how serious Michael is about not acting on whatever desire he's harbouring for this divine little creature we're both enamoured by.

"You'll get cold," I tell her, even though it's the most copout fucking excuse for a reaction I've ever given.

She looks like I've slapped her, and I feel sorry for Michael with added empathy, because I can't imagine he experienced any less of a fucking guilt rush than I'm feeling right now.

Carrie pulls up her top like I've just shit on her cereal, her cheeks flushed pink and her eyes wide, even though she's trying to force an air of confidence that's really not coming.

"They're very pretty," I tell her once they're safely out of temptation's way. "And if I were ten years younger."

She shakes her head. Sneers at me like I'm a fucking idiot.

"So *you're* blowing me out too? What's wrong with me? Why can't a girl find a real fucking man around this fucking shithole?"

I hold up a hand. "There's nothing fucking wrong with you, Carrie. But I can't."

"Can't, or don't want to?"

I make sure my eyes are right on hers when I answer. "Can't."

Her mouth drops open. "But why not?"

Because of fucking Michael. Because he fucking wants you, too.

"Because it wouldn't be right," I say. "Because you're barely eighteen and I don't do relationships."

"Why don't you?"

Because I've never met anyone who excites me. Not until you. Not until right fucking now in this kitchen.

"Because I like my own company. I'm not a man who likes to settle."

It was a stupid choice of words. She nods at me, smiling as though I didn't just see a flash of pain in her eyes.

"Well, luckily for you, I think Michael's nearly done with my housing application. I'll be out of your hair before you know it, and you can get back to your own brilliant fucking company."

I sigh. "That isn't what I meant…"

But she isn't listening. She picks up her jacket and downs her tea. She barks out she's taking a shower when she's halfway down the hall, and the door slams at the top of the stairs.

I'm a cock.

A cock with a hard fucking cock, and a mind to sprint upstairs after her and pound that tight little pussy until she screams for me.

And I will.

Just as soon as I've cleared my own fucking conscience first.

I grab my car keys.

MICHAEL

I barely even know this temp. It's like we're having a bastard leaving party for everyone these days, even if they've only been there five minutes. Drury's is busy with Friday night drinkers, and I'm huddled in a corner, wedged between Pam and Julie as they recount office stories from ten years ago.

They were boring the last three times I heard them, and my nerves are on edge as the clock ticks, counting down my window of opportunity in which I can legitimately turn up at Jack's to see Carrie.

She can't freeze me out forever, even if she's doing a mighty fine job of it this week.

I'm not usually jealous, that isn't my style, and I definitely shouldn't be jealous of Jack, given that he's been my best friend for almost a lifetime, through thick and thin and everything in between, but I am.

I'm jealous of the way she doesn't snipe at every word he utters. I'm jealous of the way he goes to sleep in the room next door to her every evening.

I'm jealous of the closeness they're developing right before my eyes.

And I'm jealous of the Friday night they're undoubtedly spending together in my absence.

We've been in Drury's over two hours and the party shows no sign of slowing down. I keep eying my watch in an attempt to rustle up an excuse, but every time I do, Pam pats my wrist and tells me to lighten up.

I'm about to drop Jack a text to scope out a late-night beer at his, but the minute I pull my phone from my pocket the bleep of a message comes through.

Our thoughts must have crossed in the ether, because it's from him.

We need to talk. Meet you in Drury's car park.

My blood runs cold.

Talk.

We need to talk.

There's only one thing he'll be wanting to discuss with me in Drury's car park with no prior warning, and I wonder what crazy shit she's done now.

Surely nothing worse than the crow incident.

The idea he's had enough of her, both horrifies and thrills me in equal measure.

I get up from my seat and squeeze through Pam's side, offering up excuses about having an urgent call that needs attending to. They groan and roll their eyes, telling me the night is still young, and I do the polite thing of insisting I'll be back soon, just get me a nice cold beer to come back to.

Jack's already in the car park when I step outside. His engine is still running as I climb into the passenger seat.

"What's she done now?" I ask before he can speak.

His hands are on the steering wheel. His fingers give it a frustrated squeeze before he cuts the ignition.

"She's fixed my fencing," he says. "She's done a great job. Worked like a trooper."

It takes me a moment to register his words. "She's fixed your fencing? On her own?"

"On her own."

"And that's good, right?" I prompt. "That's good news?"

He sighs. "And she showed me her tits. Pulled her top right down in front of me."

My throat dries up. "But why did she…"

"Because I told her to. Because she showed me a dodgy selfie that she definitely wanted me to see, maybe even both of us, and I called her out on it. I said if she wanted me to see her tits she should have just showed me, not dicked about playing stupid games with a fucking camera."

My gut lurches. "And what did you do?"

He sighs again. "What do you think I fucking did? I told her it couldn't happen. That it wouldn't be right."

The relief floods through me until I see the guilt on his face.

"So what's the problem?" I say. "What are you trying to say?"

He twists in his seat to face me and I know shit's about to get serious.

"Man to man," he says. "Are you serious about not going there? Because if you are…"

I hold up a hand. "Serious about not going there with Carrie? She's eighteen years old, of course I'm serious. She needs stability and support, not a–"

"I think I'm falling for her," he says over me, and my words shrivel in my throat. "I think I'm falling for her, and I don't know how long I can hold back from acting on it, because I'm a fucking dick who can't keep his dick in his pants. But if you want her, if you really want her and this is a load of politically correct bullshit morality you're spouting and nothing more, then I'll…"

"Then you'll what?" I ask. "Then what will you do?"

131

He tips his head back against the window. "Then I don't fucking know what I'll do. I don't fucking know what either of us will do."

And neither do I.

My heart is beating in my ears. My stomach twisted up as I contemplate the cold hard reality of my best friend falling for the girl I'm in love with.

I can't lie to him. I don't want to lie to him.

And I don't want to lie to myself, either.

"I'm in love with her," I admit, and it sounds despicable even as I say it.

"Fuck," he says.

"Fuck," I agree.

He takes a deep breath. "Well, fuck. That's really put us up shit creek."

I close my eyes. "When she showed you her–" I pause. "Does she want you? Does she… have feelings?"

"Fuck knows what the girl wants," he says. "She doesn't think you're interested. Says you blew her out and don't give a shit about her. She probably thinks the same about me."

A wave of regret washes over me. "She really thinks that?"

I open my eyes and he's staring right at me. "She's not as confident as she thinks she is. It's all bluster. I don't think she has any idea how attractive she is."

"And she thinks she's not good enough…"

"Yes, that's what I'd suspect." His fingers tap against the steering wheel. "Not gonna lie to you, Mike. She's under my fucking skin."

I laugh, because what else is there to do?

"The Carrie Wells effect. Welcome to my world."

"We need to work out what we do from here, because she's in my house, Mike. She's in my house and I can't stop thinking about her."

"And neither can I," I admit. "I haven't been able to think about anything else for months."

"Fuck," he says again.

"We can't act on this," I tell him. "She needs to know she can count on us. She needs to know she's safe, and supported."

"She doesn't need pandering to, she needs discipline. She needs to feel part of something, and to feel part of something she needs to know there are ground rules."

I sigh. "Jack, it's not that simple. Carrie has behavioural issues, she's been let down by the system and –"

He shakes his head. "She pushes away everyone that gives a shit about her. She tests people and they always fail. They fail because they refuse to stand their ground and pull her up on her bullshit. They expect her to behave like a fucking nightmare so she does. But not in my house. Not with me."

"You've known her a couple of weeks," I tell him.

"And you've been working with her five months and she speaks to you like you're a piece of shit."

His observation smarts. "What's your point?"

He shifts in his seat. "My point is that your approach isn't working, not with her. If we're going to get her through whatever crap she's got going on in that pretty head of hers, we need a united front. She needs to know that she can't just throw her fucking toys out of the pram without consequences."

"And you plan to do that by fucking her? Is that what you're saying?" My tone is more brutal than I intend.

"I'm not saying anything about fucking the girl, Mike. I'm just making an observation. Whether I fuck her or not is incidental."

"Incidental?"

He nods. "Yeah, incidental. One of us is going to end up fucking the girl.

Now or in six fucking months, it doesn't matter. The question is, how do we make sure this situation works in a way that doesn't fuck one, two or all fucking three of us right up." He pauses. "We've been friends a long time, Mike. Never has a girl come between us so far, I don't want it to start now."

My laugh is low and mainly for my benefit. "You've never been interested in a girl long enough for her *to* come between us, what makes you think Carrie is going to be any different?"

"Because I think I'm falling in love with her," he says, and my heart fucking stops. "When I said I'm falling for her, I meant it, Mike. I mean I'm falling for her hard."

"And I've already fallen," I tell him. "Hard."

He nods. "So what do we do now? Where the fuck do we go from here?"

I shake my head. Sigh, then take a breath.

"I have no fucking idea."

CARRIE

I hear Jack's car pull away and it breaks my heart.

He's running from me.

He's running because he doesn't want me. He's running because I made a stupid fucking mistake and showed him my tits and he hated them.

He hates me.

I try to calm myself down because things never end well when I get freaked out. I try to tell myself that I didn't just fuck up so bad that I have to leave this place. That Jack isn't like the others.

They let me stay because they had to, because I was a kid and they were obliged to care for me. Jack let me stay because he wanted to, and he hasn't kicked me out yet, not even when he thought I was being a lazy bum all day.

Maybe he won't throw me out for showing him my tits either.

I take a shower to get rid of the mud, and hope I can wash the embarrassment off with it. My plans for a passionate encounter in the kitchen seem so fucking silly now. He didn't even touch me.

I thought he wanted to, but he couldn't have. Not someone like Jack.

Jack's the kind of guy to go for what he wants, I know him well enough to know that. And he didn't.

He couldn't drive away fast enough.

The more I think about it the angrier I feel. Two guys and neither of them want me. And why?

Am I hideous? Am I too fucked up for them to want to touch with a bargepole?

Eddie Stevens didn't seem like that.

Bill didn't seem like that.

Neither did Luke, or Eli.

They all wanted to fuck me.

They may not have wanted *me*, but they wanted my pussy.

But not Jack or Michael.

I guess my pussy just isn't good enough for Jack or Michael, no matter what I do.

No matter if I spend all fucking week trying to prove to the both of them that I really can be good and work hard. No matter if I show Jack a hundred fucking pictures of how hard I work, it doesn't matter.

They still don't think I'm good enough.

I feel the anger brewing. Stupid anger that makes me act like a crazy bitch. Stupid anger that protects me against getting hurt and upset and pushed away.

I throw some clean clothes on and check out of the window.

He's still gone.

I can't believe they've both gone out and left me here on a Friday evening, like they think I'm just going to sit around and do nothing while they're off having a good time or doing whatever fucking important shit is worth leaving me home alone for.

I don't have any money, and once upon a time I'd have dipped into the envelope of cash I know Jack keeps in the kitchen drawer next to the tea towels. I'd have told myself I'd earned it with all the fucking manual labour I've been doing this week.

But I have no Eli demanding money, not this week, and I don't want to take any for myself, either.

I don't want to take anything from Jack, not now he's been so kind to me.

Not now I care about him.

So I don't.

I pull on my boots and head out the front door without so much as a penny in my pocket.

But this time I do have my ID.

Fourteen

MICHAEL

J ack and I stare at each other for what feels like an age. My palms are
clammy as I think the unthinkable; that I might have to watch my best
friend become romantically involved with the girl I'm in love with.

It's not that I'd resent Jack being happy, or Carrie either. Of course I wouldn't.
But fuck, the thought makes me feel sick as a dog.

"If you want to be with her, I'll back off," Jack says. "You saw her first."

"How could I make a move now, knowing you want her too?"

"I'd deal with it," he says. "I'd have to deal with it."

"And *I'd* have to deal with it if it was you she wanted to be with. And it
might be. She's barely spoken a word to me in days."

"But she wanted you first. She almost certainly still does."

"She showed you her tits less than an hour ago. I'd say her interest in you
is pretty current, Jack."

He shakes his head. "I can't believe this is happening. Both of us going fucking crazy over an eighteen year old girl."

"She's not like other girls," I say and he laughs.

"No, she fucking isn't. She's a whole fucking whirlwind of trouble."

"I could lose my job," I tell him.

"I'd be more worried about your bloody mind than your job, man."

He's got a point. I think of my colleagues back inside the pub, imagining their faces if they discovered I'd made a move on Carrie Wells.

Shit like that never ends well, especially around here. And it shouldn't.

Professionals shouldn't abuse their position. Professionals should never discard their moral ideals and pursue girls that were once in their care. Professionals definitely shouldn't be sitting in a car outside a pub on a Friday evening trying to work out which one of them is going to make a move on a girl with a whole raft of behavioural issues.

But here we are.

"What is it you like about her?" I ask him.

He takes a breath. "Her spirit, her smart mouth, her wildness. Her laugh. Her smile. The sweetness in her when she lets her guard down. Her pixie nose. The way her hair moves. The way she argues the toss about every fucking thing in the world."

His words make me smile. He's right. She's really quite something.

"We shouldn't even be contemplating it," I say. "Neither of us. She's too young. She's unpredictable. She needs stability."

"She needs discipline." A pause. One of those long pauses I've come to know means someone's about to spit something out. "And love. She needs love too."

Love.

It's strange to hear the word come out of Jack's mouth. He was evasive on the topic even after he got down on one knee for Diana, answering my questions on whether she was really the one with nothing more than a shrug of the shoulders and an *it'll do*.

"What the fuck are we gonna do, Mike?"

I have nothing. Nothing but an uneasy churn in my gut as I contemplate the potential outcomes. Jack and her, me and her. Neither of us with her.

Losing my job.

Losing our friendship. My best friendship.

Losing Carrie.

"You've known her for weeks. How do you know this wouldn't be like the others?" I ask.

"She's already nothing like the others."

"She's nothing like anyone."

He smiles. "You got that right."

I've a suspicion I've got everything right, and this whole setup is snowballing into disaster in front of our eyes.

He sighs. "She should choose. It's not our call."

Even the concept makes me edgy. Choosing me, choosing him – and I suspect she'd choose Jack, because who wouldn't? The guy's great. He's my best friend for a reason.

"We need to think on this," I tell him. "We need considered judgement. Her welfare has to be our top priority. Her security comes first, beyond anything else."

"Agreed," he says.

I look beyond him to the lights on in Drury's. "I should get back. I've got to get through this leaving party before I can find my bearings. You've dropped quite a fucking bombshell on me."

I'm expecting him to speed off back home to hole up with Carrie just as soon as I make a move, but he doesn't.

He gets out of the car when I do and bleeps the central locking. "I think I need a drink after all this. Think prissy Pam will mind if I gatecrash?"

The prospect is a good one. Having Jack at my side in Drury's will be a strangely comforting norm amongst the turbulence.

"I'm sure you'll be very welcome."

There's a smile on my face as we cross the car park. A friendly slap on the back as we head in through the rear entrance.

But an ache in my heart that no amount of rational thought will ever make go away.

JACK

I feel like an absolute prize fucking asshole as we head into Drury's. Mike might be putting a thoroughly gracious front on it, but my confession has him reeling and I know it.

That's the thing with Mike – he's always trying to be the reasonable one. Always trying to do the right thing, for everyone. Not least for me.

And certainly not least for Carrie Wells.

If he was a lesser man, I'm sure he would've fucked the girl already. If he was a lesser man, I'm sure he'd have told me to fuck off with my stupid fucking confession after one paltry week of knowing her.

But he's a better man than I'll ever be, and in my gut that's why I know he should be the one to make a move on Carrie, even if I'm the one in danger of recklessness.

Even if I'm the one who's seen her pretty little tits.

The thought crosses my mind that maybe the little minx is playing both of us for a fool, but I doubt it. If Carrie Wells is playing a game, she's playing a good one. She seems too sharp to risk pitting the two of us against each other, not least because she seems awfully settled at my place.

It's like she belongs there already.

I wave to Mike's colleagues as we step inside the pub, cringing as prissy Pam Clowes jumps from her seat and grabs Mike by the elbow. I think she's always had a thing for him, even if he's always been oblivious.

I have to stifle a laugh as she presses her mouth to his ear, as though I'm about to witness another confession of devotion that will leave his brain spinning even faster than it is already.

Pam's whisper is ragged and harsh and nothing like I was expecting. It's loud enough that I hear it over the chatter from the leaving party table.

"Carrie Wells is here!"

My eyes widen as his do.

"Carrie is here?" he asks and she nods.

"Smoking out the front with Eddie Stevens. They just came in and got tequila. I'd have stopped the barman if she wasn't legal." She pulls her phone from her handbag. "We should call Rosie and Bill, or maybe the police."

I'd leap into action myself, but he's already on it. His hand lands on hers, stopping her as she scrolls through her contacts list.

"No need," he says. "I'll handle this."

"But they'll want to know…" she counters.

Mike shakes his head but doesn't elaborate, and it's the look she gives him, bewildered speculation that has me jumping in to save him the unwanted scrutiny.

"She's staying with me," I tell her, just like that.

Both of them stare. Pam takes a minute to find her words.

"Carrie Wells is staying with you?!"

"She's doing some work on my land," I elaborate. "She's good with fencing."

"Fencing?"

I nod. "Fencing."

"Fencing," Mike confirms with a grimace.

I don't hang around any longer, prising Mike from Pam's grip and asking him for his assistance outside.

We leave her open-mouthed as we march our way through the packed pub. I hope for some reason Pam's losing her fucking marbles and Carrie is safe back at home where I left her, but I hear her wild laughter before we're even out through the door.

She's had more than one tequila, that much is certain. She sways outside the window with a cigarette in her hand, laughing along with Eddie fucking Stevens as he recounts some idiot fucking story that he probably made up on the spot.

His eyes are all over her, his tongue practically lolling as she braces herself against him for balance.

I have the strange urge to rip the bastard's head off, but I think Mike is gunning for him even more than I am.

"What's fucking going on here?" he asks, heading right between them to break the contact.

"Having *fun*," Carrie sneers and laughs right through it. "You guys were long-gone, why should I stay home alone on a Friday fucking night?!"

Eddie is a stupid cunt, I see his challenged brain slowly turning as he registers the implication.

"You're staying with these guys?"

She slaps his arm as she cackles. "Yeah, they're my new fucking foster daddies. Daddy Jack and Daddy Michael."

I reach a new personal low when my cock twitches.

A really low fucking personal low.

Daddy Jack and daddy fucking Michael. The gleam in her eyes tells me she's not entirely joking either.

There are no words for the clusterfuck she's bringing into our once quiet country life.

"You're coming with us," I tell her.

She shakes her head. "I'm fucking not, *Daddy Jack*. Go fuck yourself."

I grit my teeth and take a step forward, shunting Eddie out of the way as Mike takes hold of her arm. "You're coming with us," I repeat. "Right fucking now."

"She's my girl tonight," Eddie protests, and this time it's Mike that loses his fucking cool.

"You're done here," he says to the kid. "Take your drink and get back inside that fucking pub, before I tell the police you're dealing again."

"You fucking wouldn't..." Eddie says, and if I wasn't so pissed that Carrie was trashed on tequila in his company, I'd be amused at how Michael's changing in front of my eyes.

Once upon a time he'd have defended Eddie to the ends of the earth, just as he defends all those kids whose paperwork lands on his desk.

But not anymore.

Not now Carrie Wells is involved.

"Get back inside," Mike repeats and Eddie does.

He stubs out his cigarette and shrugs his shoulders at Carrie, and then he's gone.

Good fucking riddance.

Carrie struggles in my grip.

"Get the fuck off me," she screeches. "You've no fucking right to order me about!"

But I don't. I don't get off her and I don't pander to her kicking and screaming either. I take one elbow, and Mike must have finally heeded my bastard advice about discipline, because he takes the other and together we drag her back to my car and bundle her into the backseat, be damned who sees the spectacle.

She tries to climb back out no sooner as I've shut her in, but I raise a finger and my voice with it.

"Don't even fucking think about it," I tell her, and she backs away.

I climb into the driver's seat and check out her expression in the rearview mirror. She's scowling, her arms folded across her chest as her foot taps furiously.

Difficult. Little. Bitch.

It's about time this little cow learned some manners.

And I'm about to fucking teach her.

CARRIE

can't believe those two assholes were in the pub having a drink without me. I can't believe they manhandled me into the back of the car like I'm a naughty fucking kid.

"Eddie Stevens is a stupid little shit," Jack barks from the front. "And you'll be staying away from him. He deals fucking coke."

"Oh, I will, will I?" I snap. "Says fucking who?"

It's Michael who turns to look at me through the gap in the seats. "Says fucking me, Carrie. And Jack. We both fucking say it, so shut your fucking mouth and be thankful we were there before you ended up more shitfaced than you are already."

I stare in shock at the man who's always been so kind to me, not recognising the angry guy who glares at me as I shut my mouth and settle down with a sneer.

The tequila has gone to my head. I downed way too many before stumbling out into the cold to have a cigarette, courtesy of Eddie and his plan to get his dick inside me. Any more and I'd be on my ass right now, most likely with Eddie's slimy tongue down my throat.

I can't keep my mouth closed for long, it's not in my nature. "You've got some fucking nerve, both of you. You can't fucking tell me what to do."

And then Jack says it, he actually says it.

"While you're under my fucking roof, you'll do as you're fucking told. Any more backchat and I'll put you over my fucking knee and slap some fucking manners into you."

Fuck, how a thrill zips through me. Fuck, how the tequila makes me want to slip my hand down my knickers and touch myself at the thought of Jack tearing my jeans down and spanking my bare ass.

I should be pissed at the humiliation of being dragged away from the pub in front of everyone – so many nosey gawping faces staring through the windows at the commotion.

I should be bailing out of this car and telling those sonsofbitches to get fucked, that I'm not doing what either of them tell me, because I don't have to. I'm a woman now, a woman with her own fucking mind.

And her own fucking needs that neither of these two assholes are willing to fulfil.

Even though I'm drunk, I see the look pass between them. It's one I can't read, and that's not something I'm used to. They're conspiring without words, and it makes me uneasy, nervous…

Excited.

"I mean it," Jack continues. "I'll spank your insolent little ass until you've learned your fucking lesson. And don't think for a fucking second that I won't."

I lean forward in the seat until my head is on Michael's shoulder. He smells amazing. Like musk and man and rage. He stiffens in his seat as I breathe into his ear.

My voice is loud when it comes out. "Why are you letting him speak to me like that? You're supposed to be my fucking caseworker."

"Not anymore," he says. "So I'd mind your fucking manners and sit back nicely in your seat, if I were you."

But I don't.

My thighs are closed tight, my muscles tense as my hips rock back and forth. My pussy is tingling, just like it does when I think about Michael and Jack in bed at night.

"You two are totally fucking out of order," I hiss. "You're not my fucking daddies. I'm not some little kid who'll do what she's told."

"You *will* do what you're told," Jack barks. "And if we have to be your fucking daddies to knock some sense into you, then we'll be your fucking daddies. I don't give a shit."

I suck in my breath so they don't hear me gasp, and I can't help it. My fingers slip between my thighs in the darkness of the backseat. And I'm wet. I'm really wet.

I've never had anything like a daddy before, not since my first foster family all those years ago. Not since Eli ruined everything for me.

I've never had anyone threaten me with a spanking before either.

I circle my clit with my drunk fingers, trying to steady my breath as I speak right into Michael's ear.

"What about you, *Daddy Mike*? You gonna let him spank me? You gonna watch?"

"He'll spank you his fucking self," Jack snaps. "Won't you, *Daddy Mike*?"

Michael's so stiff in his seat. I can hear his breathing, and it's fast. Nearly as fast as mine.

"Just shut your mouth, Carrie, and you won't have to find out." He shifts his position and I wonder if he's hard. Surely not.

Not Michael.

Not the man who said he doesn't want me.

I want to sink into the backseat and play with my pussy in the darkness where they can't see me, but I can't. I can't because I *do* want to find out if Michael will slap my ass. If I shut my mouth and act like a good girl, I may never get to see where this is going.

And I want to.

I really want to see where this is going. Even if it hurts.

Especially if it hurts.

"I'll never shut my mouth," I snap to seal my fate. "You two pricks can threaten all you like, you're too fucking pussy to lay your hands on me."

Jack laughs. "Just keep talking. We're nearly home."

My heart races as we pull into the lane by the house. I wait until we're on the drive until I take my hand from my knickers.

I'm surprised when it's Michael who opens the car door for me and takes hold of my wrist. I fight him, because that's what I do best. I kick and scream and lash out and call him filthy names from my filthy mouth, and I kick and scream some more as Jack joins him and wrestles me from the car.

"Shout all you fucking want, there's nobody around to fucking hear you," Jack says, and I do. I shout and scream and kick out at them, but they're strong and I'm drunk and they take me easily. Jack grips me tight as Michael opens the front door, and I feel his breath on my cheek. I feel him, too.

I feel the swell of his dick against my ass and it makes me squirm.

"You're fucking hard, you dirty bastard," I hiss. "Does it get you off to be my daddy? Is that what you like, you filthy cunt?"

I feel a shiver up my spine as he lifts me over the threshold, and his voice is low and dirty and like nothing I've heard from his mouth before.

"You have no fucking idea what I want to do to a little brat like you." His fingers twist in my hair and tug my head back and I gasp. I actually fucking gasp. "You don't know me and you don't know Mike, either. I think you're in for a big fucking surprise."

I stare at Michael staring at me in Jack's arms. I squirm and wriggle my ass against Jack's hard dick and I want him.

I want both of them.

And I want whatever it is they're going to give me.

"You've been a rude little bitch to Mike all this week," Jack continues. "You think he doesn't realise you need to learn some manners? You think he's going to let you get away with being this much of a brat, just because he had a job to do once?"

"He's too chicken shit," I hiss, watching how Mike's jaw tenses. "He's too fucking nice to teach me a lesson."

Jack lets me go and I'm so surprised I stumble. I catch my balance in no man's land between the two of them, feeling so unsteady under my bratty act.

"We can do this the easy way or the hard way," Jack tells me as he heads past me into the living room.

"Then I guess it's gonna have to be the fucking hard way," I say.

It's Michael who grabs me from behind and walks me on in after Jack. It's Michael whose breath is in my ear as Jack takes a seat on the sofa I trashed just a short week ago.

"This is for your own good," Michael tells me and tugs my jacket from my shoulders. "Sometimes people need tough love. Fuck, Carrie, I've tried everything else."

"So stop fucking trying," I snarl.

"Never," he says and it takes my breath.

It takes my everything.

Never.

He'll never stop trying.

It knocks the wind out of my sails.

"I'm sorry," he whispers. "But Jack's right. You need discipline."

I shiver as he pops the button on my jeans and slides them down around my thighs. My eyes meet Jack's as he stares up at me, glaring at me despite the fact that I can see the jut of his cock standing up. Michael hooks his fingers in the elastic of my knickers and I moan as he slips them down. Their clammy and they stick and I wonder if he can tell how wet I am.

"Over my knee," Jack says, and I can't believe I'm doing this. I can't believe this is really happening as I drop myself over his lap.

His palm feels hot against my skin. My hair hangs down to the floor as I balance myself. I can feel his swollen cock against my belly and I like it.

"Remember," Jack says. "You brought this all on yourself."

I cry out as his palm lands hard and square. "Fuuuuuuuck!"

MICHAEL

Carrie Wells has officially driven me insane.

I'm not even drunk but I feel heady. Intoxicated by the way she pushes everything to breaking point.

My cock is so hard it's uncomfortable, and it takes every scrap of restraint not to drop my pants and jerk myself off right in front of her, regardless of the fact Jack's right in front of me too.

She looks beautiful spread across his knees. He rubs his palm around her sweet little backside and I wish it was me delivering the first blow.

"Remember, you brought this all on yourself," he says, and she did.

I saw it in her eyes.

I saw the devilment in her as she pushed it too far.

He hits her hard, landing a smarting blow right on her ass. She cries out and squirms on him, and he rests an arm firmly across her back.

He hits her again and she squeaks but doesn't move. Again and she grunts.

Over and over his palm lands hard on tender skin until she's pink and sore.

"Say you're sorry," Jack orders.

She doesn't say a word, not until he's landed a couple of extra strong slaps across her thighs.

"I'm sorry you want to be such a dirty fucking daddy," she whispers, and I hate myself for the man I'm becoming in all this.

I hate the way her words make my balls tighten.

This isn't me.

None of this is me.

But it is.

I feel more like me than I've felt in years, as though the perfect shell of monotony is cracking and falling away before my eyes.

"Say sorry," I tell her, and she stares up at me with piercing eyes.

"Sorry, *Daddy*," she hisses.

How I'd love to drop my pants and stick my swollen cock down her throat. How I'd love to hear her squeal with her mouth full. I don't recognise the thoughts in my head, and I don't recognise Jack, either.

I've known the man for a lifetime and I've never seen this side of him. I've never seen his jaw gritted in the way it is now. I've never seen the sternness in his eyes as he administers a lesson to a girl who so desperately needs it.

I never thought for a second I'd want to jerk my cock in front of a man I've known since we were boys. I never thought for a second we'd be queuing up to spank the same crazy girl.

"Be glad this is my hand," Jack snarls. "Back in my day you got the fucking belt."

I see her shiver, but more than that I see the way she spreads her thighs open.

Fuck.

The girl wants him.

She's putty in his hands, even though she's playing the brat.

Even through all her bluster I can tell it's starting to hurt.

She flinches as he lands another slap, hisses under her breath as he catches her good across the thigh.

"I'd think carefully about when you want to apologise," Jack tells her. "Michael's waiting to teach you a lesson for himself next."

She grunts as another slap makes her wriggle on his knees.

She takes three more before she screeches at the unfairness of the world and everything in it.

And then she says it.

"Sorry!" she snaps. "I'm sorry, alright?!"

But no. It isn't alright.

"Say it like you mean it," Jack says.

She's looking at me as she speaks again. Her eyes are hooded and horny as she opens her mouth and gives Jack what he wants to hear.

"I'm sorry," she says. "I'm sorry I got drunk with Eddie Stevens."

"And what else?"

She takes a long breath. "I'm sorry I was... a brat..."

"Good girl," he says and the way he strokes her hair takes my breath.

The way she arches her back on his lap and twists her head for more, sends my pulse into overdrive.

I don't want to stop watching.

I don't want them to stop.

And it's all kinds of fucked up, but I can't change how I feel.

I can't change how filthy I am for wanting this.

I'm about to excuse myself to go to the bathroom and relieve myself before I say or do something I regret. My balls are about to explode and I don't think I can hold back from doing something insane.

But I have to.

Because no sooner have I determined that I'm well out of control with this craziness, Jack lets Carrie up from his knee.

She stands meekly. Demurely. Her jeans and knickers still gathered around her thighs as she twiddles her thumbs in front of her.

And, oh fuck, her pussy.

I've never seen such a pretty little pussy in all my life.

"Your turn," Jack instructs me, like I need it. "Make sure you give her the punishment she deserves."

I nod.

Take a breath.

And then I take a seat in the armchair.

Sixteen

CARRIE

My ass is burning and so is my face. I'm still floaty from the tequila, but I'm horny as hell and reeling and I really want this. I've never wanted anything so much as I want this.

I can't believe it as Michael takes a seat in the armchair and beckons me over with open arms.

"Be a good girl now, Carrie, and take your punishment."

I nod, because this is how it should be.

This was always how it should be.

All those sessions in Michael's office, sitting across from him in that chair, thinking about how much I wanted him as he tried to help me any way he could.

Any way but the way I really needed.

He should have put me across his knees right then and there in his office. He should have made me take my punishment and shown me that bad behaviour has consequences other than getting thrown out of yet another home.

I didn't know it then, but this was always what I wanted.

I take a breath as I shuffle my way across to him, loving the way my dropped jeans restrict my movement. Loving the way his eyes are on my pussy. Loving the way his breath hitches as I let myself drop across his lap.

His hands are kinder than Jack's. His fingers tickle up my stinging thighs and I wish he'd put them inside me, but he doesn't.

"I hope you realise we're doing this because we care," he says and I find myself nodding again.

I squirm until I feel his dick underneath me. I gasp because I know for sure now that he really does want me.

They both do.

Jack's voice is gruff when it sounds across the room.

"Tell him you're going to be a good girl. Tell him you know you deserve this."

I've never felt the way I'm feeling right now, so small and raw and vulnerable.

It feels so nice to let go of the fight in me. It feels so nice to have two men who care enough to work through my shitty attitude.

"I'll be good," I whisper. "I'm sorry I've been bad, but I promise I'll be good now."

"Jack got you pretty bad," Michael comments and my tummy tickles as his fingers spread my ass cheeks. I burn up all over again at the thought of him staring at my asshole, but I like that too. "You're so pink."

I want him to see just how pink I am, so I wriggle until my jeans slip down around my knees and spread my thighs as wide as they'll let me.

I wonder if I'm leaving a wet patch on his trousers. I wonder if I left one on Jack's.

My pussy is tingling and desperate to be touched. If I didn't need my arms to balance myself I'd struggle not to reach back and rub myself.

Michael runs his fingers up the inside of my thighs. I moan for him but he stops too soon.

I stare across at Jack and moan again when I see he's palming his dick through his trousers. I want him to touch himself. I'd love to see him touch himself.

I don't think Michael is going to hit me as hard as Jack did, but he surprises me and hits me harder. His slap is loud and stings and sends me jerking forward on his lap. He takes my hair in his fist to stop me and I love the way it pulls at my scalp.

"You've been rude to me for a whole fucking week," he says, and hits me again. "You've been rude to me for five whole fucking months."

And I have. I tell him so and he hits me again.

I tell him I thought he was a pussycat and he slaps my thighs so hard I squeal.

I stop saying anything just to concentrate on how my skin is on fire. It burns a nice burn – one that blooms at my ass and travels right through me.

I love the rhythm as he lands his palm right on all the sore parts. I love the way his breath is raspy.

"I showed Jack my tits," I tell him. "I took a picture of them and I wanted you to see. Both of you."

"I know," he says. "Jack told me."

"I play with myself in bed at night and I think of you. Of both of you."

Jack's palm rubs against his dick through his trousers and his eyes are wild and dark. I hope Michael's are too.

"Shh," Michael hisses, but I don't want to.

"I wanted to fuck Eddie Stevens to make you jealous." The words sound so raw as they come out. "I wanted you to get angry."

"It fucking worked," Jack says. "If you'd have let that loser inside your pretty little pussy I'd have ripped his fucking dick off."

I cry out as Michael speaks through his hand. Harder now. Much harder. His slaps tell me everything.

"Stay away from Eddie fucking Stevens," Michael growls and he slaps me again and I squeal like a pig.

"I don't want Eddie," I tell them, panting for breath. "I want you. Both of you."

"You're too young," Michael snaps and Jack's hand stops palming his cock.

"I'm eighteen," I argue. "I'm more than old enough."

"We're in our fucking forties," Michael says, but I know that.

I like that.

I tell him so and he lands me a good one, right between my ass cheeks.

"I'm sorry," I whisper. "I'm sorry for all of it. Just don't make me leave… don't send me away… not even if you have to do this every night, not even if you have to wash my mouth out with soap…"

"It's not fucking soap I want to wash your mouth out with," Jack growls, and Michael stops hitting me.

He lets go of my hair and helps me to my feet.

And then he pulls my knickers and jeans up.

I feel sick as I see the guilt in his eyes. He feels guilty. Uncertain. I know it and I hate it.

"I was a good girl, right?" I ask, hating how much I need reassurance.

"You were very good," he says. "Be even better and go to bed now so I can talk to Jack."

I look at Jack and he nods. "Make sure you take a glass of water up with you, you need to hydrate yourself after the tequila.

I want to stay and hear what they're saying, but I daren't.

My heart is in my throat as I look between them one last time before heading out to the kitchen to grab a drink of water.

I make sure my footsteps are loud on the stairs and that I slam my bedroom door so they'll hear it.

And then I crouch, like a little mouse on the top of the stairs, loving the way my ass burns from where they hit me.

And relieved how good it feels to slip my hand down the front of my jeans.

JACK

Michael looks mortified, and I can't say I blame him. This wasn't exactly on the menu as his ideal way to handle one of his waifs and strays.

But it was the right way to handle *her*.

I've no doubt we've done the right thing, even if things veered dangerously close to the edge.

"She needed that," I tell him and he nods even though I'm unsure he believes me.

"She needs to stay away from Eddie fucking Stevens," he says and I've no argument there.

"She *will* stay away from him. She has us to keep her on the straight and narrow."

He lowers his voice. "By spanking her every time she does something we disagree with?"

"By spanking her every time she deserves it."

"It's wrong," he says.

"No," I argue. "It worked. How can that be wrong? The girl is crying out for discipline. She's crying out for people who'll stand up to her shit and stay firm through it."

"And that's us, is it? We're going to be the ones to do this?"

I shrug. "Unless you have any better ideas?"

He runs his hands through his hair. "I wanted to fuck her, Jack. I was so fucking close to fucking her. Her pussy was right there by my fingers. I could've just…"

"Maybe you should have," I tell him, and I know how fucked up it sounds. "Maybe we both should have."

He shakes his head. "No, Jack. No fucking way. This is so fucking fucked up."

I haven't smoked in over a decade but I'm gagging for a cigarette right now.

"One of us is going to fuck her," I say.

"And what about the other one?"

I shrug, because I have no fucking idea. We're both in deep. Too fucking deep.

"Unless we don't work out which one," I think aloud. "Unless we just let it run its course."

"Like it did tonight, you mean? With both of us on the edge of fucking the girl. I nearly got my fucking dick out when she was over your knee."

"I nearly got mine out when she was over yours, what's your point?"

His mouth flaps and I have the strangest urge to laugh at all this.

"My point is," he says finally, "that we can't do this. It's wrong."

"Probably," I agree. "So what next? Ask her who she wants out of the pair of us?"

The thought of rejection scares me and I can tell a mile off it scares him too.

"She said she wants both of us," he says, like I'm not perfectly aware of that. "She can't be serious, and even if she were, that would never work. It's insane."

"Everything about this is insane," I tell him. "Everything about this whole fucking spectacle is insane."

His eyes widen as he stares at me. "Don't tell me you're even contemplating it."

It surprises me to find that I am. It surprises me to find that if I had it my way, I'd drag her back downstairs and we'd take it in turns right here and now to fuck that tight little pussy.

She wants it.

We want it.

But the horror on Mike's face tells me he's not nearly so sure.

"I have to go," he says. "I've got to think."

I nod. "Sure."

"I can't believe I'm involved in this."

I get to my feet. "I'm pretty sure none of us fucking can."

I've the strangest urge to ruffle that scruffy hair of his, like I did when we were kids and he was getting stressed about some shit or other.

I'm two months older than Michael and it counted back then. I was always the daring one. Always the one who'd cross the rickety bridge first, just as I was today.

"It's Saturday tomorrow," I say. "We need some normality. How about you come over for some beers in the evening, we'll try to wind this shit-storm back down to some kind of decency. A few drinks, maybe a film. Absolutely no spanking." I laugh but he doesn't laugh with me.

"I'll let you know," he says as he gets to the door.

"You can stay if you want," I tell him. "You can take the sofa," I add hastily, in case there was any confusion.

He's already halfway down the drive when he raises his hand in a *thanks but no thanks*.

It appears he doesn't want a ride home either.

He's turned the corner before I've even found my keys.

Seventeen

MICHAEL

I **walk fast, head down and** hands in my pockets, guilt rattling through me at the thought of how badly I've desecrated my professional judgement. This should never be. This thing with Carrie was bad enough, this craziness with Jack involved is nothing short of criminal.

But it's not criminal.

It violates the moral code of my career, but it's not criminal. Not on paper.

She's of age and willing. Definitely willing.

And we mean her no harm, Jack and I. Quite the opposite.

But that matters not. I feel sick to my stomach at the thought of what nearly went down in there, and sicker still to know that my cock is still rock fucking hard, no matter how harshly I condemn myself.

I could have fucked her then handed her over to Jack to do the same. We could've taken turns all night long. I could still be there now, buried deep inside the only girl who's ever made me lose my fucking mind.

Would I have still been hard as I watched him take her? Would I still have wanted her pretty little pussy in my face if he'd been inside her first?

Yes.

It sickens me, but it's the truth of it.

Me and Jack are close, close enough to weather anything. But this? How can we possibly come through this unchanged if one of us ends up hooked up with the girl we're both insane about?

And if we don't come through it?

If we can't?

It doesn't bear thinking about. Neither does losing Carrie after coming this far.

The memory of searching for her day after day, night after night, is still terrifyingly vivid. The fear of never seeing her again still palpable.

The fear of watching her fall in love with my best friend should be a walk in the park after all that, but it isn't.

Jealousy isn't me, it never has been, but it feels that way tonight. Sharing her seems a better option than being left out in the cold, but sharing a girl isn't something that any sane man in my position should ever consider.

No. We can't share her.

We shouldn't even be considering the possibility. Neither of us.

We should never have broken the boundaries we've already ploughed through tonight, but it's too late for that now.

I'm almost back to the main stretch of town when I just can't hold it any longer. I slip behind the old oak we used to scale as kids and pull down my zip. My cock is throbbing as I wrap my hand around the length, my breath coming in grunts as I jerk myself off.

Fuck, it feels so much better than it should.

I remember how she wriggled against my lap, the feel of her smooth ass against my palm. Her clammy thighs, the pretty swollen pink of her pussy. The way she looked at me after Jack gave her a good hiding, the way she so willingly dropped herself over my knees.

The way she looked over his knees.

The way he spanked her.

I slam my head into the trunk of the oak, eyes screwed tight as I shoot my load. My dick twitches as the rush floods me. I'm lightheaded and disoriented, open-mouthed at the filthy pleasure of sharing that girl with the man who's been at my side my whole fucking life.

I stuff my cock back in my pants and catch my breath, stumbling back out onto the main road to continue my walk back to regular civilisation.

This isn't me.

I was never like this with Molly, but Molly wasn't anything like Carrie Wells. Molly never let me indulge any of my darkest fantasies, she never wanted any of them.

The only person who's ever known the shit I'm really into is Jack.

Trips to visit him at University. The mad thrill of going along with his wild hedonism without the pressure of social standing back home. Without the gossip and the whispers, and the fear of everyone in the corner shop knowing about your kinky sex life.

Jack's a dirty sonofabitch. It's one of the reasons he's chronically single.

Jack knows what he likes, and he likes pretty much everything.

He goes for what he wants, and he wants Carrie Wells.

I think he even wants her as much as I do.

It's a relief to stride through the high street and arrive on my own doorstep.

Pam's light is on downstairs and I see the curtain twitch as I turn my key in the lock.

She knows Carrie is staying with Jack now. She knows I knew about it, too.

Fuck knows what questions I'm going to have to answer at work on Monday, but I've got bigger fish to fry right now.

I've got tomorrow night to get through yet.

And Carrie may well have a decision to make which doesn't go my way.

The thought doesn't bear thinking about, but the fucker won't leave me alone.

JACK

She's not quick enough to dart away from view when I head through to the living room with a fresh cold beer from the fridge. Call it instinct, but I used to do it when I was a kid and my parents were arguing – sit myself down on the top stair and hope people would be too caught up in their row to notice me.

I prop myself against the bottom bannister and call up to her.

"You can come down if you want. Michael's gone."

She pokes her head around the top rail. "I wasn't–" she begins, but I shake my head.

"Don't even think about lying to me, you've been there since we sent you out."

She shrugs. "It's not eavesdropping if the conversation is about you. It's called not being a stupid fucking idiot."

"It's called poking your pixie nose in where it's not fucking wanted. What Mike and I talk about is for our ears and not yours."

She folds her arms as she heads back downstairs. Good manners seem to fade awfully fucking easily with this girl.

"Even if the shit you're talking about revolves around me?"

"Especially if the shit we're talking about revolves around you."

"He's freaked out," she says and it isn't a question.

"Mike takes things hard. He's very considered." I pause. "Usually very considered."

A flash of insecurity shows in her eyes. "I guess I'm messing things up for him a little, right?"

I have the strangest urge to pull the girl into my arms and hold her tight. I saw one of those sickly sweet graphics on the internet once. It said *one day someone's going to come along who'll hug you so tight that all of your broken pieces will fit back together again.*

It made me roll my eyes at the time, and yet here I am years later considering whether maybe it's not quite so grotesque an idea after all. If I could hug Carrie Wells that tight I would.

I'd love to feel her broken pieces fitting back together again. Hell knows there's enough of them. The girl has a list of issues a mile long.

"My ass hurts," she says and I can't help but smile.

"That's the idea. I trust you'll think twice next time you get the urge to drink tequila with a coke-dealing loser."

She shrugs, and there's that devilment in her eyes again. "Maybe."

"Maybe you won't be able to sit down for a week if you do it again. I'd count yourself lucky."

I head back through to the kitchen and she follows me, arms wrapped around herself as her feet pad softly across the floor tiles. I get her a coffee, not a beer, and she doesn't argue.

She looks thoughtful, pensive even. It's not an expression I usually see on her.

"Why did you let me stay here?" she asks, and the question takes me aback.

"You needed somewhere to sleep. Mike would lose his job if he took you to his."

"But the hotel. Mike said he'd take me to a hotel."

"And I had a spare bedroom."

Her eyes meet mine for just a second before she stares down at her coffee. "I'm glad you let me stay," she says.

"So am I," I tell her. "Even if you are a pain in the fucking ass." I smile to let her know I'm joking, and she smiles too.

"Can't help it. Born that way."

"We'll knock the spiky edges off you, young lady. Just give it time."

Time. It's only been a week, but it feels so much longer. It feels like Carrie Wells has been a whirlwind in our lives for an eternity already.

I finish up my beer as she finishes up her coffee and I'm done for the night.

Exhausted enough to sleep for a week, even if my balls are still tight enough to blow.

"Goodnight, Carrie," I tell her. "I'll see you in the morning. Tomorrow night is movie night. Me, you, Mike and some popcorn."

She raises an eyebrow. "I don't like movies. I don't even like TV."

"Then I guess you'll have to make an exception, won't you?" I smirk. "You can choose since you're likely to be the awkward whiny one."

She groans like I've just told her she has to shovel shit for a week and I'm smiling as I make my way upstairs.

Life feels strange in this house all of a sudden. Strange but not unpleasant, far from it. Even if I'm in some absurd triangle with my best friend and his runaway gypsy girl.

I finish myself off in the shower and it's one of the best hand jobs I've ever had the pleasure of giving myself.

I put that down to the Carrie Wells effect, just like everything else this week.

I'm beginning to feel glad it was contagious after all.

C A R R I E

I can't get settled in this squeaky bed. My belly is filled up with nerves, and I hate that. I hate the fear of losing people, so I've learned that the best way of going through life is not to get attached in the first place. It's lonely but it's safe. But this time is different. This time I'm already in deep.

I pushed them and they didn't walk away. I made them mad and they don't hate me for it. At least I hope they don't.

Finding Michael was a lucky break I never thought I'd stumble into. Finding Jack too is more than I ever hoped for. Having both of them in my life is a crazy dream beyond anything I've ever dared dream before. Losing them? Well, that would be more than I could bear.

I toss and turn until I'm sticky and uncomfortable, thinking about what happened, wondering what happens now.

What if Michael doesn't come back? What if he's really had enough of me now?

What if Jack is in the room next door regretting ever offering me a place to stay?

I know my heart is playing tricks on me, making me doubt all the kindness they've shown. I know the thrum of nerves in my belly is just the end result of pushing people away over and over again and still crying when they finally give up on me. I know I brought a lot of this on myself. I know I always do.

But for the first time in my life, I'm daring to hope that this road leads somewhere else. Somewhere good.

And maybe, just maybe, in this house with these two men who've given me so much time already, I'll find something for keeps.

When I was still a little girl being passed from one home to another, I'd get nightmares so bad they'd wake me up. I'd tiptoe out of my bedroom in the middle of the night with my heart racing and tears streaming down my face, and hover outside the bedroom of whichever new *parents* I had that month, and I'd want to knock so badly. I'd want to tap on that door and ask them to make the nightmares go away, just to feel someone there. Just to have someone's arms around me and tell me I wasn't alone.

But I never did knock on that door, not with anyone. I'd take a couple of deep breaths and remind myself that I was all alone in this world, and I'd pull my big girl panties up and go back to bed without a word.

I take a deep breath in the darkness tonight, and it feels different somehow. Everything here feels different.

And maybe I'm different, too.

Maybe tonight's the night I can finally knock on that door and reach out. Maybe tonight's the night someone will actually be there.

My heart is in my mouth as I slip out of bed. The springs creak as I leave, and I wonder if Jack's been able to hear me tossing and turning through the wall every night this week. I'm really quiet as I turn the door handle, steps light as I tiptoe along to his room.

I press my ear to the door and listen. There's no light showing around the edges, and I can't hear any movement in there.

I don't know whether I can really do this, not knowing if he's going to freak out and order me back to my own room. Maybe he'll think I'm coming for sex, which I'm not.

It's weird to find that I'm not, but I'm really not.

I press my forehead to the door, frustrated that my fingers are shaking and I'm not brave enough to knock. I think of all the times we've sat together with a beer in the evening. All the times he's seemed pleased to have me around.

What's the worst that can happen?

It can't be any worse than Michael blowing me out with some bullshit *friends only* excuse, right? Right?

So I knock.

I knock loud but only once, and then I step back, recoiling as though my fist is on fire. My muscles are wired and ready to bolt back to bed, skin clammy at the thought of reaching out where I'm unwanted. I'm about to bolt when the door swings open, and my eyes are wide as they meet Jack's sleepy ones. He's naked. Stark bollock naked. But he isn't shy and he shouldn't be. He looks amazing.

He's broader than I pictured him under his clothes. Solid and muscular with a dark line of hair under his belly button leading down to a…

A really big dick.

Really big.

"You okay?" he asks and I nod like a dumbass.

"Yeah, I'm just…" I dither for words, suddenly so aware I'm in knickers and a vest top and nothing else. "Sometimes I can't get to sleep…"

I feel like he's staring right inside me. His eyes are thoughtful and kind and they make my stomach do weird flips.

"You wanted some company?"

"Yes," I blurt, and then panic, in case he thinks I'm a slut looking for a ride, but I'm not and I tell him so. I tell him so fast that my words are garbled, and then I close my eyes and take a breath. "Sorry," I say, "I'm crap at this stuff."

"You think you're crap at a lot of things," he says. "But you're not nearly so crap as you think you are."

"You think?"

He nods. "I know."

"Thanks," I say and I wonder what happens now. I feel like a tit stood here outside his bedroom door begging for someone to talk to me. To hold me.

"I'm tired," he says. "But if you want some company you're welcome in here."

"Please," I reply before he thinks better of it.

He steps to the side to let me through and I brush past him into a room that smells of him. I love the way it smells. The lamp is on at the far side of his big bed, so I guess that's his side, if he has a side. I slip into the other and hug my knees to my chest, heart racing at being in someone else's personal space.

He slips into bed on the other side and flicks off the lamp. I can hear him breathing.

"That stuff earlier," he begins and I feel him move closer. "You know that it's because we give a shit, right?"

I nod, then realise he probably can't see me in the dark. "Yeah, I know."

"Good," he says. "We give one hell of a shit about you, Carrie. Both of us."

My heart pangs when I think of Michael walking away. "Do you think he's okay?"

"He'll be fine. He just needs to work things out."

I roll to face him in the darkness. "You think he'll be back?"

He laughs a little. "I know he'll be back. He can't stay away. The guy's besotted with you."

A ripple of shock runs from my head to my toes. "He's what?"

He laughs again. "He's crazy about you. Always has been."

"But he said…"

"He said what he thought he should say. He's being noble because he thinks that's what a better man would do."

"There is no better man," I whisper and I hear him take a breath.

"I know. He's my best friend," he says. I feel the heat from him even though he feels a million miles away. The space between us feels like a gulf. "I guess he's the man you want, right?" he asks and I've never heard him sound nervous before, but there's something there. Just a little something.

"The man I want?"

"Of the two of us. It's about him, right?"

My heart flutters. "You mean my favourite?"

He sighs. "Yeah, your favourite."

"I don't have one," I reply honestly. The silence is heavy. It makes me fidget, like I've said something wrong. "I don't have to have a favourite, right? Why do I have to choose? I can't choose. I don't want to."

His voice is low but warm. "Well, that's uh, kinda how things work, no? You meet a guy, you hook up, it becomes a thing…"

"You want me to choose one of you?"

He sighs. "Fuck, this isn't how this conversation was supposed to go."

"But you do, right? You want me to choose?" I hug my knees tighter, because I can't. I always wanted someone to give a shit, and now there are two and I can't lose them. Not either of them. "I'm not choosing," I tell him. "You'll have to work it out between you. I love you both."

I suck in breath as I realise what I've just said, every muscle wired as I wait for him to freak out. But he doesn't. He really doesn't.

"You mean that?"

My body is on fire with nerves. "Yeah. I mean that."

And then he touches me. I flinch as a warm solid arm reaches out for me and pulls me close, but it feels good. It feels amazing. My body presses to his and his legs wrap around mine, my head fitting so perfectly against his shoulder.

"And we love you, both of us. We're both fucking crazy about you, Carrie

Wells, you little shit."

I smile against his skin, and I could cry. I could really cry.

His cock is hard, I can feel it pressing against my leg, but he makes no move to fix that and I make no move to fix that either. I wrap my arms around him and hold him tight and he holds me.

"Sleep now," he whispers. "We'll sort this crap out another day."

I nod. Yawn.

And eventually I fall asleep happy.

Eighteen

CARRIE

Jack tries to act *super* normal next morning, even though I wake in his arms with my hair all over his pillow. He gives me a smile and disentangles himself and heads off for a shower like this is just any other day.

But it isn't.

Now I've slept in his bed I don't want to sleep alone again.

It felt too good to feel someone's body against mine. It felt too good to have someone hold me for the first proper time in my life.

Now I know how it feels to be safe and warm in someone's arms I can't let it go, and I won't.

But I can't choose, either.

I can't choose either man over the other, they both mean too much to me.

When I was being passed around foster homes like a bad smell, all I ever wanted was one person to give a shit about me. Now there's the chance I have two. Two men who care enough to give me a chance. And they love me, he said so, and Jack isn't the kind to lie.

I'm eating a bowl of cereal when he joins me in the kitchen. He pours himself one and takes a seat opposite, smelling ocean fresh with a navy-blue t-shirt over jeans.

"You don't have many clothes, do you?" he asks, but it's not a dig. I look down at the top I'm wearing, another basic cami, and one he's seen already this past week.

"How many do I need? I can't wear them all at once."

He smiles. "It was an observation. Most girls I've ever met love clothes, can't get enough of them."

"I'm not most girls."

"You got that right."

He digs his wallet from his jeans and I put down my spoon as he counts out a load of notes. He slides them across the table at me. "What's that?" I ask.

"For you," he tells me. "I was thinking of buying you some things, clothes, boots, whatever, but you earned the money, you should spend it on whatever you want."

Nobody has ever given me cash before. Gifts, but not cash. Nobody trusts me with cash.

"I don't want it," I tell him all the same. "I won't be bought."

He raises an eyebrow. "You think I'm trying to buy you for a hundred quid? Please. I'm hardly that much of a miser. I'm paying you for your work on the fence."

"But I don't want it," I tell him. "I did it for me, not you."

"Then I'm paying you for *our* fence, Carrie. Take the money please. A good job is a good job and worth paying for."

I stare at the notes like they could bite me. "That's too much."

"Hardly. It's not even minimum wage."

"But what if I spend it all?" My eyes are so guarded when they meet his.

"I hope that you do. You need some new boots if you're going to be trekking through fields every day, those old things are a health hazard."

Slowly, so slowly I reach out and take the money. "Thanks," I say, trying to play down how touched I am. Not just for the money, but because he trusts me enough to have it.

"I can take you into Gloucester if you like? Take you shopping?"

I shake my head quickly, much too quickly. "I'll get the bus."

He nods. "Okay, suit yourself. Be back in time for movie night though, yes? I'm getting in the popcorn."

I turn the notes over and over in my fingers. One hundred pounds. A whole hundred pounds.

I think of the things I could buy. New underwear and boots and maybe a pack of cigarettes of my own, to smoke in the fields after a hard day of fencing. Maybe I could buy a new hairbrush and a lipstick. I've only got one lipstick, not that I ever wear the stuff.

"Carrie," he says to call me back to my senses. "You'll be back in time for movie night, yes? Don't let us down."

"I won't," I say. "I won't let you down."

And I won't.

I'm never going to let him down. Nor Michael, either.

MICHAEL

I slept a lousy sleep. It's my phone that wakes me up, bleeping away on my bedside table.

I rub my eyes before I reach for it, and realise the daylight is blazing through the crack in the curtains.

"Wake up sleepyhead," Jack says at the end of the line. "It's almost midday."

I check my alarm clock. He's right.

That's what a night pacing around your living room does for you.

"Guess I overslept."

"Guess you did. You should've stayed over."

I sigh. "I hardly think that would've been a good idea."

"She loves you," he says, just like that, and I sit bolt upright.

"What?"

"She loves you, she told me so. And she loves me, too."

A mix of relief and nausea floods through me. "She said that? Love?"

"Uh huh, yeah. She said it. Love."

I can't fight the zing of nerves. "And were you... when she said it?"

"Was I fucking her?" He sighs. "No, Michael, I wasn't fucking fucking her. How much of a cunt do you take me for?"

"I'm sorry," I say, and I am.

"She did sleep in my bed though. But not like that. Just sleeping." He groans. "Fuck, this is awkward. It's just..."

"Fucked up," I say, "yes, I know."

"I mean, she was in nothing but a scrappy little top and knickers, and she is fucking divine, and I did have my fucking hard on pressed against her ass all night."

176

His laugh is low and easy. "But I didn't stick her with it, and she didn't ask."

"I'm supposed to say thank you, am I? That's how this goes? Thank you for not fucking the eighteen-year-old girl we're both infatuated with. Well done, have a gold star."

"Thank you for not fucking the eighteen-year-old girl we're both infatuated with *without me*. That's how this goes. Gold star for me."

I shake my head, even though he can't see me. "This isn't happening. Forget it."

He laughs. "Suit yourself, but she doesn't want to choose and I don't want to let this go."

"Then I'll back out gracefully," I tell him.

"And she'll hate us both for it if you do."

"You're a cock," I say.

"Yes, I am," he says. "But you brought her to my doorstep, and she isn't like other girls. She's nothing close."

I lean back into the pillows. "Your point being?"

"My point being that your concrete sense of morality is going to have to take a bashing if you want to live in Carrie's world. Your call."

"I'll bear that in mind," I say.

"You do that," he replies. "I'll see you later. Don't be late for movie night."

He hangs up the call before I can argue.

CARRIE

I've been in Gloucester city centre a thousand times, but never with a hundred quid in my pocket. I feel uneasy to have it there, like someone is going to take it from me. Someone like Eli or one of his loser mates.

That's why I didn't want Jack to bring me here. I didn't want to risk running into any of them. I didn't want them to see me with someone. Someone they could speak to, someone they could scare off me.

Eli is the only family who's ever stuck by me. He ruined my life, but he came through at the other side, tracking me down when I was fourteen and telling me he was still my brother.

He's never even mentioned what happened all those years ago, and I was always too scared to bring it up in case he dropped me again. Sometimes he's kind and tells me about my old mum and dad, and sister, too. He says they don't want to see me and never will, but I still care.

I still like hearing about them.

I guess he knows it and that's why he's always used it to take things from me. Whatever he wants. Money, favours.

Me.

I shiver at the thought of how much I've given him, and I've never really minded before, because family's family, even if it is fucked up, but now that I have things I'm really not willing to give up for him, I hope he just stays well away from me.

I came to Gloucester because I don't know my way around anywhere else, but it makes me nervous.

I want to get my shopping as quickly as possible. I head over to the shoe store on South Street, the one with the boots I've always ogled, but even though they're reduced they're still almost sixty quid. That would leave me forty for some underwear and some other bits I need.

But I really wanted to get Jack and Mike something, so I put a hold on the boots until I've done that first.

Choosing a present for Mike is easy, I know exactly what I'm going to get him.

I've only ever seen him in three ties for work, and I know he likes weird slightly zany stuff, so I head into a suit shop in one of the posher streets and choose him a nice deep green one, to match his eyes. I smile as I picture him in it, because it'll look good on him. I know it will.

It cost me twenty, which is a chunk of my money, but at least I can still get Jack something and get my boots. The other stuff will have to wait.

There's a boutique homewares shop next to the tie place, and I've never even looked in here before because for one I've never had a home, and secondly because I've never had any money.

But then I see it, in the window. A big coloured glass sculpture thing with flecks of blue and green right through it.

It's not like the thing the crow smashed, but it's not too dissimilar. My heart races at the thought I could replace it for him. My stomach is in knots at the thought that I can really make up for what I ruined.

I dash inside and ask the snooty shop assistant how much it is, then gulp as she says it's eighty-five.

I only have eighty.

My heart breaks.

I step outside defeated, not giving a shit for my boots anymore or the hairbrush I can make do without. I just need a fiver, that's all. One measly fiver.

Once upon a time I'd have considered stealing it, but not now. Now I only want to take what I earn and nothing more.

I should walk away and get my boots and work out a way of getting it another time, but I can't. I really can't.

I want nothing more than to see Jack's face as I get him another sculpture, Michael's too as he tries on his tie.

That's the reason I head into the backstreets to find Eli. That's why I trek into an area that makes me shiver and knock on his front door.

He's not happy when he answers. His eyes are dark and angry, beard dishevelled as he yanks me inside by my wrist. He squeezes hard as he pulls me upstairs and this time I don't fight because I don't want to explain the bruises.

He throws me into the living room and jabs a finger at me. "You took off!"

"You were being a cunt to me!"

"If I'm so much of a cunt, then why are you fucking back here, you little skank?"

I fold my arms. "I need to borrow a fiver."

He laughs a mean laugh. "A fucking fiver? Why? You already fucking owe me."

I owe him for a fucking sandwich and not much else, but I don't say that.

"I need it for a friend," I say and he sneers.

"You don't have any fucking friends."

"I have friends now," I say proudly. "Are you gonna give me the fiver or not?"

"Are you gonna fucking bail and ignore me again if I do?"

I shake my head. "I'll give it back."

"And the rest?"

There is no rest, not really, but I still want the updates on how everyone is doing and I really want this fiver so I nod. "Yeah, and the rest."

He reaches into his pocket and pulls out the note and I'm so happy my heart soars. I rush towards him, but he holds it out of reach.

"Kiss first."

He stinks of weed and I hate it, but the fiver is so close I can smell the happiness more. I brace myself for it and when it comes it's sloppy and gross and makes me feel sick.

His hand paws my tit through my top and pinches my nipple even though

I twist away. I daren't break off the kiss before he's ready, because then I'll never get the fiver, so I hold my breath and let him do it, just like he always does.

"You really wanted that fucking fiver," he laughs when he's finally had enough. I wipe my mouth on the back of my hand then snatch the note from his fingers.

And then I'm outta there, as fast as I can before he causes me any more shit.

"You owe me, remember," he calls down the stairs after me.

"How can I fucking forget," I yell back and flip him the finger at the bottom.

JACK

"She'll be here," I say, "she said she wouldn't let us down."

Mike is pacing. Nervous as fuck.

I'd like to say I'm not, but I'm more tightly wound than I'd like, even if I'm hiding it pretty well.

"You gave her a hundred quid, Jack. She could be fucking anywhere right now."

"She won't be," I tell him, even though I'm not entirely sure. "We're having movie night, she'll be here."

"Or be drunk in an alleyway somewhere."

I sigh. "You've got to have some faith in her."

He flashes me a horrible stare. "I've got faith in her, Jack, it's us I've got the issue with. Last night we slap her ass, today she's taken off."

"She's gone shopping, Mike."

"You don't know that," he insists, and he's right. I don't.

I hope my gut is making the right call on this one. Not just on Carrie being back in time to spend the evening with us, but on this whole crazy situation we're involved with. I thought teaching her some discipline was the right call, just as holding her tight in my bed felt the right call.

Paying her for a job well done also seemed the right call.

But there's a chance I've been off the mark with the whole lot of it.

The clock is ticking and she's not back. Six p.m. and there's no sign of her, and there isn't another bus until gone eight.

I'm about to call defeat at six thirty and suggest we go take a drive to look for her, but the sound of the front door has both Mike and me jumping to our feet.

Carrie tries to catch her breath in the hallway, cheeks flushed pink as she doubles over.

"I... I'm sorry..." she wheezes. "I lost my fucking bus ticket and I had no money for another... my phone was out of credit... and I didn't have money to make a call..."

I hear Mike sigh and I slap him on the back in unspoken victory.

"How did you get home?" I ask and she holds up a finger for a moment while she catches the rest of her breath.

"Hitchhiked," she says, "and walked the rest."

I feel Michael leap up the fucking pole. "You hitchhiked?!"

She shrugs. "Yeah, was alright."

"Could've at least put your new boots on for the walk," I comment, gesturing to the same old pair on her feet.

She looks so uncertain as she stares down at them. "I didn't get any," she admits and Mike flashes a glance at me.

Carrie heads on through to the kitchen and we follow her, staring on in interest as she pulls a box and a little bag from her backpack.

She hands the little bag to Mike. "For you," she says and her smile is nervous enough to break my fucking heart.

He opens it slowly. "For me?"

She nods. "Yeah, for you. A present."

He looks so touched I can't stop grinning. A tie. A decent one too. He runs it through his fingers.

"Do you like it?" she asks and he nods.

"I love it."

Her smile makes my heart stop.

"That was a really nice gesture," I say to her, but she won't look at me. She picks up the box and hands it over to me but she won't meet my eyes.

"And one for you. A present, and a sorry. That's why it's bigger. It's two in one."

"Two in one?" I repeat and she nods.

I open the box with clammy fingers, surprised at how fucking excited I am. And I should be. I really should be.

The glassware inside the box is no auction piece, but it doesn't matter.

It's beautiful and stylish with perfectly coloured flecks of aqua and green.

I stare at Mike and he's staring at me, and I knew it. I was fucking right about everything.

I was right about trusting her with money and timekeeping, I was right about how a little discipline would help her feel loved.

It feels so fucking good to be right. Mike nods and he knows it too.

"It's beautiful," I say. "I'm really touched, Carrie."

She breathes out a sign of relief. "Phew," she says. "I was crapping myself that you'd hate it."

I hold the sculpture in my hands, admiring every facet and curve of it. It may not be a one-off designer piece, but there's no doubt about it. I love it more than I ever loved the original.

"What did you get for you?" Michael asks and I take a step forward to see what else she bought, but she's already dropping her backpack to the floor. Empty.

"I didn't," she says. "I spent it all on you. But that's cool. My boots are fine."

"Hey," I say, and finally she looks at me. "You did good."

She smiles. "I did?"

"Yes," Mike says. "You did."

She shrugs like it doesn't mean anything, but it does. It's written all over her pretty face.

"Shit, you guys. Getting all emo."

I place my new sculpture on the top of the cabinet where it belongs, before any of us get too fucking gushy and make a tit of ourselves, and then I grab the beers from the fridge.

Nineteen

CARRIE

I did good.

It feels so good to do good. Buying presents for Jack and Michael was everything I hoped it would be. It's not just in the way they say thanks over and over, and it's not in the way I feel so proud as Jack places his present up on the cabinet where the other one used to be. It's not even in the way Michael looks so fine as he tries his new tie on over his shirt.

It's in the way they smile, the way they look at me.

The way their appreciation makes me feel so loved.

I do feel loved here. I feel accepted and wanted and bothered enough about that they work through my shit rather than give up on me. I feel safe when I wake up in the morning, and like I belong right where I am as I walk through the fields behind the house.

I never want to let this go, not any of it. Not this house, not this life, not

Michael, and not Jack, either.

I've never liked TV, not shows nor films, but after a couple of cold beers in Jack's kitchen, laughing and joking through a load of old jokes they have to fill me in on, I think that maybe watching TV with these two guys won't be so bad.

They say I can choose what we watch and it takes me an age, but they don't seem impatient. I sit between them on the big white sofa Jack spanked me on last night, and I try to stop thinking about it but I can't. Michael's still wearing his new tie. I like that he is. I like it a lot.

Jack slumps back easily, his legs spread and his knee touching mine. It burns a nice burn.

So did my ass last night.

I try not to fidget as I scroll up and down the listings, but my jeans are stiff and need a wash and my bra is itchy where my backpack rubbed my shoulders earlier.

"Ants in your fucking pants," Jack laughs as I shift position for the millionth time, and I grumble about everything, about all of it, finally losing my shit as I admit that I've no clean clothes and I don't know how to work his shitty washing machine.

And then I fold my arms and say I quit film night after all. Everything can go fuck itself.

It's Michael who squeezes my arm and tells me to stop being so melodramatic.

I tell him I'm not, and hope he spanks me for it all the same.

My cheeks burn as I realise that's what I want now.

I want them to pull my jeans down and put me over their knee. I want to feel their hands on me and their swollen dicks against my belly.

"Get your clothes," Jack says. "I'll show you how to work the machine."

"But then I'll have nothing to wear," I grumble, still acting up even though there's no need and I know it full well.

"I'll find you something," he says. "Your clothes will be clean and dry before you know it. You should have said something by now."

Yes, I should have. But I hate looking like a stupid idiot who can't take care of herself.

It's been over a week and the machine is one of those fancy ones with a million bastard settings that make no sense whatsoever.

Jack beckons me upstairs and I follow. I get tingles as I walk into his room after him, remembering how nice it felt to be in his arms this morning.

He opens a drawer from the chest and pulls out a baggy white t-shirt which makes me smile.

"Planning on dumping water on me?"

He raises an eyebrow. "Not unless you ask for it. Be good and you won't get hosed."

He turns his back to me as I change, and I wish he hadn't. I wish he was looking at me.

I pull down my jeans and tug off my cami, unclipping my bra and dumping that down with them. I've only got one bra but I don't want to say anything, so I have to go naked under his t-shirt. Luckily it's so big on me that I don't think it's obvious. I'm quite possibly wrong on that.

I keep on my knickers but nothing else, and the shirt comes halfway down my thighs, so that's no big deal.

I gather up my dirty clothes and the others from my room, embarrassed at how small the pile is.

"Is that it?" Jack asks and I nod.

"Like I said, can't wear them all at once."

"Next week's wages are being spent on you," he tells me and I get tickles right through me. *Next week's.*

Surely not. Surely he won't pay me every week?

At least I'll be able to give Eli back that fiver and he can fuck off and leave me alone for good.

I follow Jack downstairs and he opens the washing machine for me. I throw the clothes inside without bothering to separate them, but he pulls out the whites and leaves them in their own pile. I squeeze my thighs together at the sight of my dirty knickers in his hands, and I'm damp already without jeans on. I can feel it.

He shows me the controls and I make a mental note of them. It's really not as hard as the settings make it look.

"Thanks," I say and he grins.

"My clothes suit you."

I roll my eyes. "Don't think I'll be going outside like this somehow."

"No," he says. "You fucking won't." He points back through to the living room. "Movie night. No getting out of it."

I mock groan as I head on back through, and Michael startles as I enter, as though he's been caught doing something he shouldn't.

I wonder if he's been thinking about last night, just like I was. I wonder if it makes him feel guilty.

Or horny.

I hope it makes him feel horny.

I slump back down between them and pick up the remote control. All the films look much of a muchness to me. Action, thriller, horror, yada yada.

And that's when I see some dirty thriller thing with Keanu Reeves in it. I read the synopsis and put on the trailer, and it looks really dirty.

"This one," I say. "I want to watch this one."

I'm suddenly glad I dicked about for so long choosing, because it's getting dark outside and Jack has to put the little lamp on. He gets us a fresh beer before we settle down and heats up the popcorn in the microwave, even though I don't like popcorn anyway.

I like it in the low light between them both. I like the way they move closer to me as the film starts up. Michael's arm rests casually along the back of the cushions and Jack's hand is on his knee next to my thigh. I pull my knee up onto the sofa and he moves his hand from his to mine.

It gives me flutters.

The beer isn't strong but it's going to my head. Jack's t-shirt is only flimsy and the heat of the guys makes me burn.

I rest my head on Michael's shoulder as the film starts, raising my knee even further to press against Jack's thigh.

And it's good.

The film is really fucking good.

The girls in it are filthy as they convince poor Keanu to have an affair with them. They're all over him in the shower and the sight of all three bodies together makes me blush in the darkness.

I try to keep my cool, but I can't. My clit is tingling between my legs and it makes me squirm. I have to clench my hands into fists and ball them at my sides not to touch myself, because I want to so bad.

Michael keeps clearing his throat in a way that's definitely got to be nerves, and his legs are still crossed tight.

Jack's fingers tickle my knee. Round and round in little circles which only makes my clit flutter worse.

And then the film gets all kinds of fucked up.

The girls turn wild and crazy and I feel wild and crazy with them. They kidnap Keanu in his own house and tear it apart in front of him.

And then one of them puts on his daughter's school uniform.

I hold my breath as she rides him and calls him Daddy. Because I can't. I just can't stand it.

Of all the things Michael and Jack know I've done wrong, they don't know the half of it. They don't know how I've tried to tempt every fake daddy I've ever had. They've no idea of all the times at Bill's I left my bedroom door open and played with myself when I knew it was only him in the house. Not because I wanted him, but because I wanted him to want me.

They don't know how horny I felt when I knew he was watching, even though I never saw him.

They've no idea how fucked up I am, not really. And it scares me that they might not want to.

But then I see it. Jack shifts next to me and I'm sure there's a swell in his jeans. I feel Michael's breath quicken, and as fucked up as it is, I know they're as horny as I am.

Maybe we're all more fucked up than we'd like to be. Maybe we make each other more fucked up than *any* of us would like to be.

I don't want them to notice as I slip my hand between my legs. I hope maybe I can rub myself so slowly they won't even see me, but when I start I can't stop. I hitch my foot right up onto the sofa between Jack's spread legs and bury my face in Michael's neck, and my fingers slip inside my knickers.

I can't stop. I don't want to stop. And neither of them try to stop me.

Jack moves first. He takes my ankle in his hand and presses my raised foot to his crotch. I feel him there, big and hard. I rub him with my heel and I hear him grunt under his breath, and Michael turns his face slightly in my direction, his breathing as shallow and desperate as mine.

I know he can see me now, they both can. They both know my hand is down my knickers. I can hear the wet noises I'm making and so can they.

I close my eyes when I realise they're staring at each other over my head. I don't want to imagine the thoughts passing between them as they register what a dirty girl I really am.

My voice is a breath when it comes out, so quiet it sounds like I'm begging. Maybe I am.

"Touch me…"

And they do.

Oh my God, they really do.

Twenty

MICHAEL

O h fuck, the noises she's making. Her breath on my neck in little
gasps, her fingers frantic inside her knickers. I can hear how wet
she is. I can feel how desperate she is.

And I'm desperate too.

One look at Jack and I realise we both are. His eyes meet mine and stay
there, waiting, and I know he's pinning this all on me.

My call.

My filthy fucking call.

My dick is throbbing like a sonofabitch, and that filthy scene on screen is
everything that should turn me off but doesn't. Far fucking from it.

"Touch me…" she whispers, and it's enough to break me.

I give Jack the tiniest nod and he drops his eyes. His hand slides from her
knee to her thigh and she spreads her legs for him, hitching one right across

my lap as his fingers slide over her wet knickers. He moves his fingers over hers until she pulls hers away, and then his hand dips inside the lacy elastic and rubs her there.

She moans into my neck. Right into my fucking neck.

I part my thighs and her leg drops perfectly to press her calf against the bulge in my pants. She lifts her face just a fraction, just enough that I feel her breath on my lips.

Her eyes open into mine and they're hazy and hooded. Horny. So fucking horny.

"Touch me, Michael..." she whispers, and I take one last steadying breath before I'm all in with this craziness.

My fingers land on her shoulder and trail down her arm. I'm slow as I make my way across, my palm flat against her stomach before I inch my way up. Her nipples are pretty little bullets poking through Jack's old t-shirt. I brush one with my thumb and she moans for me.

She arches her back as I take her tit in my hand and squeeze. She offers them up for more as I roll her nipple under my thumb, moaning as she lifts her t-shirt. I tug it up and over her head, her hair swishing as I pull the shirt free and toss it to the floor.

Our beautiful Carrie bares me her beautiful naked tits, and they're perfect, just like she is. Sweet little pink buds against pale skin. A birthmark just underneath her right nipple. She smiles as I run my hand from one to the other, closes her eyes as I roll her soft little tits around my palm. I grip those hard little nubs between my fingers, and she groans.

"Kiss me..." she breathes. "Please, Michael. Kiss me."

Her lips are soft and sweet and open. I press my mouth to hers and her tongue reaches out for mine. I take her hair and hold her tight, kissing her with the pent-up frustration of every time I've wanted to kiss her but couldn't. I suck her bottom lip, and she twists her fingers in my hair as she murmurs for more, urging me down to her perky little tits.

And then she reaches for Jack. I hover with my open mouth just a breath from her beautiful nipple, staring up as Jack's open mouth crashes into hers.

Their kiss is wet and frantic. Their grunts make my balls tighten.

I fix my mouth over that pretty pale tit and I suck. I suck with my eyes closed, soaking in everything.

And then a firm hand lands on my wrist. His fingers are wet. Wet with her.

He guides mine where his have been and I rub that wet little slit as he smears his fingers all around her other nipple. And then he's sucking too.

His face is next to mine, his mouth fixed over that pretty tit as we both suck and nip and slurp on her. Her fingers in my hair hold me tight, him too, shoulders back as she asks for it harder.

I suck harder.

I circle my thumb around the nub of her clit until she rocks her hips and wish I could see her there. I'm desperate to see her there.

Harder, please harder… she moans again and I pin her nipple between my teeth, my cheeks hollow as I give her what she wants.

Jack tugs her knickers down over her hips and I help him, wriggling them down over her ass until she squirms her way out of them. We hitch her up between us, breaking away from her tits in perfect synchrony to stare at each other. His lips are puffy, mine must be too.

I move to take a look at that pretty little pussy; swollen pink and glistening, tightening as she rocks her hips.

Jack and I must get the thought at the same time, because no sooner has the question crossed my mind than he voices it.

"Carrie, are you a…" he begins, then takes a breath. "Have you done this before?"

She nods. She's done it before.

Maybe I shouldn't be surprised, but I am.

I wonder who she's been with. I wonder who the lucky guy was that took her first.

It matters not. He'll never take her again.

Carrie positions herself evenly between us, slipping her hands down over the bulges in our pants and palming us both.

"Clit or cunt?" Jack grunts at me, and I'm sure I should be bothered by this, but weirdly I'm not.

"Clit," I say and he spreads her glistening lips wide with his fingers. I wet my thumb before I press it to that dark little bud and she shudders.

I stare down in fascination as he hooks two fingers and pushes them inside. Pushes them deep and she takes them with a sweet little moan.

"Tight," he growls. "You're so fucking tight."

I want to feel it too, and he knows it. He smiles as he pulls out and I push mine straight in after him and she moans all over again. She is fucking tight. Perfectly fucking tight.

Her foot thrashes as I stretch her with a third finger.

"Give me cock," she hisses. "I want it…"

It's Jack who takes hold of her and twists her in my direction. It's him who drops her backwards until her head is in his lap, his wet fingers grasping at her tits in a heartbeat.

"You saw her first," he growls, and I did. I did fucking see her first.

Her eyes meet mine. "Fuck me, Michael…"

I loosen my tie and tug it off. She helps me unbutton my shirt and drop it to the floor, rubbing my dick through my trousers as fumble with my belt.

I take them down and my boxers with them, far beyond giving a shit about Jack's eyes all over me.

"Big." Carrie smiles like a filthy little pixie as she wraps her fingers around my shaft. "I want it inside me."

So do I.

But not until I've tasted that pretty little cunt. I have to shunt down to bury my face between her thighs, licking in her long slow sweeps until I've tasted all of her. I dip my tongue inside and she's gloriously fucking slippery in there. Slippery but fucking tight. She bucks against my face.

"Suck my clit…" she whimpers. "Make me come…"

I suck that hard little bud until she squirms. Until she moans for me. Until I feel her feet grappling against my back.

I suck her clit as Jack tugs his t-shirt over his head. He pulls his zip down and frees his big meaty dick from his jeans, trailing precum across Carrie's cheek until she opens that filthy little mouth of hers wide for him. He pushes inside her cheek, and the noises, oh the fucking noises.

She comes against my face, her moans stifled by his dick as her body shudders.

It's violent and wet and fucking beautiful.

She's still shuddering as I lift her legs up and slam my way inside her. Her pussy takes me all the way, but it's tight, milking me like a fucking glove with every fucking thrust.

I'm losing myself.

Losing every scrap of resistance to this crazy fucking setup.

I'm staring at the girl I love slavering over my best friend's dick and I like it. I fucking like it.

I want to watch him fuck her.

I want to watch him fill her up right after me.

I want to be the one in her mouth as her pretty little cunt struggles to take him.

She gurgles and Jack groans.

My balls slap against her ass as I pound the fuck out of the gorgeous little brat underneath me.

And then I come.

I come hard.

So hard I see white behind my eyes.

I come without even thinking about protection. I come with no fucking scrap of sensibility left inside me.

I'm still twitching inside her when Jack tells me it's his fucking turn.

CARRIE

I'm grinning wide as they swap positions. My face already twisting to suck Michael's salty dick into my mouth. I can taste his cum. He's still throbbing as he rubs his cock against my tongue.

My eyes are all on Jack. Broader than Michael's toned leanness. His dick maybe a fraction shorter, but thicker. Thick enough that I know he'll hurt, even now I've opened up for Michael.

Michael hurt too. It was the best hurt in the world. I'm glad Jack's going to make me feel it all over again.

I feel him spread me and look inside, and I feel so fucking dirty, still squelchy with Michael's cum in me.

I can't believe he came in me, but I like it.

I want more.

I want Jack's in there too.

"You came inside her," Jack says as I open wider for Michael's dick.

"I'm hardly fucking thinking straight," Michael says and Jack smiles.

"Wasn't a fucking dig. You can have sloppy seconds next time, but what's good for the fucking goose." He thumps his big dark cock against my clit and I squirm.

And then he pushes inside.

Michael stuffs his dick in my mouth as I try to cry out. I gurgle-snort spit and cum, dribbling down my cheek as Jack bottoms out in me.

It aches a perfect ache right the way inside. I feel the ache in my belly and I want more.

I want hard.

I grind myself against him, scissoring him with my thighs and urging him on.

"We've got a dirty little girl here," Jack growls. His eyes are dark. Dark and fierce. He looks on screen to where the credits are rolling, movie be fucked. "You liked how she called him Daddy, didn't you? That's what made you touch yourself, isn't it?"

I feel my cheeks burning even as I splutter on Michael's dick.

"I thought you were just being a smart-mouthed bitch when you called us Daddy, but you like it, don't you?"

My heart is racing, hammering in my chest at being discovered.

Michael's dick throbs in my mouth and he swears under his breath, and I know for all his trying to be sensible and sane and professional, he's as fucked up as the rest of us.

"Fuck," Jack groans. "Your tight little cunt is going to be the fucking death of the both of us."

I don't recognise the Michael that takes hold of my neck and tips my head back until I retch on his dick, but I love him.

I don't recognise the Michael that tells Jack to fuck me harder.

I don't think Jack does either.

"Fuck her," Michael grunts again. "She wants it. She's wants all of this. Just fucking give it to her, Jack."

And I do want all of this.

I want all of them.

Jack's thrusts are brutal but they hit just the right spot. I'm gagging around Michael's dick, pulling at my own nipples when Jack's voice sounds out filthy and low, just as it did in the hallway when he told me I had no idea what he wanted to do to a brat like me.

"Call him Daddy," Jack growls, and I choke in surprise. "Call him Daddy fucking Michael and tell him how deep you want him down your pretty little throat."

Michael pulls out, but not all the way. The head of him is still in my mouth as he lifts my dirty, wet face up enough that I can look at them both.

"Do it," Jack says, and brushes his thumb over my clit as he pounds me. "It'll sound even fucking dirtier with his dick in your mouth."

My senses are on fire, my stomach in knots as my clit goes fucking crazy.

They're right inside me, not just in my body but in my mind, too.

And we're right on the edge. Right on the edge of toppling over forever, once I say it I'll never go back, I'll never be able to go back.

"Daddy," I gurgle with Michael's swollen dick between my lips.

"That's it," Jack says as my body betrays my secrets. My toes curl, my whole body trembling as I lose control. "Again," Jack growls, and I'm done. All in for everything.

"Daddy Michael," I whimper. "Love me, Daddy Michael, please."

Thick globs of cum splatter my tongue as Michael swears under his breath.

I cry out as my own orgasm rushes through me, and Jack's on his way too, I feel it in his thrusts.

"And me," he growls. "Fucking say it."

I look him right in the eye, knowing I'll love him forever, no matter what.

"Daddy Jack," I whisper.

And he comes inside me.

Twenty-One

JACK

Not once in all the sex I've ever had, have I ever shot my load deep inside a woman's pussy, no matter what contraceptives they've been using.

Commitment scares the shit out of me.

But here, still catching my breath with my cock throbbing between Carrie's spread thighs, there's nothing more thrilling than watching my cum dribble out of that tight little cunt of hers.

The fact that Michael's is in there too, and certainly smeared all over my dick, matters to me surprisingly little. I feel like I've conquered the fucking world.

I don't know what the fuck is happening to me – fuck, to either of us – but I like it.

I just hope Michael does too.

"Are you okay?" I ask Carrie as her breathing calms.

She nods. Smiles. Giggles a giggle that barely sounds like her.

It's light.

Free.

"I'm great," she says.

She slides a hand down her belly, palming her swollen clit before dipping a finger inside herself.

"I'm full of you," she says, piercing eyes right on mine. She looks up at Michael after me. "Both of you."

I'd stare at that dripping pussy forever, but she lifts herself up to sit between us.

I was fucking livid when she traipsed mud all over my cushions, but cum smears I can live with all day long.

I feel surprisingly mute on the topic of contraception. The urge to dash out to the chemist for a morning after pill is non-existent.

The Carrie Wells effect. Michael wasn't joking when he said she sucks you in deep.

I look over at him, focusing on his face and not the dick he's holding absentmindedly. He looks as spaced out as I feel.

"You alright?" I ask, and his eyes clear.

Carrie reaches out for him, tugging on his arm until he settles at her side. She nestles into the crook of his shoulder, her cheek against his clammy skin.

"I'm fine," he says. "As fucked up as this is, and it *is* fucking fucked up, I feel like a cloud's lifted."

I get it. I've been feeling it too. Days of tension as this cart veered off the rails.

Now it's crashed and toppled, we at least know what we're dealing with.

Carrie's voice is timid when she speaks. "You're not going to run off now, are you?" She snakes an arm around his waist as though she'll fight him every step.

What she means is she doesn't want him to leave her, and I get that, too. I don't want him to walk off into the night with a head full of regrets, any more than I want to erase what happened here.

I have no regrets. Not a single one.

I don't regret taking Carrie Wells and filling her full of my cum, and I don't regret sharing her with Mike, either.

One of us was going to lose out big time, I didn't want it to be him, and I sure as fuck didn't want it to be me.

"I'm not going to run off," he tells her. "I'd never run off from you. I'm the one who came running after you, remember?"

"Nobody's running off anywhere," I say. "Not us, and not you."

She nods. "So, what happens now?"

I meet Michael's eyes and his are as clueless as mine.

"We go to bed," I improvise. "Sleep on it, see what we work out in the morning."

"Bed?" she says. "All of us?"

I hadn't even thought about the logistics. The prospect of me in an empty bed with Carrie in the guest room and Michael roughing it on the sofa seems less than ideal.

The prospect of Carrie choosing to share a bed with either of us individually seems a recipe for jealousy and nothing more.

"I'm happy to bunk up if you are," I tell him.

He's quiet for a minute.

"Three of us in one bed?"

"Unless you've got a better idea?"

"I like that idea," Carrie chips in. "Please can we go with that idea?"

Michael shrugs. "I have no better option to counter."

"Bed buddies it is," I laugh, hoping the humour carries through to all of us.

Carrie laughs along with me, Mike manages a smile at least.

She winces as I reach out a hand and pull her to her feet. "You got me good," she says, laughing as cum drips down her thighs.

We did that, alright.

I wrap my arms around our beautiful dirty girl and squeeze her tight. I breathe in her hair and she melts against me, her warm fingers clammy against my back.

"You're not such a bad little bitch as you like to make out," I whisper. "I think, in fact, you're a good girl, you just hadn't found the right guys to bring it out of you."

Her eyes are mischievous as she stares up at me. "You think?"

I smirk and then I kiss her to answer her question, long past caring that she's had another guy's dick in her mouth.

Her kisses are sweet, genuine, without even a hint of the hissing banshee who railed on me for letting a crow fly out over my head.

"How about you grab us all a coffee while Mike and I clean up in here?"

"Sounds good," she says, padding away from the living room with that delightful little ass of hers swaying every step. I'm gonna ride the fuck out of that asshole, but not tonight.

Soon, but not tonight.

Mike tugs his pants back on when it's just us left in the room. I don't bother with mine. Who really gives a fuck for modesty after all that?

He collects up the beer bottles and gathers the scattered popcorn from the carpet while I grab a wet cloth from the kitchen to wipe down my poor ravaged sofa. I give Carrie's ass a playful slap on the way through and she pokes her tongue out.

Fuck, I love that fucking girl.

"You alright?" I ask Mike as I rub over the wet patches on the fabric.

"I don't know what I am anymore," he says, but he doesn't look about to go anywhere, and I doubt he ever will.

I doubt either of us ever will, because this thing we have – the contagious Carrie Wells effect – I'm pretty damn sure this shit is terminal.

"I can't find a way to justify why what we did feels so right," he tells me.

I tip my head. "So stop trying. I have."

"It can't be right," he says, but he's lacking the conviction he's been so desperately clinging onto.

"Maybe it's right for *us*," I offer. "Maybe it's right for *her*. Fuck, Mike, neither of us have a stellar fucking track record on the relationship front. Forty years old and both single? Maybe we're not fucking destined for a twee little life with neat little tick boxes."

"Maybe not." He looks so fucking pensive.

There's that urge to ruffle his hair again. To pull him into a friendly headlock and slap his back and make this all about two guy friends again.

But I'm naked and he's not far off either, and that crap still feels a little weird around the edges.

I'm worried about him, I'm worried about how his mind will play over all of this. But most of all I'm worried he'll try to climb back up the cliff we've just tumbled over.

There's no fucking way to scale back up that motherfucker, we're well and truly all in.

"Coffee's up," Carrie calls from the kitchen, and we head out, him before me, dumping the cloth and the leftover movie-night supplies by the draining board before taking a seat at the island.

It's when I see him look at her that I know he's gonna be just fucking fine.

His eyes are warm, fingers reaching out to rest on her back so tenderly.

Because he loves her. He really fucking loves her.

I love the way he loves that girl.

I love the way she smiles right back at him.

I love the way she sips her coffee and smiles at me, too.

We're gonna be just fine and I know it, even if I do have to share my bastard bed with a naked guy.

I finish my drink and head up before them, tugging the bedcovers into some kind of order before I flick the bedroom lights down low.

I'm already in my en-suite shower as I hear Michael and Carrie reach the bedroom. The bathroom door is open in invitation.

Carrie has her hand in Michael's. She tugs him along after her as she heads in my direction.

I slide open the shower door and she steps inside, turning back to face him as he ditches his boxers on the tiles.

I'm glad I'm a man who prefers opulence over budget, because it's just as well I opted for a shower big enough for three. Carrie grins as she joins me under the water, tipping her head back and closing her eyes as the warmth lands on her face. Mike presses up behind her, his arms around her waist as I grab the body wash from the rack. I squeeze a load into my palm and slap it over my chest, lathering it up before I offer the bottle to Carrie.

She laughs as she dribbles it over her tits, the filthy little minx making quite a spectacle of soaping her nipples. I brush her hands away and take over the job, soaping her nice and good before dipping my fingers between her legs. I lather up that delicious little pussy, washing our stickiness off her as she rests her head back against Michael's shoulder. His hands palm her tits, his hair nearly as dark as hers under the showerhead. He kisses her wet hair and I browse the bottles on the rack for the fancy shampoo one of my last female guests left here.

I hand it to him and he gets to work. Her expression is one of wonder as his fingers work her scalp, and under all this, under all the dirtiness and the sex and the come-ons she's been giving us, I'm reminded again that this girl hasn't really known tenderness before. She's never been looked after before.

It's never been more obvious than it is right now. Never been more obvious than it is in her pleasure at having her hair washed by someone else's hands.

Her eyes are closed in rapture, mouth open as she tips her head back for him. He gathers her hair up onto her head, soaping her with surprising skill as she murmurs under his care.

"That's so nice," she whispers, like it needs saying. She moves exactly as he guides her to let him wash out the suds. She turns to him when he's done, her clean hair hanging in perfect wet waves against her back. She takes the shampoo and reaches up to him, and my heart flips as she mimics what he did in perfect concentration.

I suddenly wish I had more hair than I do.

She soaps him right down, her eyes on his in nothing short of adoration as she works her hands over his body.

I should feel jealous, but I don't. I should be weirded the fuck out, but I'm not.

My cock is hard again, but that's secondary to the wave of devotion I feel to this beautiful creature in front of me.

It's secondary to the pleasure I feel in seeing my best friend so enamored by the girl he's been in love with for months.

When she's done, she shoots me a glance over her shoulder. Her eyes are hooded but twinkling. I love the way the water droplets glisten on her eyelashes.

"You next," she tells me, and I press in closer. She turns between us, a fresh load of soap on the skin I already lathered, but I don't care.

My mouth dips to her neck and I lick up the water from her throat. She runs her soapy fingers between my ass cheeks and guides my thigh between hers.

She must be tender but she doesn't show it. She wriggles between us, wrapping an arm back around Mike's neck to steady herself as he grinds against her from behind. We pin her, wet bodies rubbing wet bodies, soap and fingers and groans as our tender little wash session descends into another wave of hard dicks and needy pussy.

"This is love, right?" she asks as I hitch that sweet little pussy tighter against my thigh. "We love each other?"

The nervousness in her eyes breaks my fucking heart.

My answer is easy, even though it's been impossible with every other woman I've ever had in my bed.

"Yes, this is love," I tell her.

Her smile lights up the world.

Mike's lips press to her temple, his eyes closed as he trails his fingers down her throat.

"I love you," he says. "I've always loved you."

She turns her face to his. "And Jack, you love Jack, too? We're in this together, right? The three of us?"

Her breath comes in little rasps as she grinds against my thigh.

I save him the self-consciousness.

"Yes, he fucking loves me," I tell her. "He wouldn't be sharing if he didn't."

She seems happy with that, and so am I.

"I want you inside me," she groans. "I want it again. I want us to love each other again."

It seems now Carrie Wells has opened up to the love word she can't get enough of it.

It's sweet. It's beautiful.

It's more than enough to convince me that this crazy train ends somewhere worth the ride.

Guiding her back onto Mike's dick comes so naturally. Sucking her dripping tits while he fucks her from behind is a beautiful pleasure.

Wet slaps of flesh make my dick throb. The judder of her tits as he thrusts inside is fucking divine.

She braces herself against the wall, arms tense on either side of me, balancing like a fucking ballerina as Mike lift her leg to take her deeper.

Water drips from her hair onto the hard dick in my hand, and her glazed eyes focus on mine.

"It's just bodies," she whispers. "We're all just skin and bone and muscle. Just people. All three of us. Three people who love each other."

I don't know what she's getting at until she presses a hand to my scalp. She pushes me down, urging me onto my knees before her.

I hear Mike's balls slapping against her ass so loudly down here. I'm bizarrely fascinated by the way his dick thrusts inside her.

"Just bodies…" she says again, and spreads her dripping pussy lips with her fingers. "Kiss me, Jack. Kiss me there."

But I don't know if I fucking can.

The swollen bud of her clit is ripe for sucking, and her taste is everything I want.

But my shoulders are tense, and my stomach is fucking twisted up, and I don't know if I can put my mouth so close to another man's fucking dick.

She grunts as Mike angles deeper. "Please…" she hisses. "Kiss me, Jack."

I squeeze my dick in my fingers, work that motherfucker hard as I contemplate the fucking unthinkable.

"Just fucking bodies," I grunt under my breath, grip her thighs and fix my mouth over that sweet fucking clit.

It drives her crazy. Her hands are in my hair and the noises from her dirty mouth are everything.

And it's enough. It's enough that I don't care that another man's balls are slapping so fucking close to my chin. It's enough that I don't care that my tongue is just an inch from tasting dick.

I don't fucking care.

And I can't believe that one crazy girl is worth stepping over boundaries I've never considered crossing in my whole fucking life up until now.

But she's worth it.

I just hope she's worth it for Mike too, because as he grunts and groans and tells her he's on the fucking edge she tells him to stop. She tells him not to come yet.

And I've got a sneaky fucking suspicion he's about to toe the line right after me.

CARRIE

They love me.

I feel it in their touch and in their kisses. I feel it in the way they soap me down and hold me tight.

I feel it in every look that passes between them, between us. Between all of us.

They love me and I love them.

But they'll have to love each other too if I'm gonna keep them both.

I so wanna keep them both.

More than want. *Need.*

I need to keep them both.

And if love is really love then it has to be free. If three is gonna work then love has to go all ways.

I know these guys don't love each other like *that.* I know they don't wanna touch each other or kiss each other, or stick their dicks inside each other.

I know they're only doing any of this because they love me enough to share.

But I want them to learn that love is love and bodies are just bodies. I want them to learn that love doesn't come in neat boxes, and it doesn't have stupid rules about how close someone else's dick can be.

I don't know much about love, but I do know that.

I know I'm pushing Jack hard when I ask him to kiss me down there while Mike's dick is inside me. I feel how tense he is when he gives into the moment and presses his mouth to my desperate clit.

But he does it.

He does it because he loves me. He does it because he loves Mike, too.

And now it's Mike's turn. It's why he can't come yet.

It's why he needs to be throbbing hard when I ask him to kneel between my legs and kiss me with Jack's dick inside.

He knows what's coming, I know he does.

His eyes are closed as I turn to face him and Jack gets to his feet behind me.

"I'm not sure I can," he says, but I know he's wrong.

I've seen the way he looks at Jack's dick when he fucks me. I've seen the way he can't stop looking.

"Try?" I ask and he sighs.

I wrap my hand around his dick as Jack pushes his way inside me. It makes me groan.

My words come out on their own, and even though they sound dirty, I don't care.

"I'll be a good girl," I tell him. "I'll be a good girl for you, Michael, I promise. I'll do whatever you want, love you however you want. I'll love you forever, Michael, I swear, no matter what. I'll do anything you say. But kiss me down there. Kiss me so I know you can love Jack too."

"Fuck," he says. "This is fucking insane."

I spread my pussy lips for him. Jack fucks me hard. Really fucking hard.

I love the way it aches.

I love the way my pussy wants to take him, even though I'm sore inside.

"It's not so bad, Mike," Jack growls. "Just do it, man."

"Fuck," Michael says again, and drops to his knees.

I take his hair in my hands before he can change his mind. Guide him to my clit before he can think himself out of it.

And it's perfect. His mouth is perfect.

"We're gonna make you take whatever we want after this," Jack growls and I smile. "You fucking owe us."

I sure hope so. I hope they make me take everything.

Michael doesn't stay down there long. Just a quick suck and he gets back to his feet.

I take his dick in my hand and rub him, moaning under the water as Jack fucks me hard.

And then Jack stops. I groan as he pulls from my pussy, taken aback as he manhandles me onto my knees.

"Open that dirty little mouth nice and wide for us," he barks, and I do, I open nice and wide.

They stand under the water, both of them side by side, working their huge fucking dicks as I stare up through wet lashes.

"We love you, you filthy little minx," Jack says and spurts thick cum right onto my tongue. I let it dribble to the back of my mouth, angling my face to Mike as he groans.

Mike comes hard, splattering my whole face as his dick spurts. It goes up my nose and in my eye and it stings like fuck but I don't fucking care.

I wipe my eye and lick my lips, giggling like the dirty little whore I feel.

A loved, spent, dirty little whore.

Their little whore.

And this little whore is just about ready for bed.

Twenty-Two

MICHAEL

don't know who I am anymore as I wake up in bed with my best friend and the girl whose pussy we both pounded last night.

My dick is already at half mast, even though my stomach is churning at the thought of it all.

Carrie is still asleep between us, her face resting on my arm and her ankle over mine. She looks peaceful in the warm morning light, nothing like the dirty girl who begged for dick last night.

Sleeping next to her was beautiful. Her limbs tangled in mine after so long sleeping alone was exquisite.

Having Jack on the other side of her really shouldn't seem like such a big deal after what went down in the shower, but it still has me reeling.

Fuck, the shower.

My cock twitches at the thought and I grimace, not sure whether to jerk myself to hardness or jump right on back in to hose myself down cold.

I don't know how this happened, and I don't know why I can't stop.

I don't know why I'm tumbling down the rabbit hole without so much as an attempt to slow my fall.

That's a lie. As soon as Carrie yawns in her sleep and her nose wrinkles I know exactly why I've fallen so willingly.

Jack props himself up on an elbow and stares over. The guy's hair is too short for bed hair and I'm jealous because mine feels like a nest on my head.

I flash him a look, conveying just how many variations of fucked-up I'm feeling right now.

He gestures to the bedroom door and I nod, freeing myself so gently from Carrie's grip as I slip out of the covers and follow him.

My fucking clothes are nowhere to be seen, just a pair of boxers that I scoop up from the bathroom floor.

I have to traipse downstairs in my underwear after my naked best friend like this isn't the weirdest fucking setup we've ever been in. He pulls on his t-shirt in the living room and I step into my discarded trousers with a sigh of relief.

"Let's get a coffee before we say anything," Jack says, and that's probably for the best.

He sticks the kettle on and I take a seat at the island, amazed at the fact that it's tiredness, not a hangover, that has me feeling like a bag of shit. I can't even say I was drunk. I wasn't even close.

And neither was he.

"Thanks," I say as Jack puts a hot mug of black in front of me.

"The Carrie Wells effect," he laughs. "You weren't fucking joking."

"Glad you're finding this hilarious."

He raises an eyebrow. "Isn't it?"

"We did filthy things to an eighteen year old girl with serious behavioural and emotional challenges last night. A girl who was on my books until a matter of weeks ago."

He shrugs. "I think you'll find her behavioural challenges are improving. Her emotional ones, too. Our therapy has been far more successful that anything you did with her on the books, if you don't mine me saying."

"That's not the point."

"I think it is," he says. "She's happy. We're happy."

"Are we?" I ask, shaking my head about the whole thing before I take a swig of coffee. It goes down like a dream.

"*I'm* fucking happy," he tells me. "You seemed pretty damn happy too last night. We hardly dragged you up there kicking and screaming, you were the one who gave me the nod before we even touched the girl." He pauses. "Is this about your job?"

My eyes burn his. "Of course it's not about my job. This goes way beyond my job."

"Then what's it about? Being too close to another man's dick? Because truth be told, I'm not too stoked on that bit myself, but I'm getting over it."

"It's not about your dick," I tell him, even though the memory makes my heart pound.

"Then what? Wasn't it as good as you thought it would be?"

I shake my head. "It's got nothing to do with how good I thought it would be." The memories pile in and I'm embarrassed at how much I enjoyed it. All of it.

"So enlighten me, because I'm missing a puzzle piece here. She wants us, we want her, she's perfectly legal and perfectly willing, so we took her, we came a lot, she came a lot. The end." He glugs back his coffee. "Now we need to work out what happens from here on in."

"I can't do this," I say, even though my dick hates me for it. "This isn't who I am."

"You don't know who you are," he laughs, as though I'm the one who's fucking crazy here. "Ever since you holed up with Molly you've been going through the motions of some cardboard cut-out ideal of normality. You think being nice has to make you a fucking saint, man. And it doesn't."

"Just as well, isn't it? Because I wasn't exactly on my best behaviour when I was balls deep inside a girl I'm supposed to be taking care of."

"You *are* taking care of her. She's more loved than she's ever been." He sighs and I realise he's as churned up as I am. "You have to tell me what you want to do here, Mike, because I'm drawing a fucking blank."

And so am I.

I stare into the coffee like it holds the answer to this whole fucked-up scenario.

"I love her," I tell him.

"I know," he says. "So do I. And you're my best friend, so I love you too. Not in a gay way, before you think this is a come on. It's not a fucking come on. I've no intention of putting my face any closer to your dick than it's already been, regardless of what that dirty little minx upstairs has to say about it."

His stupid smile makes me smile back, and I remember again that this is Jack. My Jack. The Jack who's always been on my team, no matter what.

"My balls were on your chin," I tell him, and he laughs.

"Yeah, well, I'm pretty sure mine were on yours too. Who's fucking counting?" His expression turns serious. "Tell me honestly that you don't want to do it again, and we'll draw a line under it. We'll never do it again. She can choose one of us, or live with both of us entirely platonically. Whatever. If you're really serious about this not being for you, then it's not viable for any of us."

I stare at him.

I think about it.

Contemplate the reality of calling time on all this.

And I don't say another word.

CARRIE

They aren't there when I wake, and it cripples me. My heart races as I pull my knees to my chest, all alone in way too much bed.

I scared them away. This whole crazy thing scared them away.

I have to take a breath before I force myself out of bed. My hands are trembling as I grab a spare t-shirt from Jack's open drawer. I tug it on and prepare myself to face the news.

Prepare myself for the crushing blow of having them both change their minds and throw me away.

It wouldn't be the first time.

I head downstairs slowly, being so quiet on the stairs. I peek around the corner at the bottom, listening out for any sign of them.

The kitchen door is open at the far end. I hear low voices and wonder what they're saying about me.

If they're working out how best to let me go.

I could cry as I head closer, teeth gritted tight so they don't see me break, but when I reach the open doorway it's not a load of *thanks but no thanks* excuses waiting for me, but smiles and open arms and a fresh pot of coffee.

"Hey, sleepyhead," Jack greets. He pulls me in tight and I take a deep breath against his chest. "We thought we'd let you rest."

"I thought you'd left me," I admit, and he grabs my shoulders.

His eyes are fierce. "Never," he says. "You're too under our skin to get away from us that easily."

It's all I can do to smile, anything more and the relief would come out in stupid tears.

Michael kisses my cheek on his way past to pour me a coffee. "You look cute in your sleep," he says, and my words come back.

"I look cute all the time, even when I'm being a bratty little cow."

"Keep on telling yourself that," Jack says and pinches my nose.

I hitch myself up onto the stool between them and take my coffee gratefully. I don't know what to talk about so I don't say anything, for once in my life trusting my fate to other people.

I'm tired of guarding myself so hard all the time.

"What do you want to do today?" Michael asks.

I don't think I've ever been asked that question before.

My answer is surprisingly easy to find. "I want to show you my fences," I tell them. "I want you to see how great it is out there."

Jack raises an eyebrow. "The great outdoors. It's been a while since I went out trekking."

"It's hardly a trek," Michael says. "You have a few fields, not a national park."

"It's quite a few fields," I tell him. "Plenty enough for a load of sheep and some goats, and maybe some ponies too."

"Or plenty enough to let the grass grow just fine without them," Jack says. "I'm hardly much of a farmer."

But I am, at least I want to be. I really want goats and sheep and maybe some chickens. And ponies. Dogs, too.

I'm getting carried away but I don't care. Anything feels possible here.

"Maybe Carrie can be a farmer," Michael says and I smile to remember how well he's gotten to know me over the months.

"Maybe I can," I grin.

"Forget it," Jack says. "One crow was enough." But his eyes linger on mine, and I wonder.

I daren't even hope.

"Right," he says and finishes up his coffee. "You'd better get dressed, missy. I can't wait to see your handiwork."

That's good, because I can't wait to show it to him either.

JACK

Sheep and goats and ponies.

Fuck that.

I can only imagine the chaos if our sweet little Carrie had a whole menagerie to take care of. And yet the thought makes me smile to myself as we leap across the brook after her.

She's so alive out here, our gypsy girl. Her wind-whipped hair flies wild and her cheeks are rosy pink. She's nimble on the banks and quick over the fences, putting us to shame as she scrambles up and over in a flash.

She belongs out here. This land is more hers than mine, even though it's my name on the deeds.

I make her wait for the praise, eyes like saucers as she watches me examine her new fence panels.

"Well?" she asks finally. "Are they good or what?"

I take a breath as though I'm about to deliver bad news, but Michael blows my ruse.

"He's dicking about with you," he says. "He's impressed."

"I'm impressed," I admit. "You did great."

My heart flutters like a fucking sap as her chest puffs up proud. "I told you," she says. "It's in my blood. It's all in my blood."

"Goats and sheep and chickens, too?" Michael adds.

She nods. "And ponies. And dogs."

I tip my head. "Maybe a couple of chickens, for the eggs. You can clean the fuckers out though, they're vicious."

Her shock is intoxicating. Almost enough to tell her she can have the whole bastard farm if she wants it.

"Really?! I can have chickens?"

"A couple," I say. "Enough for the three of us to have eggs in the mornings."

I don't realise what I'm saying until it's out there in the air. Michael stares at me and I stare back, and Carrie stares between us with her pretty mouth open.

"I mean, when you stay over," I add, but it's too late for that.

I curse my big mouth when he doesn't say a word, convinced that this may be the straw that breaks his sensible back and sends him running back to normality.

But it doesn't. Credit where it's due, the guy is adapting much more readily to all this than I thought he would.

"I like eggs," he says. "I could be persuaded to muck in with the shit-shovelling if there was a hot breakfast on the other side of it."

"Deal," Carrie says.

I start walking before I can say anything else dumb, skirting the edge of the field as they follow behind, checking out Carrie's hard work until I come to the spot on the bank that she must have taken her slutty selfie from. I recognise the tree down below, the line of hedge running off to the right.

"You took it here, didn't you?" I ask. "The dirty photo."

Her eyes are full of devilment. She marches up to me and plants her boot in the mud about a foot away. "Here," she says. "I stood right here and I thought of you."

"What did you think about?" Michael asks, and I'm sure there's a thickness to his voice.

Carrie laughs before she answers. "I thought about showing you the selfie. I thought about how angry you might be if you knew I was flashing my tits around the countryside."

"There's nobody about to see them," I counter.

But she grins.

"There is today," Michael says, and she nods.

I think I'm beyond surprises at this point, but I'm not. The way he closes the distance between them and unzips her coat is nothing short of ferocious. She gasps as he tugs down her nice clean cami and her bra with it, offering up her pretty tits without hesitation.

"I want you out here," she says. "I want you both out here. It's where I belong."

Mike takes her jeans down to her knees. He drops her onto the mud and guides her onto all fours like a man possessed.

I don't understand it until I hear him speak.

"This is how I dreamt of you," he tells her. "With your knees in the mud and the wind in your face."

I can't help but grin as he takes out his dick and he's rock hard.

Carrie flattens her tits to the floor, the ground against her cheek. "Take me," she hisses and he drops down behind her.

I dig my dick out of my jeans and gawp like a fucking idiot, but this is their time. Their moment.

She lets out a moan as he pushes inside her, and he grunts like a starving man over dinner. He drops his weight onto her, crushing her flat to the ground as her thighs struggle to open wide enough.

"You're so tight like this," he says, and his movements are slow and deep as he savours it. Savours every fucking second.

"Never stop loving me," she hisses, like there's any fucking chance of either of us giving this up.

The girl's pussy is the Holy Grail.

She stares up at me as he fucks her, smiling as I work my dick in my hand.

She stares up at me like she can see inside my soul, and I remember what a little mind-reader she is.

And in that moment, I know that she sees how much I like watching him fuck her.

This is way beyond sharing for me.

This is way beyond a needs must situation.

This is about the three of us now.

Michael fucks her, blissfully unaware of my changing emotions. He fucks her until she squirms underneath him, whimpering and mewling as he slams into the right spot.

She comes loud, and she's filthy when she's finished, her cheek smeared with mud, her cami top green with grass stains.

And Michael's fresh cum dribbling down her thighs when she gets up.

Twenty-Three

CARRIE

It's warm in the middle, wedged tight between two hot bodies in Jack's bed. I love it here.

I try not to remember it's Sunday night and they'll be back at work again in the morning.

Jack's hand is on my stomach, Michael's is in mine. One of my legs hooks Jack's, the other hooks his.

I should be exhausted but I'm not. I should be ready for sleep after an afternoon trekking through fields, my pussy sore from taking Michael again earlier.

But I'm not.

I want them both again and I want them now. I can't get enough of them.

I can't get enough of them loving me. Wanting me. Taking care of me.

I can't get enough of the way I know they'll pull me back in line whenever I get too much, either.

Rough. That's what I want.

Rough and strong and dirty.

My two dirty daddies.

I must manage an hour or two of trying to sleep before it gets too much. Jack's rolled onto his side, facing me, his breath even against my cheek.

Michael is still on his back, rigid as he stares up at the ceiling.

I know he's awake. I know he's still churning with all of this.

His hand is still in mine until I pull free and run my fingers up his arm.

I don't speak, not with my mouth anyway. It's my hand that glides across his body, feeling every ridge of him, as though I'm trying to prove to myself he's really here.

The months I spent thinking about him come flooding back. Nights of playing with my pussy until I couldn't take any more. Months of imagining him naked under his suit.

And now he's here.

This weekend he's really here and he's really mine.

His breath quickens as I stroke my hand down his belly. His muscles are tight and lean, tightening further as my hand moves lower.

Jack was right, I'm a dirty girl. My clit is already thrumming for more, my nipples sensitive, even against the soft cotton bedding.

I can't stop squirming, and it's a relief to find Michael hard when I reach him. He rolls onto his side without a sound, and his mouth finds mine in the darkness.

Slow kisses. Soft kisses. Wet kisses.

My hand moving slowly up and down the length of him.

His breath in my mouth, his tongue lapping at mine. His finger teasing my nipple so softly I think I'll explode.

"Love me," I whisper.

"I do," he breathes and mine hitches.

He dips his mouth to my neck and his lips feel so nice there. His tongue finds my ear and drives me insane. I'm panting and I can't stop, squeezing his dick as he rocks his hips.

"Jack," he whispers, "we have to wake Jack."

And he's right. We do.

It's how we are. All three of us together.

I wake him in the best way I know how. My hand gripped around his cock as I find his mouth with mine. Mike's still kissing my ear, his thumb still teasing my nipple as I squirm for him.

I'm desperate. Needy in a way I've never been needy before. Warm in bed between two men I love.

Jack hardens in my hand, his breath shallow as he moves his hips in rhythm. He doesn't say a word as he kisses me back, just pushes his tongue inside my mouth and hitches my leg further over his.

It's gentle. Torturous. Everything a tease as two dicks shunt slowly in my grip.

Two sets of fingers slip down between my legs. Fingers brushing over each other as two men play with my clit. Two fingers push inside me and I don't know who they belong to, but I don't care. Another two line up against them and I moan that I want it. In and out, first two and then a different two, and then both. Four fingers stretching me. Two men inside me at once. Two men kissing my neck at once.

Two mouths on my tits.

Two dicks thrusting.

One mouth on mine, then another. Over and over. Open-mouthed kisses that set me on fire. A thumb on my clit that drives me insane.

I want this every night. I want the three of us in a bed from now until the end of time.

It's Jack that rolls me to face Michael and guides my leg up and over. It's Jack that urges us on as four fingers make way for one hard cock.

He slides his hand down between us, fingering my clit as Michael pushes his dick inside me. His hand is wedged tight, fingertips pressed right on target.

Slow thrusts, all the way in and all the way out again. And then Jack, hitching up tight behind me with his big dick pressed against my ass.

I want to tell him I like it. I want to tell him I've done things. Dirty things. Things I know I like already.

I want to tell him to do them to me, but I don't know how to say it.

I'm going to come already, fucked so slowly by Michael as Jack circles my clit. Only Michael stops before it gets that far. He pulls out and urges me to back up on to Jack.

Jack takes his place without hesitation.

A few deep thrusts and he passes me back.

Michael, Jack, Michael, Jack.

The distance between us closes. My body is pressed tight between two. They fall into a rhythm, taking turns on my pussy as I wriggle and moan in the middle and it's fucking heaven. It's Jack who pushes his fingers into my mouth when Mike's inside me. It's Jack who whispers in my ear to make them nice and wet for him.

I'm a good spitter. I show him so. And it's just as well I am, because it's my spit he uses to lube up his finger as he squirms it against my asshole.

Relax, he says, but I'm already there. I'm already desperate.

"Fuck," I breathe. "Please…"

"You really are our dirty little girl, Carrie," he whispers.

His finger pushes in and I groan. I moan like a dirty bitch, like I've always moaned when something goes in there. I can't help it.

It's tight with Mike's cock filling my pussy. It's so tight I suck in my breath as he pushes in another finger.

Mike groans too, and I know he can feel it.

He pulls out and Jack thrusts to take his position, but I squirm.

"Not there…" I hiss, and he stops. I wriggle to illustrate and he takes a breath.

"It'll hurt," he says. "Your ass is tighter than your tight little cunt."

"I don't care," I tell him.

He moves away from me and rustles at the side of the bed. I press into Mike while he's gone, rubbing my pussy against his leg as he holds me tight.

There's a squelch as Jack comes back to me, a cold wetness between my ass cheeks. I hear him lube up his dick and I rub against Mike all the harder.

Three fingers in my ass and I grunt. "Still want it?" Jack rasps in my ear.

And all the gentleness has gone now. "Yes," I hiss. "Fuck me."

I love how dirty I feel with his fingers in my ass. I love how raw it feels. I love how it hurts before it gets better.

"You want to be stretched by two big fucking dicks?" Jack growls and it's too much. "That's what you want, isn't it? That's why you want two? You're a greedy little girl who wants two dirty daddies all to herself."

I'm a whimpering wreck as I tell them I want it. I'm a wriggling mess as I beg them both to give it to me.

"Put your fingers in her cunt," Jack barks, and Mike grunts as he does. Two at first, and it's tight, so fucking tight. Then three.

I curse under my breath, teeth gritted as both men work their fingers deep.

"You're too fucking tight for two," Jack says. "Not tonight, but we'll fucking get there, I promise." He pauses. "Take a deep breath like a good girl," he tells me and I do.

I hiss it out as he pulls his fingers from my asshole, and gulp it back in as he drives his cock in there instead.

I'm tense, wired as Mike stills his fingers in my pussy.

"Take it," Jack breathes. "Take it for Daddy like a good girl."

I'm glad he says it. I'm glad he likes it too.

And I do take it for Daddy Jack. Oh, fuck I do.

"Fuck me, Daddy Jack!" I beg. "Fucking fuck me!"

And he does.

He fucks my ass so hard I see stars behind my eyes.

"Keep those fingers in that horny little snatch," he barks to Mike, "make her take it."

"Fuck," Mike grunts, and I feel his cock throbbing against my belly.

"You're gonna come inside her after me," he growls. "It's your turn for sloppy fucking seconds tonight."

Mike fucks my pussy with his fingers as Jack pounds my ass, and I love it. I fucking love it.

Mike kisses me harder than I've ever been kissed and I fucking love that too.

"Dirty girl," Jack breathes into my ear. "Look what you're doing to us. Look what you're doing to poor Mike. I should put you over my fucking knee for being such a filthy little bitch."

I gasp in air as Mike breaks the kiss, and I don't know myself. I don't know the little slut between these two men, but I like her.

"I'm gonna make you do everything," I hiss. "I'm gonna make you do filthy fucking things to me, and filthy fucking things for me. I'm gonna make you do it all."

"Promises," Jack says.

And they are promises.

"Come in my fucking ass, Daddy Jack!"

"My fucking pleasure," he replies, and slams me hard, once, twice, three times before he's grunting in my ear.

And I'm coming too, coming around Mike's fingers as he wriggles them inside me.

I'm still going as Jack pulls out and rolls me right over onto another man's cock.

He rubs his wet dick against my clit as Michael shunts his whole fucking length in my dripping asshole.

I'm stretched. Used raw between two men, and I've never felt so wanted as I do right now.

It's in the desperation of their touch, their rasping breath, the way they can't get enough of the fucking crazy. *My* fucking crazy.

I've dreamed of one dirty daddy for as long as I can remember, and now I have two.

Michael surprises me when he lifts me up and onto him. I gasp as he wraps his arm around my neck and fucks me hard from underneath. I bounce on top of him, speared by his long hard fucking dick, powerless to fight it, even if I wanted to.

I like it that way. I like being their powerless little girl.

"Fuck, yes," Jack says and climbs right up after both of us.

I flinch as he turns on the lamp and spreads my legs wide open so he can watch Michael's dick pound the fuck out of me.

"We're gonna fuck you two at once," he says. "But not today. Soon, but not today."

And then he sucks my desperate clit until Michael's cum fills my ass after his. I don't even need to ask him this time.

Twenty-Four

MICHAEL

The whole town knows Carrie Wells is staying with Jack. Three different people question me on my way to the office, three nosey fuckers without anything better to be worrying about.

Yes, she's staying with Jack. Yes, she's working for him.

The gossips will talk, rumours will ripple. Maybe some of them will even be close to the truth.

I know I'm going to have to face Pam, but I head to my desk first and turn on my PC. I've no idea yet what I'm going to say to her, and I've never been a man to lie – that's not my style, but I'm not about to offer up the full, honest truth to her either.

Not when I'm still coming to terms with it myself.

If I weren't so invested in helping the poor kids on my books that need someone to fight their corner, none of this would bother me.

But there's no arguing the fact that I've stepped over professional boundaries, even if Carrie Wells is a case all of her own. I've stepped over lines that would be impossible to justify to co-workers, and my board, and the agencies I work with.

I contemplate resigning, but the thought pains. I'm good at what I do. I work damn hard, give it everything I've got.

I care more about my job than anyone else in this building, but that won't be enough.

Pam heads right on through before my day officially starts. She takes a seat opposite me, her back bolt upright as she clutches a file of paperwork in her lap.

"When did you know about Carrie Wells?" she asks.

I look her straight in the eye. "It moved fast, a couple of days ago. Jack came back from business and she was already at his. She said his fencing was a disgrace and he gave her a shot at fixing it."

"I see." She nods. "You didn't say anything."

"Rosie and Bill didn't want to know. The police weren't interested in locating her, not now she's an adult, and officially she's off our case list. I didn't see what relevance it had."

"It doesn't," she agrees. "But I'm still surprised you didn't mention it."

I don't break the eye contact. "Well, now you know."

"And this is permanent, is it? Her position on his property?"

"She's doing a good job, he certainly has no complaints."

She sighs. "Poor sod. I hope you've told him what he's letting himself in for."

And that's it. I can see it in her eyes. She's no more interested in Carrie Wells than anyone else around here beyond having someone to sigh and gawp over.

"Jack's making good progress with her. We both are."

"I'm glad to hear it," she lies. "I hope the girl sorts herself out." She taps her fingers on her paperwork and I wonder what it is now it's obviously not my official written notice. "You haven't been home this weekend, I take it that you're helping Jack with Carrie?"

"I am."

She smiles. "You really do take your work seriously, Michael." The smile disappears as she flips open her file. "Which is why it pains me to say that the official quarter's budget has been released. It's another cut, I'm afraid. I only got the memo this morning."

I raise my eyebrows. "Another cut? But they slashed it to bits last quarter."

She sighs. "And they're slashing it again. Donations aren't what they once were and you know what the state of services is like around here. At this rate we won't get any funding at all by the end of this financial year."

Fuck.

It's not that I haven't seen the cuts to services. In a rural community like this they affect all of us. I've seen the local police cutbacks, I've watched smaller charity organisations fold under the pressure or merge with other branches. I've been at local school fundraisers, giving my time to fund things that should never have to be funded with private donations.

"We knew it was coming," she says.

I shake my head. "I didn't think we'd get hit with cutbacks twice in a row."

She shrugs. "Yeah, well, me neither." She hands the file across my desk and my mouth drops open as I see the scale of the deficit and the proposals in place to handle our existing commitments.

"No," I say. "It can't be."

"It can be, and it is," she says. "Two months tops with each of our cases from here on in, fortnightly sessions instead of weekly. I'm going to have to let a few members of the team go. I'll break it to them after our morning catch up and call a team meeting later in the week to announce all this officially."

"Fortnightly sessions for two months isn't going to do anything to help these kids," I tell her, like she doesn't already know.

"My hands are tied," she says. "All our hands are tied, we're just going to have to do our best."

But my best will never be good enough, not under these conditions.

My career is turning to dust before my eyes, not because of any dubious choices I've made this weekend, but because our whole funding infrastructure is going to the dogs.

"I'm sorry, Michael," she says again. "I know how much this job means to you, I know how much you care about your service users."

Service users.

She means kids. Kids without prospects. Kids who need us.

Kids who have been let down by the system.

Kids who've never known anyone to be on their side.

"We can't work like this," I tell her but she shrugs again.

"It's not my call," she says. "Please keep this to yourself until after the official announcement."

Luckily, I'm good at keeping confidences.

I try to think of ways to reverse the funding decision right up until my first meeting.

But I have nothing.

Pam's right, we can only do our best.

But my best isn't going to be enough any longer. It's going to be nowhere close.

JACK

It's the same old office with the same old team in it. The same old faces asking me about my weekend out of politeness.

I give them the same old bland answers and wonder how I didn't realise my life was so flat and dull before Carrie Wells came tumbling into it.

I normally struggle to give too much of my time to this business, but right now, with that delicious girl waiting at home for me, I'm struggling to give it any time at all.

I've never been so pleased to jump back in my car at the end of the work day. I've also never been so pleased to pull up onto my driveway to find Mike's old car already parked in my space.

I'm grinning as I step through the front door, whistling a stupid tune as I head straight through to the kitchen.

"Someone's happy," Carrie says, but it seems like I'm the only one. She gestures at Mike, head resting on his palm as he flips through the local newspaper.

He looks like he's had a pig of a day, but as I step closer it looks like it's even more than that.

He's on the job pages.

My mouth dries up. Surely Pam Clowes didn't grill him that fucking hard about Carrie being here. Surely the prick didn't fess up to fuck knows what.

"What's going on?" I ask and it takes him a moment to meet my eyes. "What did you tell them?"

"Nothing," he says. "None of this is about Carrie, it's about the quarterly budget."

I take a seat. "But they cut it last time round, they said it would hold for at least another six months."

"Yeah, well they changed their mind. We're forty percent down."

"Forty?!"

That's fucking ridiculous. That office is strapped enough for investment as it is. We've talked it through plenty of times. Mike's even considered giving up some of his retirement fund to help out a little.

But this. This is something else.

"They're letting George and Diane go at the end of this week."

"And what about their workload?"

"Client funding is down from a six-month plan to two. Fortnightly instead of weekly. We'll have to take on the backlog between the few of us left."

"What do they expect of you? You'd have to be a miracle worker to get anywhere in that kind of window. You won't even be able to liaise with the agencies, the conversation chain will be over before you've even had a chance to action the paperwork, you'll be starting afresh each time."

He sighs. "I know."

Of course he knows. I feel like a jerk for pointing out the obvious.

Carrie looks worried for him. She's dithery as she flits about the kitchen, making up a fresh pot of coffee as we talk.

I smile to see the mud stains on the knees of her jeans. They suit her.

"What you gonna do?" I ask Mike, and he shakes his head.

"I don't know," he says. "What *can* I do?"

"You can quit," I tell him. "Find something to do where you don't have your hands tied with crappy budgets and tick boxes."

He holds up the job page. "That's exactly what I'm doing, but there's not much out there where I'll be genuinely able to make a difference for a living. In fact, there's fuck all."

Another job's not quite what I mean, but he carries on scanning the ads obliviously.

I watch Carrie as she pours the coffee, noticing the way she glows after a good day of work on the land.

She's nothing like the hissing little bitch I walked in on just a few weeks ago. She's nothing that any of her previous carers would recognise.

And that's not from Jack's little sessions with her every week, talking her through her options in a stuffy little office.

It's this place, it suits her. *We* suit her. And as much as I'd like to think it's a good hard fucking that brings her in line, that has little to do with it.

Trust, responsibility, hard work and a little bit of freedom along with a healthy amount of discipline. Those things have everything to do with it.

And love.

That has the most to do with it of all.

Love and respect.

I have an idea exactly what Michael can do with the rest of his career, but I don't blurt it out right then and there.

It's going to take some careful thinking about first.

"You'll sort something out," I tell him and he smiles sadly.

"I'll have to, I can't work under those conditions, and I won't."

I nod.

He closes the newspaper as our beautiful girl brings us coffee, and the topic is officially closed.

Twenty-Five

CARRIE

I **hate seeing Michael so sad.** I don't understand all of it, but I know it's bad, and I know it's about work.

I also know how hard he tried to work with me when I was sitting across his desk every week. He's good with people. He cares.

Even if that place is stuffy and snooty and no good for people like me.

I don't think now's the time to tell him that, so I keep my mouth shut and do what I can do, which is mainly make coffee.

He closes his newspaper and pulls me tight against him as I dish out the drinks, and it's nice to feel him smile against my cheek.

"I'm sorry," he says, "I don't mean to seem miserable. I've been looking forward to seeing you."

I nod. "I've been looking forward to seeing you, too." I look over at Jack. "Both of you."

I love how Michael's arm feels around my waist. I love the smell of him in his suit.

He's wearing the tie I bought him and it makes me feel proud.

"Did they say anything?" I ask. "About me, I mean? Did you get into trouble for helping me?"

"No, it's all good," he says and I'm relieved.

I'm glad I'm not going to cost him the job he loves, not yet anyway. But from the gist of their conversation, it seems as though it's on the rocks regardless.

I'm sure I'm the only one in this room who wouldn't think it a tragedy if he couldn't do it anymore, but they don't see what I see.

They don't see the snooty looks as you walk through reception, or the way you're so aware the clock is ticking every time you try to talk through something.

Being here, on this land, holds more value to anyone than that office ever will, but I don't think Michael will see that right now.

"You came straight back," I say to him. "Does that mean you're staying for good now?"

"I don't have my suits here," he says and Jack answers before I do.

"Pack a case then," he tells him.

"And move in?" Michael laughs, but Jack isn't joking, and I'm not joking either as I nod.

"Please," I say. "I want you with us. Provided it's ok with Jack, of course."

Michael shakes his head. "I think there's a bit of a road ahead before we start talking plans like that."

He waits for us to agree but we don't.

Not me and not Jack.

Michael sighs into my neck. "Enough of my shitty day," he says. "Tell me about yours."

I do tell him. I tell him how the top paddock needed some serious fixes.. I tell him how I fixed it and how I'll be done with all of the fences before the week's out.

"Time for chickens then," he says, and Jack smirks from across the table.

"She'll need to build herself a hen house first."

My heart soars at the thought. I can do it, I know I can. I just need some wood and nails and online videos.

"I'll build it," I say. "I'll build the greatest hen house you've ever seen."

"I don't doubt it," he says. "And when you have, we'll get you some chickens to fill it with. We'll go to Coleford poultry market and you can pick them out."

"And then the sheep next," Michael says and Jack raises an eyebrows.

"We'll see how the chickens go first," he says.

And I can't stop smiling, even though I'm grinning my head off, because I know that the chickens are going to go really fucking fine.

MICHAEL

Loving Carrie Wells is everything I thought it would be. More than I thought it would be.

Because the Carrie Wells who snapped and sneered at me every week in my office has transformed into a girl who's everything I knew she could be.

Even more than I knew she could be.

I know I said packing my clothes and bringing them here would be way too soon, but here, in bed, with Carrie snuggled into my side and Jack pressed up against the back of her, it feels anything but soon.

It feels like all roads led here, even if I didn't know it before it happened.

The whole town undoubtedly knows Carrie is here, even if they didn't even know where here was before now.

Jack's house will have been discussed and pointed out, questions raised over just what's going on between the man they know makes a shit ton of money out of insurance, and the mouthy little gypsy girl they shake their head at in the street.

But I don't care.

My job is the only string left holding me to any of their unwanted opinions, and that string is fraying before my eyes with every budget cut.

I think this one will be the final one I can take. I'm going to hand in my notice to coincide with my existing case load winding down, and beyond that I have no idea yet.

I'm sure something will come up, even as an interim measure.

I shouldn't respond to Carrie's kisses, because we all have things to do in the morning.

I shouldn't roll onto my side to press my cock against her belly because I'm dooming us all to a night of fucking and sucking until the dawn rises through the crack in Jack's curtains, but I can't stop.

She's addictive.

She's gentle as she takes me in her hand and squeezes. I hear Jack's breathing quicken and I know she must be squeezing him too.

Carrie Wells is insatiable and I don't recognise myself when I'm around her. I'm beginning to realise that's no bad thing.

My life is changing in every way, my career catapulting into unknown waters alongside this new crazy setup we've got going on. So many considerations to take into account, so many questions that we'll need to answer down the line.

But that's not for now.

Now is all about giving Carrie what she needs, and right now she needs two men to take her and make her theirs.

I slip my fingers between her thighs and find Jack's already there. I don't even flinch, just work my fingers along with his, teasing that hard little clit until she moans. Jack pushes his fingers inside her first, and when she's bucking under our hands and begging for more, I slide mine right along in there next to his.

Our dirty girl stretches so nicely for us. That tight little pussy sucks on our fingers, greedy for whatever we offer.

I kiss her neck in the darkness, feeling Jack's breath on my cheek as he does the same. Her hand works my dick so slowly I could go insane, but it's bliss. Absolute pure fucking bliss.

And then she tugs, shifting us closer, and I go with it, we both do.

I don't realise what's happening until it's too late, until I can feel the heat of Jack's body so close, Carrie's wriggling underneath us as she spreads her legs and asks for deeper.

I recoil instinctively as my dick touches another dick, jerking back my hips as though I've been burned.

"Please," she breathes. "I want you both inside me, both at once…"

Understanding doesn't ease the frantic beat of my heart.

Understanding that she'll want the length of my dick thrusting tight against another man's inside her doesn't make me any less hesitant as she coaxes me back into position.

I focus on the warmth of her pussy around my fingers, holding my breath as I know the point of dick on dick is just moments away.

I flinch at the contact when she touches us together, but this time I don't pull away. The head of him is hard against mine, surprisingly slippery as she grinds us together, tip against swollen tip.

I can't believe I'm doing this, I can't believe my dick is still hard, but it is.

It's only when I hear Jack grunt that I realise he's not nearly so hesitant as I am. But Jack never is.

Jack doesn't have limits like I have. Jack goes all in for the pursuit of pleasure, and right now his pleasure is in Carrie's hand as she rubs his dick against mine.

"Fuck," he says. "Peen on fucking peen. This has never been on my fucking agenda."

But he doesn't stop and neither do I.

And it occurs to me, right at the back of my mind, that maybe he wants this. Maybe he's not nearly so hung up on what all this means as I am.

The thought that he might even enjoy these blurry boundaries takes me aback, but makes my dick throb. It makes me shunt closer, giving Carrie all the leeway she needs to press us length to length and move us as one.

Oh fuck, it feels good. It feels so filthily good.

"You like it," she whispers, "I can feel it."

I don't argue and neither does he. It would be pointless if we did, since she can feel it clear as day in her dirty little hands.

Her pussy is so wet, and so are our dicks. The sound of squelching fingers is loud, even under the covers, and the sound of breath is loud above them.

I'm going to come against Jack's dick, spraying my load all over Carrie's pretty little pussy underneath, and I'm pretty sure he's going to come against mine and do the same.

"Kiss me," she whispers. "Both of you, kiss me."

Jack kisses her first. She moans for him, and the sound of wet mouths makes mine water. So tentatively I press my lips to her cheek, not caring that my face is right against his, not caring that when she turns her head and offers me her mouth, it's with his tongue still lapping at hers.

I feel the last thread of resistance snap and fall away, because there's no point holding onto something which is inevitably doomed to break anyway.

We're sharing one girl. One hungry girl who's desperate for two.

Two mouths.

Two big cocks.

Two men making her feel as dirty as I'm sure we're making her feel right now.

Two men to love her no matter what.

I kiss Carrie with everything I've got, tongues twisting with tongues, not really giving a fuck anymore. Not really giving a fuck that Jack is about to come all over my dick as Carrie comes over two sets of fingers in her pussy.

"I knew you had it in you," Jack groans. "I always knew you'd lose that stick in your ass one day."

An interesting choice of words, but I feel strangely proud at the sentiment.

I'm still kissing Carrie as she comes for us, and so is Jack.

I'm still thrusting my dick against his as he shoots his load soon after, and I do too.

And then we're a mess.

A sticky, wet, slippery fucking mess of bodies.

But I'm smiling.

No matter how fucking fucked up it feels to have had my best friend's tongue in my mouth, I'm still fucking smiling.

Twenty-Six

CARRIE

After all those years of feeling I had nothing to live for but a disgusting excuse for a brother who made me do things that no girl should ever do, I suddenly have a whole world in front of me.

I love wandering through the fields every day – especially today.

Especially since there was a knock at the front door this morning and I had to sign for a parcel with my name on it. I had to ask three times to make sure the courier was sure, but there it was in print – *Carrie Wells* – my name right over the address. I stared at it for ten whole minutes before I opened it, and when I finally tore into the box it took my breath.

A new pair of boots in just the right size. The delivery note said *from Jack and Mike, you earned them* with a string of kisses underneath. I still have it in my pocket. I don't think I'll ever take it out.

I love feeling the mud under those new boots as I set off across Jack's beautiful farmland with a load of planks on my shoulder and a hammer stuffed down my waistband. They feel just perfect on my feet, as though they were made for me. Just like Jack and Mike are.

I'm nearly done with the fencing, but that's okay now, because I've a chicken coop to make and a sheep pen to make after that, even if Jack hasn't quite said yes yet.

He will.

I know he will.

I take a breath as I check out the clouds. They're the fluffy white kind that turn into pictures the more you stare at them.

I see a rabbit, and a dragon. And a cock.

I laugh as I see a big white cock in the sky.

I laugh as I realise I've got everything I ever wanted, all right here. I laugh at how bizarre that feels, to have so much after having so little.

I laugh until happy tears stream down my face, and it's a release. A beautiful release.

I've never cried happy tears before. Plenty of sad ones, but none like these.

We could be together forever – Jack, Michael, and me. Last night chased all those final fears away – the ones that cling on tight and won't let go – because I know now that they really do love each other, and it's more than friends, even if it's not like *that*. Now I know this can work, properly work, because there's nothing left to freak them out and send them running. There's nothing more I'll ask them to do, not unless they want it for themselves, because they've touched dicks and tongues and came all the same, and what else could possibly happen by accident? Nothing.

Anything else that happens will be because they want it, but it won't be me pushing. It'll be all them.

I can breathe this morning because I feel safe. Safe knowing Michael and Jack can handle this. All of this, and all of me. Even if I can be a brat sometimes, although I don't have even half of the smart mouth I used to have.

They'd put me over their knees if I did, and that would be no bad thing either.

I drop my planks at the right spot and get to work on fixing up one of the worst panels, glad that this is one of my last ones and not the very first ones I started, because I'm so much better now than I was then.

In every way, not just with fences.

Maybe all things happen at the right time. Maybe this was the last fence I came across, because I needed to learn about the other fences first. Maybe life has a plan like that.

Maybe I had to know what it was like to have no love at all, just so I can really appreciate having so much of it.

I've got so much of it I could burst.

More than enough for Jack and Mike and some chickens and sheep, and maybe some ponies and dogs too. I grin at the thought.

This is really it. They've seen the worst of me and now they're seeing the best of me. I'll put myself on the line for them just as they put themselves on the line for me.

I breathe a sigh of relief that the nerves have finally left my belly after all this time, smiling as I feel my phone buzz in my pocket.

I wonder which one of them it is.

Maybe Jack with a stupid joke, or Mike checking how I'm doing with the fence. But it's neither.

And the nerves are back in one terrible heartbeat.

Eli.

He wants his money and his text makes it perfectly clear.

His words make me shiver.

You owe me.

The attached photo makes my heart race. A picture of the centre of Lydney. He's here.

Oh my God, he's really here.

But he doesn't know Jack. He doesn't know where I live now.

I try to force the nerves away but they won't budge an inch.

All the filthy things I did for him come back to pool in my belly. They make me feel sick. I used to think it was okay before I knew what real love felt like, but now I know it isn't. It never was.

What he did to me was cruel and disgusting. The way he made me use my body for him was a world away from how Jack and Mike make me feel.

I don't care that he's my brother anymore, or that he's holding family news over my head. I don't care that I may never get to see them again if I don't do what he wants. If they wanted me, they'd have found me long ago. If they still believe his lies after all these years then I'm better off without them.

All the years of making excuses for him in the name of love seem so stupid now. All the lies I told to protect him. All the lies I told myself because I wanted to believe he loved me.

But love isn't like that. Eli doesn't love me and never has.

I wouldn't reply even if I did have any credit on my phone. I wouldn't go looking for him if he was on fire and I had the only bucket of water.

I hammer the last of the nails into the plank I'm holding and then I stop. The countryside that felt so open and free feels too open now. I feel too exposed here. Far too exposed.

I gather up my things and head back to the house, thanking my lucky stars that I've only got a few hours left before Jack and Michael get home.

Maybe tonight I'll finally reach out and talk. Maybe tonight I'll tell them everything.

I just have to trust they'll still look at me the same way if I do.

For the first time since I've been staying here, I bolt the back door behind me. I never lock it, not even when I'm in the fields, but today's not like the other days.

I dump my new boots on the mat and tell myself that TV might not be so bad for one afternoon, just until Jack and Mike get home.

I'm just grabbing myself a coffee when I feel the shiver in the air. It's not cold. It's different to that.

A sixth sense. A shudder in my mind.

And then I know. I sense him before I smell him, and smell him before I see him, a waft of weed hitting my nose from the dining room doorway.

He props himself in the frame like he owns the place, hood up high so his eyes look even darker than usual.

"Made me fucking come for it, didn't you?"

I play it cool, just like always. "Had no fucking credit on my phone, nor bus fare either."

He looks about the room and I hate how he ogles everything. "Landed on your feet here. Fucking some posh guy so I hear. Whole shitty town is talking about it, a silly old bitch directed me right to your door."

"I'm working here," I tell him. "I'm fixing fences."

"Fixing fences and sucking dick," he sneers. "Have you missed mine? I bet you fucking have, you filthy little bitch."

"Don't flatter yourself," I snap.

"Shame," he says and takes a step forward, "since you owe me pretty big, I've been charging interest."

"I'm not paying you interest," I say calmly. "I'll give you your fiver and the money for the food when I have it, but I don't have it, so you'll have to fucking wait, Eli. You've wasted your fucking time."

"Oh yeah?" he asks and I fold my arms.

I flinch as he clears the kitchen island with one sweep of his arm. The fruit bowl tumbles and smashes on the tiles, the bottle of olive oil crashing into a stool and dribbling its contents everywhere. "Whoops," he says and laughs as I can't hide the horror.

"Don't!" I hiss. "Don't you fucking dare!"

"Just a job, is it? Doesn't look like just a fucking job to me."

He takes the clock down from the wall and smashes it under his foot. Swings a stool against the wall until the plaster chips and the legs buckle.

I clench my fists and then I go for him, screaming blue murder as I launch myself onto his back. I rip down his hood and claw at his scalp, my legs gripping him tight as he tries to shake me off.

When he throws us both to the floor I lose my advantage. He's so much bigger than me, pinning me down as I wriggle. His grip is tight on my wrists, his fingers digging in so tight I know he'll leave bruises, but I struggle all the same.

"I came for my fucking money," he snarls, "but you can pay with your dirty cunt if you like."

"I don't fucking like," I hiss. "You can fuck off me."

"You fucking want it," he says, but I don't.

Not anymore.

I don't even think I ever did.

I used to think Eli was just a boy, but the body bearing down on me is anything but.

He holds my wrists in one hand and tugs down his waistband with the other, and it's so tempting to close my eyes and pretend I want this.

Pretend I'm the dirty girl he always said I was.

But I can't.

I'm Michael and Jack's girl now, and only theirs.

I only want to be theirs.

I get one chance to strike and I strike hard, shunting my knee up full force into his crotch.

It works. He rolls to the side with his hand over his dick, cursing at me as he flaps around like a fucking fish.

"I'm your brother," he wheezes. "Your fucking brother, Carrie. I'm the only one who fucking loves you. The only one who fucking cares." He rasps another breath. "You think this guy here loves you? You think he fucking wants you like I do?"

"He wants me more than you do," I tell him. "He loves me. Properly. Not with a pathetic little sausage dick like yours." I point to the front door. "Now get the fuck out before I call the cops."

He staggers onto his knees. "You fucking wouldn't."

"I fucking would," I say. "Don't fucking try me."

He laughs. "Just as well I already found what I'm looking for. You took your time getting back."

My heart drops when I see the envelope in his hand. I already know what's inside there, but I open the kitchen drawer anyway.

"Give that back!" I hiss, but he slips it back into his pocket.

"For my time," he laughs, but it's so much more than that.

That envelope is thick with money. Thick with Jack's money.

"Give it!"

"Fuck you, Carrie Wells," he says. "No wonder Mum and Dad hate you,

you're nothing but a filthy little cunt."

Tears prick. Stupid fucking tears.

Not just for the hold he keeps over me, but for the money I know he's going to be walking out of here with unless I want to risk him slamming me down and taking my body along with it.

"I hate you," I hiss.

"You love me," he laughs. "I'm your brother. I'll always be your brother. And I'll always be your first. Don't ever forget that!"

I hate that he's my brother.

I hate that I ever fucking landed in his family.

I hate him even more when he trashes everything he can on his way out. He pulls a knife and slashes at the sofa in the living room, the curtains too. He kicks at the display cabinet and glass showers the floor along with the new piece I'd bought for Jack. He puts his foot through the big TV and laughs when he does it.

And I stand and watch without fight, because for the first time in my life I have something to stay in one piece for, even if they're going to hate me for what they think I've done to their house.

He smashes the mirror in the hallway on his way out. "See you around, slut," he says and slams the door behind him.

I don't even know where to begin with cleaning up this mess, so I don't.

I don't even know how I can begin to explain what happened here, so I think about leaving before they come back, but I can't bring myself to do that either.

So I sit.

Sit and wait and think about all the reasons I hate my twisted brother.

I don't move when a car sounds on the drive a few hours later.

And I don't move when someone steps inside either.

I'm done.

Twenty-Seven

JACK

My crazy idea for Mike's career wouldn't let go once it started. That's why I called the bank today and set up an appointment. That's why I marched in there with a hastily drawn up plan and opened a new account all ready to start.

It's crazy but perfect. Perfect for both of them.

I can't fucking wait to fill them in on the news.

I've got more money than I've ever known what to do with, and more than enough time around work to help with the practicalities of setting up something like this. I make sure I've got my folder of ideas on the passenger seat as I buckle up and head for home.

I know I'll be earlier than Mike, I'll just have to keep my mouth shut until he gets there.

There's a crunch of glass under my foot as I step inside. My brow creases as I stare down at it, and it takes me a second to realise it's the mirror from the wall, smashed to pieces.

What the fuck?

Memories of walking in on Carrie for the very first time come flooding back to me, and I guard myself against any incoming crows. But there are none.

There's chaos like I've never seen it, but no bird in sight.

I stare open-mouthed at the carnage. My TV's been put through and my sofa's been slashed to shit. A kitchen knife is sticking out of the cabinet and the frames I replaced just days ago are smashed all over again.

What the holy living fuck?

A stool's been smashed apart in the kitchen, another has oil and glass all over it. My fruit bowl is in pieces amongst it all.

I don't want to look inside the dining room but I do it anyway. The display cabinet doesn't have a single whole piece of glass in it, not in the windows and not inside either.

My breath catches in my throat and stays there at the sight of my new glass sculpture in pieces on the floor.

It takes me a moment to see her, curled into a ball by the back door in her new boots.

"Carrie–" I begin, but she shakes her head.

And I don't understand it. I really don't understand it.

"Are you alright?" I ask, racking my brain for an explanation other than the obvious, but fuck knows what that could be.

She shakes her head again, and I wonder what the fuck's gone down here.

Nothing's happened but the boots.

Surely it can't be the fucking boots.

Surely one little gift can't spin someone out that bad.

I crouch at her side but she shuffles away from me.

My voice is harsher when it comes out next. "Carrie, what the fuck happened here?"

She shuffles further but I grab her wrist. It's easy to see the bruises with her pale skin against my fingers.

I heard about the bruises. Self-inflicted, so they say.

"Talk to me," I say. "Carrie, you've got to fucking talk to me."

Her eyes are wild and wide when they land on mine. She chokes over a couple of words, her nose wrinkling as she fights back tears.

"What happened here? Did someone do this to you?"

My heart drops when she shakes her head.

"It was me," she said. "I did it."

It feels like she's kicked me in the fucking gut. "But why? Why would you do this?"

She looks anything like the brash girl who trashed my house the last time around. Where once she was cocky she looks broken. Where once she was full of backchat she has nothing.

She shrugs and that's all.

One fucking shrug.

I don't even know what to say.

"I thought you were happy," I tell her and she shrugs again. "I thought you liked it here. I thought you were happy with us."

She doesn't speak. Doesn't say a word.

"This was your home, Carrie. All of ours."

Was.

She flinches as I say it.

And with that she dashes from her spot, racing through the house so quickly I have sprint to catch her. I grab her at the front door, pulling her back inside just as she's about to launch herself from the front doorstep and bail on me. Bail on us.

I'm so fucking hurt I don't know how to handle it. My whole world spinning at the thought I could've got this all so wrong.

But I didn't.

I know I didn't.

"Why?" I ask, and my voice is raw. "Just tell me why!"

"Because I'm trouble," she hisses. "Because I bring trouble on everyone."

I shake my head because I won't believe it.

"Is this because of the boots?" I ask and all her aggression shrivels to nothing. "Is this because you don't think you deserved them? Fuck, Carrie, you more than fucking deserved them." My breath is ragged. "But I don't deserve this!"

She shrinks from me, backing into a wall as her lip quivers.

"Tell me you didn't do this," I say, but she won't. "Please, just make me understand. You've got to help me understand."

But she doesn't. She doesn't say a thing.

I'm lost. Floundering. Sick to the stomach as the whole world comes crashing down around me.

And then, before I've even managed to find my bearings and get some of this shit cleared up, I hear Mike's car on the driveway.

CARRIE

I want to tell him but I can't. Even now I can't let them throw Eli in prison. He's my brother. He was there for me when no one else was.

My heart is breaking worse than Jack's, even though I can't show him.

My heart is breaking because I know I can't come back from this, because no matter how much Jack's eyes say he wants to forgive me, I know he won't.

I know he can't.

I know he'll never trust me again.

I wish I could say I'm sorry, but I can't. Even though I can't bring myself to land my brother in the shit, I can't bring myself to confess all this either.

Jack's glaring right at me as I hear Michael's car pull onto the drive. I want the ground to swallow me up and never spit me out again, but I'm standing right here with nowhere to run and no one to turn to.

Michael doesn't even notice the destruction as he steps through the door. He sees me before Jack but he's already got questions of his own.

"Kevin Baker was asking directions to your house in town earlier, why?"

He has to crunch on glass before he comes to his senses. I watch his eyes widen in horror.

"Kevin Baker?" Jack asks. "Who the fuck is Kevin Baker?"

I have no idea who Kevin Baker is. No idea at all.

"He was on my books a few years back," Michael says. "From a broken family in Gloucester, a nasty piece of work. Violent."

Jack looks at me but I can't meet his eyes.

"What was he doing asking for you, Carrie? Do you know him?"

I shrug, because I know I'm going to have to say something. "Never heard of him."

He looks so confused. "Was he here? Is that what happened to the place? It's not the first time he's resorted to breaking and entering. His criminal record is a mile fucking long."

"I've never heard of him," I repeat again, and I haven't. I don't know what the fuck he's talking about.

He doesn't believe me, I can see it in his eyes, and I'm so fucking angry that these people want to see the best in me, even when I'm lying to them. Even when all the evidence is stacked and I'm standing right in the middle of the home they think I destroyed today.

"Well, are you sure?" Mike tries again. "He's tall, stocky, wears a hoodie with a dragon on the sleeve. He has a tattoo under his right ear, of a–"

"A snake," I say, and I don't understand. "But that's not Kevin Baker."

He tips his head, smiles just a little. "That's definitely Kevin Baker, Carrie. I'd recognise him a mile off. I saw him skulking back along the lane a few minutes ago. I'd a good mind to pull over and demand to know what the fuck he's doing round these parts." He pauses. "But I think I know now. I think it's pretty obvious. So why don't you just tell me how you know him and we can get this mess straightened out?"

Even now his eyes are so kind and calm.

"Tell us what the fuck's going on!" Jack barks, and it brings me to my senses.

I look from one to the other and know there's no running from this.

"That's not Kevin Baker," I whisper. "That's my brother, Eli. The first brother I remember."

Jack's eyes widen but not as wide as Michael's.

"How long have you known him as Eli?"

"He *is* Eli!" I yell.

"How long, Carrie?"

I shake my head, trying to block out everything. All of this. "Since I was fourteen," I admit. "He found me, came looking for me. Said he was still my brother."

"Carrie," Michael says and his voice is so calm. "That's not Eli, I swear. I have Kevin's case file, and I have Eli's too. He came for help with socialisation skills nearly a decade ago. I knew you used to live with his parents, I saw it in your file when you first arrived. He's at law school now, in Birmingham."

I shake my head. "No."

"Yes," he says. "I swear I wouldn't lie to you, Carrie. However Kevin knows you, it's not because he was your brother."

"What the fuck?!" Jack snaps, and his eyes soften. "Did he hurt you? Is that sonofabitch the one who bruised your wrists?"

Michael's eyes go straight there and I can't pull my cuffs down quickly enough.

"It was him, wasn't it?" Michael asks. "It was Kevin, all those times they thought it was you, it was Kevin."

"Eli," I whisper. "It was Eli."

But Eli isn't Eli and I know that now.

I think back to how we met.

I think back to bumming a smoke from a guy in an alleyway, and he looked so similar, so fucking similar.

And that's when he told me he'd been looking for me. That's when he told me he knew me and offered me inside.

I knew he was Eli, I just knew it. I called him Eli and he said it was him.

He said he was my brother, and I believed him.

I believed everything he said.

Because I wanted to.

I wanted to believe he really was looking for me, and I wanted to believe he really loved me.

I slip to the floor, not caring if there's broken glass there, not caring about anything.

And then I tell them everything.

Finally, for once in my life, I tell someone everything.

Twenty-Eight

MICHAEL

And suddenly all the pieces fit into place.

She's in a daze as she heads through to the living room and sits herself down on the slashed sofa. She pulls her knees up to her chest and hugs them tight as Jack sits alongside her and I drop to my knees on the floor.

"It's alright, Carrie," I say, "you can tell us."

And she does. She tells us everything.

She tells us how happy she was to find her brother. She tells us the story of what happened all those years ago in Eli's family home. She tells us how they thought it was her assaulting their younger daughter and leaving bruises on her arms, but it wasn't. It was Eli, and that makes sense too. The kid was troubled when I met him, narcissistic to the point it gave me shivers. Thoroughly dissociated from those around him.

And now he's studying law, blending into the student populous no doubt oblivious to the pain he caused the broken girl sitting before me.

He didn't mention Carrie once in all our sessions. I only saw her name in the family history section of his case file.

Kevin Baker told Carrie everything she wanted to hear, and I don't blame her for believing him. A girl who had nothing and no one. The promise of a family she loved and lost coming back to find her.

I know he was the one who took her before us before she says anything. I can imagine the details before she speaks them, but they break my heart all the same.

"I thought he loved me," she breathes, and she's ashen. A paper doll where there's usually so much life.

I look across at Jack and his jaw is gritted. I find myself glad Kevin's surely heading back into Gloucester by now, because I wouldn't fancy his chances if Jack caught up with the sack of shit anytime soon.

It surprises me how willing I'd be to teach the kid a lesson myself.

"Nobody ever called him Eli," she whispers. "He said he was using a fake identity, for the drugs." She shakes her head. "I feel so stupid."

"You aren't stupid," Jack says. "He's a cunt and you were vulnerable."

He's hit the nail right on the head there, although I'd probably have phrased it slightly differently.

"What do I do now?" she asks and her eyes are wide and scared. "He took your money…"

"Fuck the money," Jack says. "He hurt you. All that matters now is that he's never going to do it again. Not ever, Carrie."

She nods so slowly. "You thought it was me."

"No," Jack says. "You wanted me to think it was you. If I really thought it was you, I'd have had you over my fucking knee already and given you the fucking belt for it."

He smiles, and my heart races and as she smiles too.

"You wouldn't have thrown me out?"

"For the sake of a few bits of furniture and a couple of hundred quid? You'd have to try a bit harder than that, sweetheart." He sighs. "I caught you on the doorstep, remember? I was pulling you back, not chasing you off."

"I thought he loved me," she says again and brushes a tear away as soon as it falls.

I place my hand on her knee and squeeze as tight as I dare. "He didn't," I tell her. "But we do."

I can hardly believe the words that come out of Jack's mouth next. They don't sound like him at all. He pulls her into his arms, even though she's rigid and trembling, and whispers them right into her ear. "You have us now, Carrie, and we'll always hug you so tight that all your broken pieces will fit back together again. You'll see."

With a lump in my throat, I take the space on the sofa he pulled Carrie from, and I wrap my arms around her from behind, until her trembling stops and her breath is even and her arms wrap around us right back.

I don't know if a hug really can fit someone's broken pieces all back together, but we can try.

We'll never, ever stop trying.

CARRIE

I don't know how long they hold me there, but I never want to move.

I'm scared I'll fall apart without their arms around me. I'm scared I'll shatter into pieces and never pick them all up again.

I remember all the times the guy who called himself Eli touched me. I remember all the times he told me that that was what love felt like.

But love feels nothing like that, and I know it now.

I want to forget every second I ever spent with him. I want to feel how much I'm loved for real this time.

I want to feel kind hands on my body. I want to feel kisses that give, not kisses that take.

I want them. The only two men who've ever counted.

I need to know I'm still theirs and they're mine, and words aren't enough.

Words will never be enough now I know how easily a random guy like Kevin Baker could speak whatever he wanted in my ear.

I'm still in their arms as I press my lips to Jack's neck. Michael is still pressed to my back as I reach for him.

Jack doesn't respond at first as I kiss my way up to his jawline. He breathes and strokes my hair but doesn't kiss me.

"Carrie, you don't have to," he begins, but I know.

I tell him so.

"Love me," I whisper and it sounds so hollow. "I need to know you love me. I need to know you still want me. Both of you."

"We should call the police," Jack says, and I know we have to, but it can wait, just a little while. I tell him that, too.

It's Michael who gathers my hair into a ponytail and kisses the back of my neck. It's his lips that replace my frightened shivers with better ones.

"Whatever you need," he whispers, and I finally come to know how much these past few weeks have changed all of us.

There's a rawness to his words that speak to my soul. A tenderness in his touch that's outside any guideline he holds himself to at work every day.

He's more than his job. He's more than the lines they make him colour inside.

"I need you," I whisper. And I do.

I do need them.

I need them both like I need air.

Jack reaches for my arm and takes my bruised wrist in his hand. He presses it to his mouth as though he can kiss it all away, and maybe he can.

His tongue feels so good against my tender skin.

Mike tugs at my hair enough to tip my head back, and his mouth finds mine and kisses deep.

His fingers slip inside my top and his strokes across my nipples drive me crazy.

More crazy.

Jack pulls off his tie and unbuttons his shirt. He kisses my fingers and guides them to his belt, and I help him unbuckle himself, before he helps me out of my jeans.

Michael tugs my top over my head and pulls my bra off with it. I'm naked in a heartbeat with my legs around Jack's waist. His cock is big against my belly and it's a relief.

To know he still wants me like this is a relief.

I twist to help Michael out of his suit, but he's already mostly there. He sits back on the wrecked sofa and guides me half on top of him, and then tugs at Jack's arm to beckon him closer.

Jack shuffles next to Michael and I straddle the middle of them. A thigh against each dick as I rise to my knees.

It's the most natural thing in the world to present my tits to two hungry mouths. I pull my shoulders back proud, as proud as I'll ever be, offering myself up exactly as I am to the two men who mean so much.

I love the way they suck and nip. I love the way the sounds of their mouths match the squelches from their dicks as they take themselves in hand.

Tonight's the night I want them both inside me. Tonight's the night I need to feel them both make me theirs at the same time.

"Let us see you," Mike whispers and I don't understand at first. He stares up at me through hooded eyes and gestures me to stand for them.

I'm so nervous as I get to my feet. So naked in my vulnerability as I stand tall for two pairs of hungry eyes.

"Beautiful," Jack whispers, and picks up pace on his dick.

"Perfect," Michael adds and my cheeks burn.

It's amazing to watch them there, watching me.

I shift my thighs apart and dip my fingers between them. I've never felt so exposed in my dirtiness as I do right now, standing all alone as their eyes rove all over me, from the wetness they've left on my tits, to the wetness I'm dribbling between my legs.

But they love me.

I can see it in their gaze, in their expressions, in the way they work their dicks as though just the sight of me is everything.

"We're really doing this," Michael rasps. "The three of us, forever."

It sounds like more of a question than a statement.

Jack answers it.

"We're really doing this," he says. "The three of us. Always the three of us."

A look passes between them that I can't read, but hope one day I will. A look that reminds me how these guys have known each other their whole entire lives, how they've shared decades before I was even born.

"Just bodies," Michael rasps, and my breath hitches.

He lifts his hand from his thigh and hovers it between them, and I can't breathe, can't even think.

"Just fucking bodies," Jack growls and takes his hand from his dick.

"Fuck," I whimper as Michael takes Jack in his hand. My own fingers frantic on my clit as he grips another guy's dick and works him up and down.

Jack tips his head back and grunts, and then he does it.

He really does it.

He reaches out for Michael's cock and swears under his breath as he takes it.

Two men work each other's dicks as they stare at me. They work each other's dicks as I play with my needy little clit for them.

I've never been as horny as I feel as they touch each other. I've never been so in awe of the way two people can give so much.

"You'd better get back fucking over here before he makes me shoot my fucking load," Jack growls, and I do.

"I want both of you inside me," I whisper as I clamber back on top. "I want to feel both of you at once. I want you to both love me at once."

I spread my legs wide across their laps as fingers push inside and open me up. "You need to be ready," Jack grunts. "Nice and wet. Stretched ready for two."

"Stretch me, then," I moan, and they do.

Oh fuck, they do.

Wet fingers slip back to my asshole and it burns as they push their way inside.

Three fingers turn to four in my hungry pussy and I groan at the stretch, bouncing up and down to open myself up for more.

I'm gonna take them. I have to fucking take them.

It's all I want.

"Tight," Jack growls, "so fucking tight."

I hear the noises I'm making and I know they can do it. I know they can open me up enough to take them both.

"Harder," I hiss. "Please, I want this."

"On his dick," Jack tells me. "Now."

It's a beautiful pleasure to drop myself onto Michael's big hard cock. I ride him like a desperate whore, because that's how I feel inside. Desperate for dick, but only theirs. Desperate to be taken by men who really do want me.

Men who'd do anything to keep me.

Jack's fingers keep ploughing my ass and it hurts, but I don't care.

"Relax," he growls and nips the back of my neck, and I know he's getting ready. I know he's really going to do this.

I hear him spitting. I hear him rubbing it around his dick.

And then he pushes both me and Michael down flat onto the sofa and pins us underneath him.

I love how tightly I'm sandwiched. I love how my cheek is tight to Michael's shoulder as Jack's big dick presses against my asshole.

"Both of us at once," he rasps, and pushes the head inside.

Oh fuck, the stretch. It burns like white heat.

"Take us," Michael whispers in my ear. "Take us like only our good girl can."

"I'll be your good girl," I whimper as Jack pushes deeper. "I'll always be your good girl."

And I am a good girl as Jack slams home. I'm a good girl as I grit my teeth and beg for more. A good girl as I push back onto Jack's big dick and milk them both at once.

"I want you to come inside me," I tell them. "I want you both to fill me up."

"We'll fill you up with more than our fucking cum if you're not careful," Jack barks, and the thought sends me over the edge.

I come between two dicks. I come between two men I love.

And they're right there after me, grunting and thrusting and spurting inside me.

They keep me pinned when they're done. I love the warmth and the weight as we all catch our breath together.

And finally, when we've gathered up our clothes and wiped down the mess we left on the wrecked sofa, Jack calls the police.

It's the first time they've ever really listened to me.

But then again, it's the first time I've ever really told them the truth.

Epilogue

JACK

t took me a few days before I sat Carrie and Michael down and talked them through my great new vision for the future.

I waited until the police visits stopped with such frequency and all Carrie's statements were taken. I didn't take the file out of my car until we heard that Kevin Baker was in custody and the evidence was stacking up nicely.

Fingerprints, text messages, a load of druggy mates who sold him out at the first sign of a police car at the door.

He's going down for it, that's a certainty. He'd better hope it's a long sentence – I'll still be tempted to choke the life out of him if he's ever unlucky enough to cross my path.

So, there we had it. An arrest, a new furniture delivery and Michael's official acceptance of his resignation, all in one day.

It that's not a good day to make life plans, I don't know when else would be.

They'd been nervous as I sat them down at the new dining table. Glancing at each other as I cleared my throat and flipped open the file.

A charity initiative, right here on our property. Goats and sheep and chickens galore, even a couple of ponies, if Carrie wants them.

An opportunity for disadvantaged youngsters to find connection in the land. To be given responsibility and trust in an environment where they can express themselves.

"You mean a farm?!" Carrie asked. "A real farm?!"

"A real farm," I said. "And no stupid tick boxes or budget restrictions," I'd said to Michael. "Just you two and the outdoors with whoever you feel can benefit from it."

"I don't know what to say," Michael told me as he eyed up my initial proposals.

"Yes would be nice," I replied. "Yes, and when can we get started?"

"When can we get started?" he asked, and I smiled.

Oh, how I smiled.

And then I got the two Labrador pups from the crate in my car.

Carrie's face was a picture I'll remember forever, hugging them like they were the greatest treasure on earth.

"Now," I said. "We get started now, so you'd better get busy on that chicken coop, Carrie. The poultry auction is next week, and the sheep are arriving two days after Michael's finishing date."

"Fuck," Michael said as a smile spread across his face.

And Carrie didn't say anything other than a whole load of thank yous muffled by puppy fur.

It was more than enough for me.

CARRIE

The farm completes me in ways I never knew I could be completed. Helping others going through similar to the things I went through growing up makes my heart burst every day.

Michael's too.

He's good at this stuff, much better than he was ever allowed to be in the office on someone else's payroll.

My pups are older now, and our furniture is finally safe from puppy teeth. Our chickens are laying nicely and our sheep are on a decent rotation through our fields.

It's easy work when you have so many people to help you, and we have a lot. More of them turning up each month.

I finally have a wagon in the field behind the house, and a couple of gypsy cobs to pull it if I ever needed to go anywhere. But I don't. I have everything right here.

Well, almost everything.

We've been watching my cycle, Jack, Michael and me. Timing our dates so they can come inside me without any risk of additional family members on the way before we're ready.

But I'm ready now.

It turns out I have more than enough love for Jack, Michael, two pups, a herd of sheep, ten chickens, two ponies and the random collection of kids who need our help.

I know I've more than enough love for some of our own, too.

And that's what I want next.

A baby of our own.

It's Jack who broaches the subject as he sees me flipping through the wall chart and marking out another month right on schedule.

He slaps Michael on the back as he hands out our evening beers from the fridge, and then he comes right out with it, typical Jack style.

"I think it's about time we put a baby in that pretty little girl of ours."

I feel the blush on my cheeks before I've even turned to face him.

"What?" I ask and he tips his head.

"You heard me. Pregnant would be a good look on you. It's not as though we haven't got the room."

I'm almost touching twenty, but they're not getting any younger. I can't hide the smile as I nod my head.

"I think I'd like pregnant." I take a breath. "I think I'd like pregnant a lot."

Michael is the last to speak. He's always so considered.

"I'm ready whenever you guys are," he says. "I've been ready since the day we met."

So have I. I just didn't know it then.

I've thought about the question of paternity a lot these past few months, and in truth I don't care at all whose baby I have first. I'm planning on having so many of them that I'm sure it'll even out one way or another.

There's more than enough love in this house for all of them.

"Three days," I say. "The calendar says three days until I'm ovulating."

And those three days crawl by so slowly I feel like I'm trapped in a time warp, but all the best things come to those who wait.

I kick off my boots the moment we're done for the day, ditching my muddy clothes and jumping in the shower to freshen up.

I don't need to remind them what night it is, the guys are already stark bollock naked on our sofa when I head back down wearing the old t-shirt of Jack's I still walk around the house in.

Jack's dick is in Mike's hand, and Mike's dick is in Jack's, and they haven't jerked each other off in a while, but I'm glad it's a special occasion all for me.

"Come here," Jack orders and I do.

I hitch myself up between them and press my tender tits to their open mouths through the fabric, knowing full well the calendar's right. I feel it right through my body.

"You're going to have to share these with more than just each other soon," I whisper, holding them tight as they feast on me. I love how it makes them suck me harder. I love how they work each other's dicks that little bit faster.

"Let's do it," Mike moans around my tit. "Please, let's do it now. I don't want to waste any..."

It makes me smile.

They're going to fuck me all night long, until they haven't got anything left to give me, and hopefully, if fate be willing, they'll give me a baby.

A beautiful baby for my dirty daddies.

I'm already soaking wet for them. Already desperate to take them both.

Mike's guiding me over to Jack quite happily when Jack stops him. He twists me around and tells me to lay on my back with my knees up high.

I do it. Expecting him to take position between my spread thighs, but he doesn't.

He takes position at my head instead and angles my face for his swollen cock.

"You saw her first," he growls, and pushes his dick in my mouth as it drops wide open.

"Sorry?" Mike questions, pausing with the head of his dick so teasingly against my clit.

But Jack doesn't answer him, he speaks to me instead.

"Be a good girl and take it nice and deep, sweetheart. Daddy Michael's gonna put a baby in your belly."

I groan around his dick. Oh fuck, how I groan around his dick.

"...And when you've pushed it out of that sweet little pussy of yours, Daddy Jack's gonna give you one of his own."

I always wanted to read every single one of those looks that pass between Jack and Michael, but this one is another that beats me.

"Take her," Jack says, "and make sure you make it count."

"I will," Michael says. "Don't you worry about that."

He does make it count.

Hard and deep as I groan around Jack's thick dick, listening to all his dirty words as he tells me what a good girl I am for my daddies and how they're gonna make such good daddies for real.

And they will.

They'll be the best daddies in the world.

I'm just glad I have them as my dirty daddies for a little while longer first.

THE END

Acknowledgements

As always there are so many of you to mention.

John, you never let me down. That's for pulling out all the stops with editing this one for me.

Letitia, thank you for another incredible cover.

Nadege – thank you for making the inside of the paperback look so pretty.

Tracy, thank you for everything. I love your face.

Louise, for the excellent beta feedback, as always.

My dirty girls and guys in my reader group – you make me smile every day.

Isabella – I'm so pleased you're going to be in my company again when I hit publish. You know this is a regular thing now, right? Thanks for the formatting too. You are amazing.

Demi, for pushing me onwards always.

My amazing friends – Lisa, Maria, Dom, Sue, Hanni, Kate, Tom, Marie, Siobhan, Jo, Leigh, Willow, Lauren, James. <3

My family – Mum, Dad, Nan and Brad – for being such an important part of this incredible journey I'm on.

And Jon, for putting up with all my crazy and ridiculous sleeping hours.

I love you all. <3

About Jade

Jade has increasingly little to say about herself as time goes on, other than the fact she is an author, but she's plenty happy with that. Living in imaginary realities and having a legitimate excuse for it is really all she's ever wanted.

Jade is as dirty as you'd expect from her novels, and talking smut makes her smile. She lives in the Welsh countryside with a couple of hounds and a guy who's able to cope with her inherent weirdness.

She has a living room decorated with far more zebra print than most people could bear, and fights a constant battle with her addiction to Coca-Cola.

FIND JADE (OR STALK HER – SHE LOVES IT) AT:

www.facebook.com/jadewestauthor

www.twitter.com/jadewestauthor

www.jadewestauthor.com

Sign up to her newsletter here for release
announcements, special offers and giveaways:
http://forms.mpmailserv.co.uk/?fid=53281-73417-10227

Made in the USA
Columbia, SC
13 April 2025